AMBER WAVES OF GRAVES

UNEARTH THE DARKER SIDE OF RURAL LIFE.

SPEED CITY CRIME WRITERS

EDITED BY LILLIE EVANS

EDITED BY TONY PERONA

EDITED BY STEPHEN TERREL

SPEED CITY PRESS

Amber Waves of Graves

Copyright © 2023 by Speed City Indiana Chapter Sisters in Crime

Published by Speed City Press

Edited by Lillie Evans, Tony Perona, and Stephen Terrell

Front cover design by Teri Barnett/Indie Book Designer (http://www. indiebookdesigner.com/)

Ebook ISBN: 978-1-7375257-0-7

Paperback ISBN: 978-0-9963092-9-5

Any references to historical events, real people, or real places are used fictionally. Names, characters, and places are products of the authors' imagination.

First printing edition 2023

www.speedcitysistersincrime.com

ALSO BY SPEED CITY SISTERS IN CRIME

Racing Can Be Murder

Bedlam at the Brickyard

Hoosier Hoops and Hijinks

Decades of Dirt

The Fine Art of Murder

Homicide for the Holidays

Murder 20/20

Trick or Treats: Tales of All Hallows' Eve

Amber Waves of Graves

CONTENTS

FOREWORD

Twenty years doesn't seem so very long ago when my sister and a newly published friend and I decided Indiana needed a Sisters in Crime chapter. Although we enjoyed traveling to an out of state chapter, we did not enjoy the obstacles such as constant road construction, ice in the winter and accidents along the way. I contacted National Sisters in Crime and soon Indianapolis had its own chapter. Speed City Indiana seemed an appropriate name for an organization located in the city famous for racing.

Mystery lovers began joining us as soon as the word got out that a chapter was being formed. One of the chapter's first projects was to study the art of writing short stories. An anthology of short stories titled **Racing Can Be Murder** was the first book published by Blue River Press in 2007. It was a huge success, earning a spot on the best sellers list and a review in Publishers Weekly.

Many published anthologies have followed. Along the way, the chapter launched its own publishing company named Speed City Press as well as becoming an incorporated not for profit organiza-tion. It would be impossible to name the scores of library programs presented across the state, the workshops, and the radio interviews, the conferences across the country promoting Sisters in Crime.

In retrospect, twenty years must be a long time for a chapter to have accomplished so much.

Congratulations Sisters.

Brenda Robertson Stewart

THE PERFECT MATCH
BY LEANNE EDELEN

"No more fires, Henry!" Natalie said. She glared at the boy through her rear-view mirror. He squirmed and turned his brown curly head towards the car window. "I mean it. This is your third placement this year. You can't keep doing this."

"Okay," Henry said, running his fingers along the outline of the box of matches hidden in the lining of his jacket.

Natalie's shoulders relaxed. "Don't you want a family? There is a home for you out there. Yes, you've had some disappointments, but you have to let someone in."

Henry watched the trees outside rush by, the overhead sun radiating beams that burst through the upper branches. He kept quiet. He knew better than to respond when an adult was lecturing him.

He'd listened to a lot of lectures in his fourteen years. His last foster father liked to lecture on how to properly clean a kitchen, speaking so close to Henry's face that he could smell the stale Pilsner punctuating every slurred word.

Foster parents were experts in everything and in every way Henry should live his life. No one bothered to see that Henry also knew some things. For instance, he was absolutely certain that people were unreliable except when it came to fire. There was no abandoning or ignoring fire. It demanded attention, a person's complete focus. Henry could count on the fact that it was very hard to come up with reasons why your foster child is an ungrateful little jerk when flames start to lick out of the mouth of your kitchen garbage can. Fire demands the attention of others too, like firefighters who notice bruises, marks, and bad parents.

"This new home is not what you are used to. You are going to love it! It's a farm. A real honest to goodness farm, a corn farm - I think. Dorothy will be your foster mom. She is great and has taken in a lot of teenage foster children, so you are not going to get away with anything. She seems really nice. Please give her a chance. This could be the one."

Henry was sure that Natalie thought every home placement could be the one.

NATALIE'S modest sedan pulled off the paved road and onto a tree-lined gravel driveway. A minute later, the canopy gave way to a two-story white farmhouse with black shutters. Tall corn stalks with edges that were just beginning to brown surrounded it on every side.

She put the car in park, and they both got out of the vehicle. Henry looked at the corn. He could smell the sweet, withering plants in every breath. The box of matches in his jacket twitched.

A tall woman in a vintage farm dress stepped out of the house. Her dishwater blond hair was fighting a losing battle with the advancing gray. Her smile was wide and welcoming as her beefy wet hands alternated grips on a blue hand towel.

Henry smiled back at her, mirroring her warmth. He was great at introductions. Good introductions keep you in homes and out of orphanages.

"Dorothy, so nice to meet you in person," Natalie began as the woman walked toward them. "I'm so excited to introduce you to

Henry. He and I have known each other for a long time and, I must admit, he may be my favorite client."

Henry was pretty sure that every client of Natalie's was her favorite.

"Oh good. I've been waiting for another strong set of hands to help around here. Sure will appreciate you joining us, and…and I bet you might take a liking to farm life. I hope anyways," Dorothy said.

"Us?" Henry asked.

"Sure. Sunny's my other foster. He's a great kid, a little older than you. Good hard worker and the boy sure is good at drawing. You got any talents, son? I really encourage finding out what you do best."

He knew better than to tell her what he did best.

"Not that I know of," Henry answered. The last word of his sentence came out more like a scream as something warm and furry brushed his leg. Henry jumped to his left and looked down to see a mid-sized rusty mutt looking back at him. The dog tilted his head in consideration and, as if coming to a decision, raised one of his floppy ears, rolled his tongue out and drew his mouth in a wide smile.

"Oh, don't mind Red. He's real friendly. You're a good boy, aren't you?" Dorothy said.

"He's the best boy," a male voice called from behind them. Henry turned to see a tall, lanky guy walking around the back of the house with a shovel perched on his shoulder. He waved a little to Henry. Henry waved back and brought his hand back down to knee level to pet Red who was, once again, rubbing his leg.

"Henry, I'll call tomorrow and see how things are going," Natalie said. "How about noonish? I'll just see you to your room and be on my way so you can unpack and get more acquainted."

Henry walked toward the house after retrieving a large, worn backpack from the sedan. Red kept close to his side. He noticed Dorothy walking closer to Natalie and overheard her hushed voice say, "I put all my flammable stuff in the shed. It's locked up real good."

His room was plain but comfortable. It had a twin bed near the single window, a small dresser and a vintage desk that looked as if it once belonged in a country schoolhouse. After Natalie left, Dorothy and Sunny allowed him some privacy as he unpacked, but Red did not. The mutt sniffed and inspected every item that came out of Henry's suitcase. He put his extra clothes in the dresser but kept his jacket on, running his fingers again around the edges of the matchbox.

Red walked to the doorway, waiting for him to follow like a furry tour guide. Henry obliged and stepped out into the long, narrow hallway with three doors on each side. Red guided him down the hall to the next bedroom, which happened to be Sunny's. Henry poked his head in to see Sunny sitting at a small writing desk - a clothesline draped around all of the walls. Clipped to the line were at least a hundred notebook-paper-sized sketches. There were dogs, sunsets, trees, people and more. It was amazing. One person in particular repeated over and over again, a beautiful girl with shoulder-length hair, wide blue eyes and freckles dotting her nose. Henry noticed that a framed sketch of the same girl hung on the wall directly in front of Sunny.

"Wow, Sunny!" Henry said. "Dorothy wasn't kidding. You are really good."

"Thanks, man," Sunny replied. "Um and, uh, don't worry. It's not bad here. She's okay. There are some rules, like do your chores, and stay out of trouble, but that's really it. She's had a lot of foster kids come stay here, and she gets it. She only wants the kids that want to be here. Won't even stop you if you want to leave. You're only here by choice."

"Did you try to leave?"

"No, but kids before me have. They left when they were close to eighteen, and she didn't turn them in. You can imagine, being tired of the rules and the system, it's tempting to give it a shot on your own."

"Is that what you're gonna do when you are eighteen?"

"Naw man, I got nowhere to run, and that time is coming soon. I'm hoping she keeps me until I figure out what I want to do when I grow up," Sunny said with a big smile on his face.

Henry chuckled and changed the subject. "Speaking of time, what time is dinner?"

"We can eat whenever we want. Tons of food in the fridge. Dorothy's a great cook, but she's probably going to work in her shed tonight, so we're on our own."

———

THE NEXT MORNING, Henry woke up to a cold nose on his face. His room was still dark, with just a little moonlight trickling in. He turned his head from Red, but the mutt climbed into his bed and licked his face.

"Leave me alone," he croaked.

"That's not a farm life attitude," Sunny said from Henry's partially open door. "Time to get some chores done before breakfast. It's not much but we need to get moving. Meet me on the porch in fifteen minutes."

The house was dark and quiet as Henry descended the stairs. Dorothy was nowhere to be found.

He walked out on the wrap-around porch. A pink ribbon of light barely peaked over the corn stalks. The heavy scent of morning dew blanketed the air. Sunny was waiting for him, passing the time using an old rag to play tug-o-war with Red. Sunny let go when he saw Henry and smiled. The mutt shook the rag violently in triumph and trotted it over to Henry, nudging his hand with the slobbery fabric. Henry couldn't help but pet him before asking Sunny, "What do we need to do first?"

"Well, first we need to feed the ladies," Sunny said, walking off the porch and around the back of the house.

"Ladies?" Henry said walking double time to catch up with the long-legged boy, Red trotting next to him.

The ladies turned out to be a group of hens living behind the farmhouse in a wooden coop. As he threw the feed and cleaned the coop, Henry relaxed his shoulders and watched the sky paint pink and blue layers as the sun inched up the horizon.

After the chickens, he and Sunny walked the corn. He learned to look closely at the leaves for the splotchy yellow or brown spots of disease and the telltale teeth marks of thieving varmints. Red bounced along behind them, occasionally goosing Henry when he needed a head scratch. Henry always obliged.

Henry marveled at Sunny through the rest of the chores, always whistling or singing under his breath. He was appropriately named. Finally, Sunny said it was time to get some breakfast and asked Henry to grab the ax leaning up against the shed on his way in so they could cut some wood later. The matches danced in his jacket.

"The shed? Ok." Henry answered.

Henry walked to the side of the small wooden building and found an assortment of farm tools lined up in a row.

"Hey, Sunny," he called after the older boy. Sunny walked back to the shed. "What's up with the shed? I mean, all the tools are outside instead of inside. What is inside the shed?"

"Well, I know there's alcohol in there. Dorothy took it all out of the house when I got here and put it there. I came here with a fondness for it, and she padlocked my temptation away. She spends an awful lot of time in there though. Maybe she likes a drink as much as I did," Sunny said, laughing. "Anyway, inside is off limits, but outside are a few tools we need around here. Dorothy says she'd rather replace a tool than a teenager. Grab it now, will ya?" Sunny replied and headed back to the farmhouse.

Henry selected the ax and placed it on his shoulder but couldn't help walking around to the front of the shed, where he confirmed it was indeed secured by a very large padlock.

After putting the ax on the front porch for easy chore retrieval, Henry entered a much different house than he'd left. Warm light filled the living room, and the smell of bacon and pancakes beckoned him to the kitchen. There he found Dorothy working very hard on breakfast.

"Not sure what you like to eat so I just made a bunch of stuff. You can have bacon, pancakes, waffles, or grits. You can take your pick or take them all," Dorothy said, smiling at him.

Henry glanced at the kitchen table where Sunny sat, his plate piled high with all the food options.

"I'll have what he's having," he answered.

Dorothy sat down with them, her own plate piled high with pancakes, and they ate all together for the first time.

After breakfast, he and Sunny cut the firewood. Henry learned how to aim his body and follow through with the ax. When they finished, his hands and shoulders ached from the work, but his eyes danced at Dorothy's suggestion that he be the one to stuff the logs into their wood stove, amazed that catching things on fire is how this home kept warm. He could definitely get used to living here.

He had most of the afternoon to do as he pleased. Chores were done, his belly was full, so he and Red went exploring. They walked through the corn. Henry ran ahead and Red would chase him. He would hide in between the stalks, but Red would always find him. For the first time in a very long time, Henry felt a genuine smile on his face.

Henry continued to play with the dog until he ran out of corn to run in. Just like that, he popped out into a small clearing lined by thick woods. He stared at a little path cut into the forest just as Red came barreling out of the corn, playfully nipping Henry's ankle and bounding down the wooded path.

Henry gave chase, yelling, "Okay, you got me again. You better run fast."

He darted into the woods and followed the winding path through the trees. He could hear the snapping twigs as the mutt before him trampled the foliage. Soon, the underbrush and trees gave way to a very small opening. A manmade twisted-branch fence framed a large square in the center. Its lattice of gnarly limbs protected what was inside from view, except for the occasional glimpse of floppy ears bouncing over the top every few seconds.

"What are you doing, boy?" Henry said, after finding and walking through a break in the fence. "Red, what is this place?"

Red sat down in the center and smiled in his direction as if daring Henry to come tag him. Henry looked around the enclosure. It was peppered with narrow beams of sun that shone on shadowed layers of creepy, invasive vines, a perfect camouflage for reclusive snakes or rats. However, he was not intimidated. He stalked in, focused on staying calm and keeping Red in one spot. Red smiled, letting his tongue roll out of his mouth. Henry slowly advanced to the center, just close enough to reach out and touch the dog, when his foot caught on something under the overgrowth. He fell flat on his face. Red turned his head towards the ground and smiled wider.

Henry rose to his knees and turned back toward what had tripped him. He grabbed handfuls of weeds and vines until it revealed the offender. Sticking out of the ground no more than five or six inches was a little wooden cross with the word *Prissy* written across it.

Henry shook his head. "What the...?"

He couldn't finish the sentence with words, instead he started pulling at the rest of the undergrowth. In thirty minutes, he had half of the little enclosure done. His hands were stained green, and his face smeared with dirt. He didn't care though. He was mesmerized by Red sitting on the ground surrounded by at least a half dozen little crosses.

Henry couldn't help but walk up to the crosses and read the hand-painted script. The one closest to him said *Coco*. The next one said *Hunter*, then *Prissy, Pee Wee, Dozer* and *Daisy*.

"Is this some kind of pet cemetery?" he asked when the dog brushed up against his knee.

Henry spent the next hour admiring his yard work and taking in the peacefulness of his find. He stood among trees, leaves, debris and wood yet his matches were silent.

WHEN THE LIGHT in the woods turned golden, Henry and Red returned to the farm. Red darted out of the corn before Henry, still beckoning a game of chase, but Henry was tired. He walked up to the house to find Dorothy sitting on the front porch.

"What got all over you?" She asked.

He looked down at his stained hands.

"I was pulling weeds in the corn," he lied, not willing to reveal his special find.

"Pulling weeds in the corn," Dorothy said with a snort. "Ok. That's admirable. Perhaps you should work on a little smaller scale, though. We have a garden if you are interested. Maybe that's your special talent - gardening."

Henry's face grew a little pink, realizing how ridiculous his lie sounded, but he wouldn't mind pulling weeds in the garden. He really did like farm living.

He smiled wide and said, "That sounds great. I'll just go in and wash up," as he walked up the front porch and past Dorothy.

A FEW DAYS LATER, Henry started his millionth new school. From then on, his days became blissfully routine and oddly reliable. School. Home. Chores. Red. Cemetery. Dinner. Red. Bed.

Dorothy would have a snack made for him when he got home and ask him about his day. Every week or two she let him know that Natalie had called checking on him. She would often follow it with a raised eyebrow and say, "Now, I told that woman you were happy here. I spoke the truth, right?"

Henry would give her a big smile in reply. He was great at smiles, but lately they were all genuine.

Sunny didn't go to school anymore. He said it didn't agree with him and, instead, spent his free time in his room working on his art. Henry would check in with him every afternoon. After a couple of weeks, while sitting with Red in Sunny's room, Henry worked up the courage to ask him about the girl he drew. Sunny's room was filled with her.

"Her name is Ellie. There was a time I thought she was the kindest, sweetest girl I've ever known," Sunny replied, losing some of the light in his eyes, but keeping a smile. Red walked over and put his head in Sunny's lap.

"How do you know her?"

"She was a foster here too. We were something together. We used to spend every evening sitting on the porch talking about how we'd get a little apartment in town when we aged out of here. It was real love. Well, at least I thought it was real, until she took off one night with one of the other fosters. He was a big, apish guy with an even bigger mouth who always tried to dodge his chores. I have no idea what she saw in him, but one night they musta decided to make a go of it. She didn't even say goodbye." Sunny said, still holding a smile and scratching Red's left ear.

"You sure were named right. How can you still be smiling after saying something like that?" Henry said.

"Named? Oh, Sunny. Yeah. It is more fitting than my given name, Francis," Sunny answered with a snort.

<hr />

DAYS LATER, Henry was in the backyard garden lazily pulling weeds away from the heavy tomato plants. He wore only a t-shirt and jeans. His jacket was hung in a closet and his matches stored in his dresser, but he hadn't looked at either for days. He plucked a ripe tomato off the vine and sank his teeth into the flesh. Red trotted over a ball to him and they played while he ate.

"I see you indulging in the fruits of your labor before your work's done. You certainly aren't as good at chores as Sunny," a voice behind him called.

"Huh." Henry said, choking a little on the acidic juice. He stood and turned to find Dorothy looking sternly at him as she stood just outside of the garden a few feet from him.

"Um, yeah I was just taking a little break." Henry said, wiping the red liquid from his chin. He glanced around, suddenly aware of how much weeding there was left to do.

Dorothy's face broke into a smile. "Had you worried there, didn't I? You scare easier than a cat at night." She laughed so hard she had to grab hold of both her knees to keep from falling over.

Henry inhaled the stale scent of alcohol puffing into the air after each of her bellows. He didn't know what to say, so he just stood there wearing one of his best smiles.

THE NEXT DAY he got off the bus and walked up the long driveway, surprised to see Dorothy and Sunny in the front yard. They stood four feet apart, close enough to talk but far away enough not to touch. Their bodies were stiff, alert and tipped towards each other. Dorothy must have outweighed Sunny by thirty pounds, but he was a few inches taller. He was waving his arms in the air.

Henry headed directly into the house. He didn't make eye contact with the pair. Whatever was going on between them, it was not in his best interest to get involved.

"I ain't done nothing!!" he overheard Sunny wail as he hurried into the house.

Dorothy was calmer but more direct, "I think we both know that you've been where you shouldn't."

Henry found Red, grabbed his matches and took off to the cemetery. The matches, now in his jeans pocket, didn't stop vibrating until he saw the little crosses in the abandoned cemetery. Of course, it wasn't abandoned anymore. Now these little forgotten pets had a caretaker, someone who would look after them and make sure that vines and weeds no longer strangled their painted names.

He and Red waited to return to the house that evening until the light was just barely winking in the sky. Dorothy seemed herself as she was putting on a feast of roast beef, with baby carrots, red potatoes and gravy. Sunny was not himself, however. His face was dark. Henry sat next to him at the table, giving a half smile in his direction.

"I thought this place was different, but what a fool I've been," Sunny yelled to no one in particular, shaking his head. Then muttered, "Man, I miss Ellie," under his breath.

"Alright, I know what you've been up to. But sometimes there's a price to pay if you go looking for what you shouldn't," Dorothy answered.

"What I need is a damn drink and an explanation!" Sunny said, running his fingers through his hair.

"There won't be any drinking spirits in this house. See here's your milk. We will talk about this later," Dorothy said, slamming two glasses of milk down on the table.

Tension took the place of conversation for the rest of the meal. Henry had no idea what their argument was about. Did Sunny go into the shed? Has he been drinking? Is he thinking about finding Ellie? Henry knew better than to ask these questions out loud.

Red came every few minutes and bumped him with his nose wanting a pet. Henry couldn't pet him because his fingers were tracing the matches in his pocket with the force of an F4 tornado. Red, insistent for attention, pulled on the napkin in his lap. He tried to get Sunny's attention too, but that was a mistake.

"Get away, you mutt, or I'll get you away!" Sunny barked through gritted teeth. The dog backed up, lowered his head and left the room.

Dorothy and Henry turned to look at him.

"This milk is awful, tastes like it turned," Sunny said in Dorothy's direction folding his arms across his chest.

She drank from her own glass and said, "Mine tastes fine. Maybe it's not the milk that's turned rotten."

Henry chugged his milk.

"If it's alright, I may just go on up to bed. I'm not feeling too well," Henry said a minute later to avoid the horrible tension and to keep from setting the garbage can on fire. He really was trying to do better and, honestly, he wasn't feeling himself.

He flopped into bed still in his clothes, suddenly exhausted. The sound of far-off arguing voices danced around him as he closed his eyes and felt a cold nose and a warm body snuggle up to him.

The next morning, Henry woke to the sunlight piercing his head. He grabbed his face and moaned. He felt his pocket for his matches and sucked in his breath. They were there. He counted them. They were all there.

"Here, boy," Henry called, beckoning Red for pets. When he didn't come in a few minutes, Henry became concerned about the time. Had he missed school? Why hadn't Red or Sunny awoken him?

Henry staggered downstairs, still in yesterday's clothes, to find Dorothy in the kitchen with a plate of pancakes for him.

"They're a little cold but I'll microwave them for you. They'll still taste good. You feeling any better?" She asked.

"My head's pounding. Did I miss school?"

"I went ahead and called you in. You seemed off last night. Figured you could use the extra sleep."

"Um, thanks," he said, clicking his mouth a little afterwards to call the dog. His head hurt too much to whistle. Where was he? Red would never pass up the chance to beg for pancakes.

"Sorry, to start off with bad news, but I think Sunny's gone."

"What?"

"He musta took off last night to forge his own future or some teenaged dreamy stuff like that."

Henry swallowed his pancake bite but couldn't imagine taking another one.

"Took off. Where?" Henry asked.

"No telling, but we'll be fine - just us."

"He doesn't have anywhere to go."

"Don't you fret too much about it. He'll do fine. He's practically a grown man, gonna be eighteen in a month. You are easy to worry, aren't ya? I think I'm going to start calling you Fret. That's a good nickname for you - Fret."

"Do you know where Red is?"

"No. Haven't seen him all morning. Maybe he left with Sunny. Honestly, that dog seemed to like you and Sunny better than me anyways. Course, Sunny really wasn't himself last night. Hope Red's okay with him."

Henry's chest tightened in a way he had never felt before. He thought of the angry boy from last night; it certainly wasn't the Sunny that he had come to know.

"If you don't mind," he asked. "I might just get started on my chores and eat this later when my head is feeling better.

"Oh, sure thing, Fret. Could you look into doing Sunny's chores too?"

"Yes, ma'am."

He walked out on the front porch before his hands started trembling.

He called out again, "Here, boy!"

Nothing happened.

He ran down the driveway calling for the dog, but there was still no answer.

Hoping, praying that Red would be at the cemetery, Henry ran through the corn calling Red's name as loudly as he could. Hot salty tears ran down his face and into his open mouth.

"Red!"

"Red!"

"Here, boy!"

"Red!"

"Reeeddd!"

His voice was already hoarse when he popped out of the corn near the little path to their hideaway.

"Red!" he croaked, running down the path, but there was still no answer.

Henry stopped, breathless at the homemade branch fence. He put his hands on his knees and sucked in huge gulps of air. There was no dog running around the enclosure.

"Damn you, Sunny! You didn't have to take him. You didn't have to take him."

Raising his head, he gave the little cemetery another look over. In the corner, where the light filtering through the trees did not reach, he saw a mound of overturned dirt. His heart dropped to his feet.

Henry's legs carried him wobbling over to it. It was a big mound. A fresh mound of packed dirt.

He flung himself on it, picking up handfuls at a time. Henry needed to know if Red was underneath this. If he was, Henry would find Sunny and burn down the entire town he was living in. The matches in his pocket didn't move as he clawed the mound, they stood at attention.

His hands started to ache and bleed when he was barely a foot down. He needed a shovel. It would take forever with his hands. He needed to go to the shed.

Henry emerged from the brittle, dry corn stalks, his eyes just as on fire as any garbage can he lit. His feet ground down the grass beneath in perfect cadence as he rounded the house towards the shed. There were no more tears. He reached the little wooden building and grabbed the dirty shovel leaning against the outside wall. If that was Red under the dirt, he would tear this shed down with his bare hands to get what he needed. Henry kicked hard at the padlocked door as he passed, shovel perched on his shoulder.

He turned to walk back to the corn when he heard the door answer back from inside. Followed by a clear bark. Henry froze.

He called out. "Red!"

A louder, familiar bark answered him. Thirty seconds later, with two swings of the ax, Henry saw his favorite rusty smile. Red jumped into his arms and Henry let him in.

After he and Red celebrated their reunion, Henry couldn't help but peer inside the shed. His matches twitched as he walked in. There wasn't much to the little building. A shelf ran along the upper portion, it was well stocked with vodka, whiskey, and gin bottles on one side, gasoline containers, turpentine, and paint thinners on the other. It looked to be almost split evenly on Henry and Sunny's vices. About mid-way up, a counter ran the length of one side of the room. On it lay various hand tools, pots and two shot glasses with a smidge of brown liquid in the bottom. Guess Dorothy gave Sunny a send-off.

Red brushed past his leg and ran behind some milk crates under the counter. Henry bent down but couldn't see the mutt.

"Come back out here, boy. Hiding back there is probably how you got locked in here in the first place," he called, but the dog stayed put.

Henry upped the ante for him and yelled, "Come chase," beckoning him into their favorite game. Red was definitely up for play and barreled out from underneath the counter, knocking a milk crate over in the process.

Paper spilled out all over the dirt floor. Henry bent down to pick it up, not wanting to leave any evidence of being in there. He gathered up several documents in a pile and placed them back in the milk crate. A photograph fell from the bundle and landed face down.

Henry reached to grab it when he noticed the word Prissy written across the back. He remembered that name from the little pet cemetery and couldn't help to turn it over to see what animal it was. Secretly, he imagined it as a cat being named Prissy. But it wasn't a cat staring back at him in the picture, it was a girl with wide blue eyes and freckles on her nose. It was the girl from Sunny's drawings.

Why was the word Prissy written on the back of this picture?

Henry rummaged through the milk crate and found a picture of a young, strong man with brown tousled hair and camouflage jacket. He flipped the picture over and, in the same handwriting, was the name Hunter. Five minutes later, Henry found them all. He found all the names on the little wooden crosses.

He stood up. They were nicknames, not pets. The hair on the back of his neck stood up. Dorothy's voice from earlier rang in his mind "think I'm going to start calling you Fret," and sweat formed on his brow.

Henry's eyes scanned over the little shed hoping to find something to the contrary. But instead found a large wheelbarrow parked near the back with dark stains and a little wooden cross in it. The cross had the word Sunny written on it in familiar scrip.

Henry grabbed the gasoline can and headed out the door. Surely, a three-acre corn fire would bring help to the farm faster than any phone call. Once outside, he tried to call for Red, but it was stifled. A big meaty hand grabbed him by the neck, pinning him against the outside shed wall. He clawed at the hand, dropping the can to the ground.

"Well, now, Fret. What do we have here?" Dorothy said, her black eyes piercing him so hard they were almost as painful as her grasp. The warm smile he had gotten so comfortable with was replaced with a sweaty upper lip drawn into a high curl on one side.

"What did you do to Sunny?" he croaked through his closing throat.

"Sunny? Oh, that ungrateful little bastard. He found my little hiding spot in the woods and cleaned it up perfectly, like Sunny does. Probably cleaned it for his precious little Prissy. She was a good kid but just couldn't keep from going where she shouldn't, like Sunny. If she hadn't seen me in there with that ingrate of a foster, Hunter, she and Sunny would be in their little apartment in town right now. Sometimes kids just can't leave well enough alone. You know about that, don't ya, Fret?" she growled as she glanced at the gas can.

Henry tried to kick out at her but was losing consciousness. His heavy head lulled to one side.

"That's right, nighty night. Hell, this works better than that sleepy-time milk."

Henry's vision turned to blackness, but he could still hear. He could hear her raspy quick breaths, then a nearby low growl, followed by Dorothy's blood-curdling scream. He dropped to the ground, his lungs filling with gasps of air. His legs thrashed a few times, kicking the shed wall, gas can and anything close to him until his body reacquainted itself with oxygen.

He opened his eyes.

"You dang mutt! You don't bite the hand that feeds ya. You're goin' in the hole with him," Dorothy said as she bent down to get the ax. She raised it high and turned to Red, who was barking and standing his ground.

"No!" Henry tried to say but his throat couldn't make a sound.

Red danced and weaved around the woman. She took a couple of swipes, but Red was too fast for her, especially now with a large chunk missing from her bleeding calf.

Henry sat with his back against the shed. Desperate to help Red, he looked for the shovel but couldn't find it. Instead, he saw a long trail of leaking gasoline from the overturned can, leading right to where Dorothy was standing. His matches jumped out of his pocket and into his hand.

Dorothy stepped back to take another swipe at Red and slipped on the ground made wet from the gasoline. Henry pushed the can away and lit the trail. He scrambled to his feet and ran as fast as he could, whistling for Red to follow. Flames raced toward Dorothy and grabbed at her dress. She squeaked out short, panicked screams as she beat her big hands against the flames on her gasoline-soaked dress. But to no avail. She tried to get up but slipped again, adding to the flames. Henry and Red stopped at a safe distance and watched her finally get up. She looked like a giant torch now as she ran, screaming, straight into the dry cornfield, setting the three acres ablaze.

HOOSIER HOTSHOT
BY ROBERTA BARMORE

The problem with the crime scene was that it had the wrong corpse. The problem with the grain silo where they found the body was that it wasn't a silo.

Hamilton Yount called me three days after his stepson Billy went missing from the family farm outside Mertonville, Indiana. The fifteen-year-old wasn't with any of his friends. He hadn't left a note. He didn't have a phone, either. "We'd been talking about it but his mother thought he was still too young," Yount told me.

Yount had found the body while looking for the missing boy. The Colfax County Sheriff had identified the dead man as an ex-con with active warrants and a serious meth problem. They hadn't had any luck at all locating the boy. He hadn't taken a bus out of town. He might've hitchhiked but it was unlikely.

It was a sunny October morning. Yount was standing in the front yard when I drove up the lane to the farmhouse. Like so many of these old farms, the lane was paralleled by a thick line of trees forming a windbreak, protecting the house and the barnyard.

"Early, aren't you? Good." He shook my hand with casual

strength, calluses rough, quickly. He gave me the kind of up and down look I'm used to. I grinned at him.

He took me in, from my curly brown hair, short enough that it's out of my way, down my wiry build to my walking shoes. I've got a scattering of freckles, brown eyes and no jewelry unless you count my wristwatch. I dress like anyone who works a trade, sturdy slacks with a lot of pockets, plain tops and a zip-up hoodie if the weather rates it, which it did that morning.

My name is Leigh Reid Moxon. My first name is pronounced "Lee." I live in Indianapolis and I'm a private investigator, which is a pretty good way to almost make a living. I take jobs a lot of investigators won't, difficult car repos, small time skip-tracing, background checks and whatever comes along. I have to: I'm non-binary, and some prospective clients pass me up. Yount hadn't.

I saw a big old red-painted barn looming behind the house and part of a newer building across from the barn. They both had the same old-fashioned white trim around the doors.

There was a row of four silos off to the side of the barn, shiny corrugated metal with ladders up the sides. I asked which silo the dead man was found in and Ham Yount sighed.

"I thought you grew up Colfax County? Those are grain bins, not silos. Short, fat, pointy top, see?"

I was a town kid. I didn't see but nodded nevertheless, trusting he was going to tell me. He had that tractor-faced look, chin pushed out, back straight, sharp pale eyes and skin like rusted, pitted metal. He was a man who would plow through any obstacle to reach his goal. He turned and walked across his yard toward the barn. I hurried to keep up.

I spent my childhood in Mertonville and buried both parents there. I left shortly after high school graduation to be a police officer in a nearby town, but it hadn't worked out. I hadn't been back to my old hometown for years until I stumbled onto a series of murders while recovering a car in Mertonville last year. Ham Yount's sister had been one of the people I met then. She'd talked me up to him. Right now, he didn't look very impressed.

"Silos are tall, skinny – for silage. It ferments. Grain'd damn well better not. And if you fall in, it'll kill you sure enough. You sink in and the pressure of the grain keeps you from taking a breath. That's where we thought Billy was, because of the open door." I could see hatches in the roof of each grain bin, person-sized, with a ladder leading up to them.

As we got closer, I saw the silo at the end closest to us had a series of openings cut into it, the roughly-cut rectangular holes straggling down the sheet-metal side, impromptu doors. Interesting, but first things first. "Mr. Yount? About my fee?"

He took one more step and stopped. "People call me Ham."

I gave him another smile, remembering Al Capone's advice about dealing with people. "It's three-hundred seventy-five a day, Ham. Plus expenses. In advance. Like I said on the phone."

I could see him make up his mind to smile back.

I kept smiling. What I do is a skilled trade. I'm not shy about getting paid. Indiana makes PI firms carry serious insurance, and it's not cheap. My cellphone is as much of an office as I can afford.

"You're the one figured out about that crazy Marelli brother last summer, right?" Yount took his wallet out as he spoke.

"A Sheriff's deputy did the hard part," I said. I'd nearly ended up dead at the bottom of a flooded quarry. Maybe I could have avoided that without Deputy Breedlove's help. Maybe. "I hear he's the Sheriff now."

"You know Dave Breedlove?" Yount was fishing out cash and counting it, but his eyebrows went up. "He's been all over this, but he can't find a sign of Billy." He sighed and held out a thin stack of hundreds and fifties. "Here's seven-fifty to get you started."

I was happy to take it.

Yount looked away. "After the first full day, I just gave up. You know they say after twenty-four hours, the chances are real bad." He shrugged. "His mother can't bear to think of it. She was out of town at her sister's up in Washington state. She's a little high-strung ever since she was widowed. Dotes on that boy. Frantic to get him back. The two of them are driving straight through. Be here tonight."

"She wasn't here when you realized he was gone?"

He shook his head no. "Billy's my stepson. I married his mother seven years now and he still isn't much for farming. Got all kinds of notions. Fool kid. I about decided he'd run off the way some kids do, and he'd come back when he learned better. Then we found that dead bum." He gave me another up and down look. "Moxon, Moxon. I went to County Consolidated, but I knew your name was familiar. You were the track champ, weren't you, at Mertonville High?"

I nodded. "I did okay." It's still painful to remember.

He looked more at ease having placed me. "You were supposed to be pretty special, weren't you? What happened?"

Yeah, aren't we all so special. "I got unlucky on a motorcycle. You can't run much with a broken knee. Spent my senior year on crutches." And that's enough about that. "Suppose you show me where they found the man's body?"

That's how I learned the difference between a silo and a grain bin.

THE FARMHOUSE WAS on a little rise with the outbuildings and a row of grain bins stretching out behind it and to each side. There was a vegetable garden next to one side of the house, and we walked past a small fenced enclosure of clucking chickens with a slant-roofed hen house for them.

Ham Yount kept talking as we walked. "You see those blamed holes the VFD cut in that bin? Hell of a mess. Volunteer firemen." He coughed instead of swearing. "It'll be tricky welding that back. Had to open the bin up, though. About all you can do if somebody's caught in there. Tear 'em up bad if you started the auger, maybe crush a man if he was still alive."

The bins were thirty feet across and as tall as a two-story house, with ladders up the side and grain-moving hardware connected to them. They were close together, maybe six feet apart.

"This time of year, they're full of corn. Billy knew better than to fool around with them."

"So what happened to the corn?" I could see a little on the ground, like yellow gravel with hints of pink.

"Ran most it into trailers once we were sure there wasn't anyone else in there. Shoveled it back in and augered it into the trailers. All the neighbors helped out." Yount thumped what looked like a fat pipe angling up from a metal box at ground level.

I took his word for it. "So, no way the boy was in any of that?"

"Not a chance."

Nothing useful there. I asked to see Billy's room. As we turned to go, a cat with a coat marked in dark brown, orange and tan came around the grain bin and towards me. It stopped when I looked at it, then proceeded to come over and smooth against my ankles, looking up. I reached down and petted it. It seemed like the polite thing to do.

Ham Yount was still striding toward the house and I double-timed after him.

A TEEN-AGED BOY's room is predictable. This one was neater than usual, with a new-looking iron bed and a tall bureau with a mirror. Along the far wall, under a tall window, there was table the boy used as a desk. It looked hand-made, with a nicely-finished, thick top supported by four splayed legs that went all the way through, their square ends planed flush with the rest of the tabletop. A pair of blue jeans were draped over the footboard of the bed, a single poster on the wall for a play at the Methodist church back in July and a stack of textbooks on the desk. I looked in the closet: clothes on hangers in no particular order, a jumble of footwear on the floor, labeled boxes neatly stacked on a shelf above.

Ham Yount watched my search from the doorway. "That kid's crazy about theatrical stuff. Helped build the sets for that church play and was even on stage, a soldier in the background."

I said, "Is anything missing? Did he take any clothing, anything else?"

"I don't think so. How would I know? Sheriff's men already asked when they went through all this."

Of course they had. "Did the deputies take anything?"

"His paper notebook, his laptop. His mother and I don't know the password. I'd already looked through the notebook. Don't think the Sheriff saw anything helpful in there either, or they'd have said."

The headboard of the bed had a metal panel with a hand-painted monogram, WBL. I gestured at it.

"William B. Landers," Yount said. "That's his name. The boy did that when he refinished the bed frame."

You don't say. "Not Yount?"

"Not going to take away the boy's last name. He wants to use mine, by and by, that would be all right. I won't make him."

I wondered if he had tried.

YOUNT LED me through the rest of the house. It was plainly furnished, almost bare, though there were quite a few plants. The kitchen had fewer appliances than I'm used to and it reminded me of my great-aunt's home from a childhood visit. "Ham, were there any Mennonites in your family?"

He looked at me, frowning, "How could you know? Yeah, Dad's people. He left the church when he married my mom, though." He looked around the kitchen, shrugged. "I guess it still shows. You haven't seen the cellar yet, either. Think you'd better?"

It was as good an idea as any, so I followed him down and past shelves loaded with home-canned food in clear jars. There weren't any good hiding places. An old full-manual Maytag washing machine stood next to a modern washer-dryer, and on the far side of the furnace, a flight of stairs led up to the angled doors of an old-fashioned outdoor entrance. "Do those still open?"

Instead of answering, he went up the steps and hinged back the split doors, light flooding down. I followed him up and out into the back yard. The old barn stood to our right. To our left, the new-looking metal building was almost as large. I pointed, "What's that?"

"Pole barn. Machinery building. Used to have a shed extension on the big barn and a workshop. Outgrew 'em. So I got that."

"Show me around."

Yount shrugged. "Deputies did all this already, you know."

"Great. I'll talk to them later." I was looking forward to an excuse to check in with Dave Breedlove now that he was Sheriff, but I doubted he'd tell me much. "I want to see it for myself first."

<hr>

DESPITE HIMSELF, Ham Yount's pride in the new building came through. Inside, tractors, a combine and equipment I didn't have names for filled most of the building, with a big workbench along one wall next to a set of double doors. There were a lot of places where a boy could hide, but between Yount and the deputies, they'd already been checked and rechecked.

I walked to the doors. "What's in here?"

"Best part of the whole thing," Yount said, and opened the door. Beyond, a series of windows lit a good-sized workshop. I recognized a bandsaw, a drill press, and a table saw, but there was a lot more. A workbench to our left near the power tools was mirrored by a smaller bench on the right. Yount gestured towards it. "That one's the boy's."

It was more cluttered than his room, hand tools hanging on a pegboard against the wall and boards stacked underneath. A stack of papers was held down by a couple of small shapes. I picked one up and saw it was a miniature version of the mirrored bureau in his bedroom, in unfinished wood much lighter than the full-sized original. I sat it gently to one side and picked up the other one, a model of the thick-topped, angle-legged table.

"He made that little one first," Yount said. "He worked out the big one on paper, but he wanted to see how it would look and fit together."

The model desk was a pretty thing. The wood was stained the same color as the table in Billy's room. I turned it to get a better look at the top and part of the front slid out. There was a drawer built into the top. I held it up. "Is the full-sized one the same?"

"I don't know." Yount took the model from me and looked it over. "I never saw that." He sat the tiny table down on the workbench, the drawer still slightly open. "I'll be darned." He slid the drawer shut. "That boy's not much use around the farm, but I will be darned."

The papers under the models were nothing much, drawings of furniture and a half-finished sketch of a sleeping cat, well-proportioned and shaded.

That was all I found. I asked to look at the barn next, and Ham led me to an outside door, past an open door into a small washroom. He leaned in and turned on the light. "I'm real happy about this. Hooked it into the septic tank myself. Got a real shower, slop sink, stool. Don't have to come into the house muddy, you know. Real handy in the winter, too."

THE OLD BARN was set into a slope where the ground fell away. We went in through big sliding doors with the trim around them painted white. I walked across the width of the barn, where another set of doors gaped open and stopped short. The opening was a dozen feet above an area where a few cattle wandered.

"Mind yourself," Yount said. "It's a long way down."

The level we were on was partially sectioned off into stalls to our left and right but didn't have much in it other than a large lawn-mower and some beekeeping equipment. Lofts above them on each side were stacked with hay bales like green-gold bricks. The air was thick with scents, the acrid reek of tomcat spray by the doors and the whiff of cattle from below mostly covered by the tickling, grassy aroma of the hay.

A cat came striding out from one of the stalls and headed right for us. It looked like the same one from earlier. Yount saw it too. "Darned cat's lonely. It favors Billy. Barn cats aren't pets, but that boy won't believe it."

The cat investigated my ankles and then began to smooth against them. "Did anyone check out the haylofts?"

Yount sighed. "Not more than four times, between me and the Deputies. First place I looked. The boy feeds the cattle, so he's in and out of the lofts a couple times a day."

They looked pretty full. Most farmers leave huge cylindrical rolls of hay in the fields, but these were rectangular, small enough for a two-handed lift, stacked in rough stairsteps sloping up. "I'd like to take another look at Billy's room."

<hr>

THE FULL-SIZED TABLE had the same hidden drawer as the model. Opening it took a few tries: push in, and a spring-loaded magnetic catch popped the drawer out far enough to get a grip. Push it back in, and the latch reset with a click. Inside were a few of the treasures I expected: pens, pencils, half an empty robin's egg, a couple of large feathers Ham Yount said were from a red-tailed hawk. Front and center, a magazine mostly composed of car and beer ads and pictures of scantily-clad young women, the last not exactly obscene but suggestive enough to make his stepfather blush when I held it up.

"You know," Yount said, "I haven't seen his multitool."

"His what?"

"You know, pliers, pocketknife, screwdriver. Like mine." He unsnapped a holster at his belt and held up a chunky gadget. "He can't carry it at school, of course, but the rest of the time he won't be without it."

We were interrupted by a shocked sound from the doorway. A blonde woman stood there, clothing rumpled, eyes wide. Her face was puffy and flushed. "Hamilton. Who – *what* is that?"

She was pointing at me. I put the magazine down and gave her my best professional smile. "I'm a private investigator. Leigh Moxon." I took a step towards her, holding my hand out.

She flinched back.

Oh, yes, this was going well. Ham Yount moved towards her and I stepped aside. "Brenda, this is the detective I told you about."

She looked at me and looked away. "You didn't say—What even is that person?"

I sighed. My friend Fabulous Earl says I look like a conscientious objector to the War Between the Sexes and he's right. Most people just assume I'm one or the other and go with it, and I'm happy enough to let them. It saves me no end of trouble, but it doesn't always work.

Yount had his arms out, holding his wife's upper arms, reassuring her. "Leigh's the person who got the Marellis caught last year, remember? My sister met, um, met them because her boss was one of the people John Marelli killed."

There was another woman in the hall, hanging back, an older, chunkier brunette with strong resemblance to Mrs. Yount. She looked tired and frightened.

Mrs. Yount – Brenda – twisted to glance at me again and started to say something.

Ham Yount moved his hands to her shoulders. "Leigh can find Billy if anybody can."

Brenda was shaking her head. "No," she said. "No, the Sheriff will find Bill. I want *it* out of here, out of this house."

"But," Yount looked towards me and shut his mouth. Seven

hundred and fifty dollars or not, I didn't feel like adding to the discussion, either. If that's what it was.

The other woman stepped next to Brenda. "It's been a terrible drive. Why don't we sit down and let your husband deal with this?"

Neither one of them looked at me. Brenda let her sister lead her down the hall and Ham Yount sighed.

"I'm sorry about that but you're going to have to be going. I'll walk you to your car."

There's nothing to do about a reaction like that. I'd put in most of a day and I was keeping at least three hundred and seventy-five bucks. It was going to have to be enough. I was working the math in my head as we went downstairs and out the front door. Halfway to my car, the sound of a train whistle made me lose my place. It sounded close. The sound sparked a thought and I stopped walking.

Yount noticed and broke his silence. "It's not as near as you'd think. Train yard's about three miles off, but sometimes it carries."

It was about mid-afternoon. I bill a day at time. You can call that predatory if you like but I've got to eat. "I still owe you a day's work. How about I go talk to the Sheriff and see what turns up? I can call you later."

"I'm sorry about Brenda." Yount was looking at the ground. "She can be set about things. But I hadn't thought she'd, um."

Oh, brother. Other people pitch a fit and I'm supposed to make nice? Okay, seven-fifty buys you a little nice. "You still want your stepson found. She wants her son found. I have some ideas about that."

He looked up. "You do?"

"Yep." It was more like the ghost of a guess, but I wasn't going to admit that. "I'll call you this evening. When's a good time?" *When can I avoid your nut wife,* I meant.

⁎ ⁎ ⁎

Dave Breedlove looked the same as ever, comfortable behind the big desk, bushy cop 'stache and all. "Leigh! I haven't seen you since the Marelli trial!"

I'd hoped to never come back to Mertonville again. Dave was a bright spot, at least. A good policeman, he didn't have much to say about the missing boy or the body they'd found.

"I can tell you what was in the papers. Truth is, there isn't anything more, not yet."

"Nothing? The dead guy, was in the habit of, I don't know, robbing freight cars? Hopping a ride?" It'd become difficult to hop a train, and then the railroads started cutting staff. They've got video surveillance at the stations and switching areas, but the cameras can't see everything, and they have a tendency to get vandalized, even stolen. Stealing items from freight cars has become common. The thief finds a spot where the trains slow down – a curve coming up on a switchyard, for instance – bashes the door lock on a boxcar and grabs whatever's grabbable.

Dave was already nodding his head yes. What he said was, "Of course I could not say for sure, but suppose he did. What then?"

"Oh, just a thought. Guy with a habit, he's got to pay for it somehow." I was pretty sure I had all the pieces then, but pretty sure isn't good enough. "Buy you a coffee?"

Dave laughed. "Coffee. Maybe later. You're up to something."

"It might be nothing." I did my best to look sincere. "I've still got your cell number. If it is something—"

"You'll call."

"Hundred percent."

I killed time until sunset. There's a place in Mertonville over by the stamping plant that turns out an adequate corned beef on rye. I passed on the beer; water suits me better. After dinner, I thought about the fancy desserts on the menu, ordered a cup of coffee instead and got comfortable reading an old John D. McDonald novel. I never could picture myself in a houseboat. Eventually it was time to call Ham Yount and tell him what I was going to do. He had his doubts but agreed.

THERE WAS a wide spot along the road about a half-mile down from the Yount farm. It was after midnight when I coasted my car to a stop there and walked the rest of the way. I walk a lot and it gave me a chance to adjust to the dark. There was another reason, too.

I paralleled the lane back to the house on the far side of the windbreak trees where there were plenty of shadows. I managed to startle a possum. It hissed at me and trundled away instead of playing dead. I swung out and edged around the barnyard, keeping as far out of the light as I could. Getting into the barn was a risk. I eased past the open door into the shadows and stood still, waiting to adjust to the dimmer light inside, spilling in from a floodlight on the newer building.

There were two lofts, hay on each side with the center of the barn mostly open. I needed to choose one or the other. Nearest the house, probably. I was looking up when motion caught my eye. A cat, tiptoeing along a beam at loft level, on the side farther from the house. It looked like the tortoiseshell cat from earlier. That made my mind up. I worked my way to the ladder on that side and climbed.

Up on the loft, I thought about taking my shoes off, then thought better of it. The stacked bales formed an oversized staircase and I planned my route before proceeding, with as little noise as possible.

At the top, I worked my way to a spot against the wall near the center. The stack sloped away to each side and I could see all of it.

There's a Zen to stakeouts. You have to give yourself over to it, melt into the environment whatever it is. You wait without impatience, without anticipation, open to whatever happens, alert but still.

Once I settled in, the cat showed up from the darkness, utterly silent, smoothed against me a few times and curled up beside me, purring. I took it as a good sign.

A couple of hours passed. Once, a bat skittered through the air, barely visible, black on gray, jinking crazily up and out somewhere high overhead. The cat woke up, bathed itself and settled back down.

I wasn't quite asleep when something clicked, sharp and distinct. Call it a meditative state; that'll do. The sound brought me right out of it. The cat sneezed and stood up as a sliver of light appeared down the slope of bales to my right and went out again.

I waited. The light flickered again, moving upwards. I could make out a shape, climbing. When it reached the top, I stood up and said, "Billy?"

He jumped a little and lost his footing. I moved as quickly as I dared and caught the boy before he fell.

He struggled and seemed to think better of it. I was thinking better of it myself. If we tumbled down the bales and over the edge of the loft, it was going to be a long, hard fall.

"Billy! I'm not a cop!"

"Let go!"

"Will you stay put if I do?" We were both crouching down as we struggled, trying to keep balanced. I thought avoiding a fall was a particularly good idea.

"Let go of me."

I was stronger than he was but not by much. I had both arms wrapped around him, and by then he was practically sitting in my lap. "I'll let go if you promise to stay still and listen." I could feel him tensing up, ready to get away.

"Why should I?"

"Because you're not in as much trouble as you think you are."

"I'm not?" He relaxed a little.

I figured I had a chance to convince him. "Listen. I'll tell you what I think I know. There was a boy on a farm who was really, really good at things that don't have much to do with farming. His dad was gone and his mom had married someone else and left him out. So he decided to run away. Sound about right?" "Uh-huh."

"So, can I let you go? Will you stay put and listen?" Geez, I hoped so. I never wanted to have anyone sit in my lap, especially not a fifteen-year-old in need of a shower.

"Uh-huh." He didn't sound all that sure.

"Promise." Come on, kid.

"You promise I'm really not in trouble?" Hooked!

"Not as much trouble as you think you are. And it'll get worse if you wait."

"Okay."

That, I trusted. I let him go and we both sat back. "Okay, Billy, where was I? You were running away and you went to the train yard, right? And you met somebody and he talked you into taking him back home, didn't he?"

"No." Even now, there was a touch of fear in his voice. "He made me take him back here. He had a knife. He was going to rob us!"

Yeah, that added up. "Let me guess. You got back home and you got away from him. You climbed up the ladder of the first grain bin, you opened the hatch and what next? Help me out, here."

"I went around the roof and jumped to the next one. I've done it before. And then the next one."

"And where was the man?"

"He climbed up after me and he must have gone inside."

"And then what?" This part, I wasn't as sure about.

"He must've done it wrong."

"Done what, Billy?"

"There's a ladder inside. You're not supposed to step on the corn. Not ever. You can't be sure it will hold you up." There it was. "I could hear him moving around at first. I thought he was climbing out. I got down, ran to the barn and hid here. This is my hiding place. I make one every year and keep it until the hay gets low. My stepdad never finds them."

"And then what?"

"I fell asleep. In the morning there was a lot of noise. The Sheriff was there. I watched. I saw them take him out. I killed that man!"

We were sitting side by side on the top of the bales of hay. "I don't think you did, Billy, and neither will the Sheriff."

The boy and I sat there, him trying to suppress tears and me deliberately not noticing. I figured he'd been hiding out during the day, coming out at night to use the washroom in the machinery shed and probably sneaking canned goods out of the basement. The tortoiseshell cat returned and sat between us while the first birds started to sing and the sun slowly came up. In the pale light, he turned to me. "What's your name?"

"Leigh Reid Moxon. Your stepdad hired me to find you."

"Are you a boy or a girl?"

Oh, that. "I'm a private investigator."

"Like on TV?"

"Close enough."

"Cool."

I don't get hit on the head as much and I've never driven a Ferrari, but why spoil the glamour?

We made our way down to ground level. I called his stepfather from the barnyard, not wanting another scene if we showed up at the house unannounced. I called the Sheriff next.

I GOT to keep the entire fee. Mrs. Yount was torn: happy to have her son back, livid that I had found him. I walked back to my car and drove home to Indianapolis, fighting to stay awake the whole way. By then, I hadn't slept for over twenty-four hours. The two days' pay was great, but it wasn't why I was smiling the whole trip home. I grinned every time I remembered Billy calling Hamilton Yount "Dad" when his stepfather came running out of the house to hug him, his mother hurrying after with a frown.

THE FALL OF THE QUARRY CURSE

BY DIANA CATT

"I've been waiting for you, young man," Cora McCardle said as she swiveled her desk chair around to face me. "Hey, watch it. Your stompers are dripping on my good rug."

I glanced at my boots. "Sorry, Cora. It's nothing but water and mud out there today." And gloomy. A gloomy, rainy day to match my mood. I adjusted my expression to look more cheerful than I felt. "I'll get Emily to put your rug in the laundry."

Cora huffed. "More important stuff is going on. I think that new woman across the hall has serious problems. Cursed, most likely. You have something in that bag of yours, young man, to help the cursed?"

Cora is my oldest patient, coming in at just under ninety-eight. That's both age and weight. I've been her physician, seeing her once every three months on average, since she moved to Pleasant Vista Estate ten years ago.

I placed Cora's chart on her writing table and gently lifted her thin wrist. Her pulse beat a steady rhythm beneath my finger. "I haven't met Mrs. Wallace yet," I said. "And I don't diagnose cursed."

Cora is also, by far, my most famous and dramatic patient. She

35

was a celebrated writer in her heyday. Her walls are lined with framed reviews of her stories. She has a shelf over her desk to display all her works—ten novels, five collections of her short stories, and every anthology or magazine where one of her short stories appeared. Her fame recently made a resurgence after she solved the murder of her good friend, Marjorie Moore, the previous occupant of the room across the hall. If Cora was a diva before, now she's downright imperial.

"A first time for everything," she said, deepening the creases around her pale blue eyes with her frown. She slid a folded sheet of paper out of her dress pocket and spread it open on top of her chart. "Take a look at this. Harriet left it in the rec room."

I glanced at the page, then picked it up for a closer look. Multiple age-progression sketches of a tearful girl covered the paper, changing from toddler to pre-teen to young adult. A bejeweled headband held tight dark curls away from her face in each rendition. Pain emanated from her eyes, and I could practically hear sobs.

"They're all the same girl," Cora said. "See?"

"So, Mrs. Wallace is an artist," I said. "And a good one at that. Not a sign she's cursed."

"Talk to me after you meet her," Cora said.

<hr>

AFTER LEAVING CORA, I continued my rounds. I forgot all about the drawings until I made my way around the facility ending at Harriet Wallace's apartment. I reviewed her past medical history. She was here temporarily to recoup from a recent hip replacement. At only sixty-three, she was a mere spring chicken for this place. I paused before knocking to study the beautiful Fall wreath on her door. Fall is usually my favorite time of year. My wife and I would take a week off for our October anniversary and stay at one of Indiana's twenty-four State Parks. This fall would have been our tenth. Instead, I was forcing myself to just get through the season, tragically alone.

I shook off my melancholy, knocked, and entered the unit. Mrs. Wallace sat at a writing desk, her room the mirror of Cora's but with different personal touches. A large painting hanging over the desk immediately grabbed my attention. It featured the same girl from the sketches Cora showed me earlier, but here she wore a beautiful smile that radiated.

"Good morning, Mrs. Wallace. I'm Dr. Walsh. May I call you Harriet?" She shook my hand but didn't speak or meet my eye.

"Are you settling in? Meeting the other residents?" I asked to break the ice.

She shrugged but didn't reply.

"Is that your daughter?" I gestured toward the painting. "She's beautiful. Did you paint it?"

She gave a slight nod.

"You're very talented." I looked at her chart again. "It says here you have a son as well as a daughter; is that right?" Again, her only response was a slight nod. Clearly, I needed to ask open-ended questions with this patient. "What do your children do for a living?" I asked.

She squirmed in her chair, which was more of a response than she'd made to anything so far. I waited. Finally, her voice floated low, a mere tickle of airwaves. "There be but one now. Jackson. Him that put me here."

I watched her expression harden and again consulted her chart. Two adult children, birthdates putting them at thirty-five and twenty-eight. Boy and girl. "What was your daughter's name?"

A tear started down her cheek. "Eddy."

"Jackson and Eddy," I said. "Nice names."

"Named after their father," she said. "Edward Jackson Wallace, be gone eighteen year now."

"I'm sorry to hear that, Harriet. You must have had a tough time raising two children alone."

She looked at me for the first time, tilting her chin upward with a fierceness about her green eyes. "Don't be asking about that time, Doctor. Then be then, now be now."

"Fair enough," I said. "Now, Harriet, may I listen to your chest?" I interpreted the next slight movement of her head as agreement. I warmed my stethoscope between my palms and proceeded with my exam. Her heartbeat was regular and strong, and her lungs were clear. "I'm going to run you through some simple tests to see how your new hip is healing." I pulled out my reflex hammer and began.

I finished my examination, made appropriate notes in her chart, and left. My last notation was a reminder to consult our facility's nurse and Harriet's physical therapist about her mental status, as they saw her more often than I did.

———

ABOUT A WEEK LATER, as dawn was breaking over the horizon, I traveled the curvy country road back to Pleasant Vista Estate on a special call. The night nurse had noticed Mrs. Wallace was running a fever. That symptom alone would not warrant an early visit unless it spiked or forty-eight hours had passed without relief. The day nurse, however, justified the call because of Ms. Wallace's extreme emotional state, it was a Saturday, and they were understaffed.

Along the route, the trees were starting to show the beautiful reds and yellows of fall. An autumnal crispness filled the air. Memories of my beloved surrounded me, and I didn't fight them. When I reached my destination, I sat in my car for an extra beat to savor the moment. Then I trudged inside.

I checked in first at the nurse's office.

"Thanks for coming, Dr. Walsh."

"Any improvement in Mrs. Wallace?"

"No. Her fever's up, and she's showing some confusion. Keeps calling out for Eddie."

I remembered she mentioned her daughter was named after her husband, and both were deceased. She could be referring to either one. "While I'm checking on her, please pull her admission file and leave it on my desk."

"Sure thing, Dr. Walsh."

I ran into Cora in the hallway on my way to Mrs. Wallace's room.

"Well, about time they called you in. That poor woman had a difficult night."

"I know, Cora. If you'll excuse me."

"She's still grieving the loss of her husband. You, of all people, should get the grief. And I found out those kids of hers are only her steps."

"Cora, I have a patient to see. No time for idle gossip."

"Not gossip. She told me that herself, and more. The *gossip* is this: I think the boy killed his dad and sister."

"Cora." I caught myself before I snapped and took a deep breath to control my voice. "Please keep your imagination to yourself. I'll stop in to see you after I treat Mrs. Wallace."

"Just hope you can cure the poor thing's curse."

I turned away without another word.

HARRIET WALLACE LAY in her bed. Sweat beaded on her forehead and upper lip. She twitched and murmured, but I could make out a few words. "Eddy? Come back. Where's my child?"

I checked her temperature, and because of the reported confusion, agitation, high fever, and current appearance of dehydration, I called the nurse to summon an ambulance. The facility's protocol dictated that her family be contacted, and presumably, Wallace's admission file was, by now, on my desk.

I returned to my office and read through Harriet's file carefully. She was from Nashville, a small Indiana artist's community nestled in the Brown County hills. She owned a home there as well as an art gallery called The Imagination Wall. Her son, Jackson, was the only relative whose number was listed. I phoned his contact number and informed him of his mother's situation.

"There are several conditions that present with delirium," I said.

"One being Harriet is nuts," Jackson Wallace said.

"Excuse me?"

"She's bat-shit crazy. Didn't you know? She's been this way awhile, ever since my sister went missing three years ago. When they found her body this spring, it put mama dearest over the edge."

"I'm sorry. I didn't know the details regarding your sister's death. Your mother might not be crazy, as you call it, just grief-stricken. The pain of losing a child can be intolerable. I can recommend an excellent therapist for an evaluation."

"Bullshit. She's not even our real mom. Though, I think she probably cared for Eddy as much as she could for anyone, which wasn't much."

Ambulance lights strobed through my office window. I relayed the address of the hospital in Bloomington and ended the call. I reviewed my notes from my initial visit with Harriet last week and found nothing to support her son's allegation. But then, I had only seen her that one time.

After Mrs. Wallace was on her way to the hospital, I stopped by Cora's room. She was pacing between the window and the desk.

"What has you so agitated today, Cora?"

"I'm afraid for Wallace."

"Her prognosis is cautiously good," I said.

"I'm not worried about her infection," she snapped. "I'm worried about her son. I think he'll hurt her this time. She thinks he'll hurt her."

"Cora, I know Mrs. Wallace suffered a terrible tragedy..."

"You don't know diddly. Her husband and child were murdered, and she suspects the son. She thinks he'll find some paintings she did now that he has control over the studio, and he'll realize what she suspects. She has no advocate."

"Sounds like she has you."

"Like I can do anything myself. She's your patient. She needs you to look into this."

"Cora, I..."

"You can. Just get out that computer of yours and look up the deaths of her husband and her daughter. Go to the studio and snoop around. She gave me the key. Look for those paintings. I can write up a plan for you to follow."

"That's not necessary, Cora. I want you to sit down and stop worrying. I'll visit Mrs. Wallace in the hospital, and if she's able, I'll get her to talk to me. If there's any truth to that story, I'll bring in Police Chief Knoblett, and he'll get to the bottom of it."

Cora walked over, grasped my hands, and stared intently into my eyes. "Please," she implored. "She's really a nice woman who has suffered heartbreaking tragedies. She's cursed. Please help her."

"Okay now, Cora." I patted her hand. "I'll see what I can do."

She huffed. "Condescension doesn't fly well around me, you know, and it is especially unbecoming on you, my friend. I might just have to go to her studio myself."

I gave her a stern look. "You know, Cora, there's a reason you no longer have a car."

LATER THAT AFTERNOON, my thoughts returned to Cora's plea. I turned on my laptop and found the obituaries for Edward Jackson Wallace and his daughter, Eddy Wallace. Edward had owned a tree-trimming business in Brown County. He had a dozen employees who were often seen around the county trimming along electrical lines or cleaning up storm damage. Edward was murdered eighteen years ago by a blow to the head. The case remained unsolved.

Eddy Wallace's disappearance was more recent, just three years ago. My search yielded thousands of hits. Both beautiful and talented, she performed under the name Eddy Magnum. Of course, now I remembered. I'd only heard about her under her stage name.

She was a popular singer in the Bloomington area and had a huge following on social media. The news focused on her very wealthy family. Her grandfather, Abe Magnum, had built a fortune with his stone quarry, and speculation was rampant that this must be a kidnapping for ransom.

All the sordid details of Eddy's family were described over and over. It started with her parents and their scandalous love affair— the heiress, Olivia Magnum, and the poor tree trimmer, Edward Jackson Wallace. Of course, Olivia's father, Abe Magnum, was outraged when they'd eloped. Eight years later, Magnum publicly blamed Edward for Olivia's tragic death in an automobile accident when Eddy was an infant, and Jackson was only seven. Abe Magnum's anger made the news again when Edward remarried Harriet Cone.

The Magnum drama was revisited periodically until Eddy's battered remains turned up in a creek just outside one of the Magnum quarries, stirring up the rumors of a kidnapping gone tragically wrong.

I was stunned. That salacious history would cause anyone to wonder if they were cursed.

I placed a call to my officer friend, Gordon Knoblett.

"Gordy, what do you remember about Eddy Wallace, aka Eddy Magnum?"

"What about her?"

"Her mother, Harriet Wallace, is one of my new patients. I've been trying to evaluate her mental status."

Gordon sighed. "It was a bad one, that. Went missing right before her twenty-fifth birthday. We searched every square inch of the county, it seemed. A hunter finally found her remains this spring in a creek near one of her grandfather's quarries. After three years missing. The mom suffered a lot during that time."

"Did you make an arrest?"

"No. I'm still looking at some friends and family members. Forensics are still underway."

"Family members? That would only be Jackson and Mrs. Wallace, right? Surely you don't suspect my patient?"

"There's a maternal uncle, Race Magnum. His sister, Olivia Magnum-Wallace, was the biological mother of Eddy and Jackson. Alibis are hard to sort out after so much time. It's complicated by business travels that weren't straightforward."

"Well, that's cryptic."

"Sorry, all I can say right now."

"Could my patient be in any danger from Eddy's killer?"

"Well, there could be a money motive to harm Harriet. The Magnum estate is a big one, but Harriet didn't get anything when the old man passed away. His estate was split with half going to his son Race, and his deceased daughter Olivia's half was split between her two children. On the other hand, Harriet has a house she shared with her husband and is a successful artist in her own right. Comfortable income, though nothing like the Magnum wealth. Eddy's belongings are still on hold until her murder is solved, but without a will, Harriet will get 25%, and the rest will go to her brother."

"Can you think of a motive other than money?"

"You're kidding, right? Eddy was a singer with a promising future. There are loads of motives: jealousy, love, hate, fear, anger. We're considering all of them. She had a boyfriend and an agent who was negotiating a recording contract, but they both have strong alibis."

"So, you don't think the father's murder and the daughter's murder are connected?"

"Sorry, Doc. We haven't ruled anything out. But that one is unlikely. Damn, this case has been full of dead ends."

On my way home, I had the sudden urge to drive the fifteen miles to Nashville, using the excuse that my mother-in-law, who was grieving the loss of my beloved as badly as I, could use a cheering-up gift. I regretted this decision as soon as I saw the crowds lining the sidewalks and the overly decorated boutiques. Mums of yellow, purple, maroon, and white adorned the streets. Doors were decorated with wreaths of sunflowers and leaves in fall colors. This much joy for Autumn threatened to lighten my mood if I wasn't careful. I found a quiet place on a side street that sold hand-crafted yard ornaments and chose a beautiful headstone saddle full of colorful fall flowers, which I knew my beloved and her mother would both love. Then I spotted a memorial stake engraved with pine trees and the quote, "Someone we love is hiking in heaven." Perfect. I bought both. The store clerk wrapped my selections and then pointed me in the direction of The Imagination Wall. As I stood at the corner across the street from the art gallery waiting for the light to change, I spotted none other than Cora McCardle unlocking the side door to Mrs. Wallace's gallery. Emily, a nurse from Pleasant Vista Estate, was right behind her.

"Emily," I called over the traffic noise.

Cora didn't miss a step entering the building as she probably hadn't heard me, but Emily froze in place, her eyes wide. It took me only a couple of minutes to cross the busy street and get to her side.

"I...I'm so sorry, Dr. Walsh," Emily stammered. "You know how insistent Cora can be. She was planning to use Mr. Jeffrey's car when I intercepted her. I figured at least she'd get here safely if I drove."

"She told me she got the key from Mrs. Wallace, but I didn't expect she would use it."

"Oh, she has permission."

"Well then," I said with a slight bow. "After you."

We stepped into a back room filled with shipping boxes, framing supplies, canvasses, paints, and an assortment of brushes. I could hear Cora rummaging around in the display room and found my patient studying paintings that were stacked on a rack in front of the check-out counter.

She frowned and raised her eyebrows at seeing me. "Glad you could join us, Dr. Walsh."

"Cora, I must strongly object to you coming here."

"Well, object all you want, but I'm here, and so are you. Let's see what we can find." She pointed at the paintings on the walls around the gallery. "You and Emily take a look at those."

"What are we looking for?" Emily asked.

"A painting that will implicate her son in his father's murder or his sister's murder."

"Cora," Emily said with a deep sigh. "You promised this would be a quick trip. This doesn't sound quick."

"It's a small place. Won't take long if you don't stand around whining."

I met Emily's eye and nodded to the right. She slumped her shoulders but headed that way. I went left, and we slowly progressed around the room. I recognized a few local landscapes, but one dark painting of a stone quarry in a raging thunderstorm caught my attention. Looking closely, I noticed a cross at the edge of a creek. It was marked with the initials EW and a medallion on a gold chain hung from the cross.

EW—Eddy Wallace?

"Cora," I said. "Look at this."

She and Emily joined me to inspect the painting. I relayed what I had read in the papers about Eddy's disappearance and the discovery of her body near the stone quarry this past spring.

"Her son wore a medallion like that when he checked Mrs. Wallace into the facility," Emily said.

"*Tears of Magnum Stone*, not for sale," Cora said, pointing to the typed card with the title of the work. "This scene probably haunts her."

"How can she bear to look at this every day?" Emily asked. "That can't be healthy. Doc, what do you think?"

"She'll move it when she's ready," I said. "She needs closure, I'm sure."

Just then, a man entered the gallery from the back room. "Stand still, everyone. I have a gun, and I've called the police."

Cora was the first to recover. "We have permission from the owner, Harriet Wallace, to be here," Cora said, stepping toward the man. "Just who are you?"

"Jackson Wallace. Mother's in the hospital with dementia. Any permission she might have given isn't legitimate."

"Now, hold on there, Jackson. You don't need a gun. I'm Dr. Walsh, your mother's physician. I called you earlier."

Jackson tilted his head and studied each of us in turn. "Why on earth would she want you three to come here?" he asked.

"You, of all people, should know," Cora said.

"What's that supposed to mean?"

"Harriet doesn't trust you." Cora wagged her finger at him.

Jackson turned toward me. "I told you Harriet was crazy. Don't buy into her paranoia."

Cora stomped her foot. "You have the necklace. Explain that."

Jackson looked puzzled. He reached inside the neck of his coat and revealed a gold chain with a quarter-sized medallion dangling from the end. "This?" he asked. "This is a family heirloom. It's mine."

"It was your sister's. Did you take it from her neck when you killed her?" Cora demanded.

"What? No! Where did you get that idea?"

"From your mother. She believes you killed your father and your sister," Cora said, her voice booming through the gallery.

"No. God, no. The police found this with Eddy's body and returned it. I've been wearing it ever since."

"Ah, ha!" Cora said. "The police would never release evidence until the case is solved. Dr. Walsh, call that police friend of yours, Knoblett."

"Go ahead. Call," Jackson said. "They gave it to my Uncle Race. He gave it to me."

My eyebrows shot up, and I looked at Cora. Her expression mimicked mine.

"Uncle Race?" I asked.

"Yes. He knew I'd like it as a memento of my sister. He watched out for us after our grandfather died. Uncle Race took over running the quarry and manages our trust funds."

"He manages the trust funds," Cora said. "Follow the money, Doc. I always say it."

"Yes, Cora, you do. And Eddy was only days shy of getting her trust fund when she went missing."

Jackson paled. "No, you are wrong. Uncle Race wouldn't...I mean, my trust fund was okay."

I called Gordy's cell number, and he asked us to wait there. Meanwhile, Cora went to the back room and fixed us all hot tea with honey, and Jackson babbled. He'd taken off the medallion and stared at it the whole time.

"Uncle Race...you're thinking he took Eddy's money, right? He could have, I guess. He was executor. But killing Eddy? That's just too wild. He's family."

"Most murders are committed by someone the victim knows. Unfortunately, that includes uncles," Cora said, her voice softening for the first time.

"Her uncle had her medallion. That doesn't look good for him, does it?" Emily asked.

We all shook our heads.

"Are you sure your trust fund wasn't tampered with?" Cora asked.

Jackson's eyes widened. "I don't know. It paid all my college expenses with a nice pot left over. I also get dividends from the quarry business each year. I never looked for any discrepancy."

"I'm sure Knoblett can look into it for you," Cora said. "If he's not already."

"How was your relationship with your uncle?" I asked.

Jackson tilted his head and frowned. "Distant, at best. I was away for years. Dad was killed shortly before I left for Yale. I only came home from school for Christmas. Some years I didn't even see Uncle Race. After Eddy went missing, I moved back here to help search for her. Poor thing."

"Was Race in Eddy's life?" Cora asked.

"Honestly, I don't know. We rarely ever talked about him. Harriet would know. But we might not get much out of her now." He waved his finger in a circle around the side of his head.

"Don't give up on Harriet," I said. "Her thinking should clear up once this infection is under control, and she can go home and resume her life."

"How old was Eddy when your father died?" Cora asked.

"Ten or so. Just a kid. Before I left, I tried to talk to her about it, but she assured me she was fine. I don't think she really grasped what death meant."

As a physician and a lot older than ten, I didn't really grasp death either.

"If good-ol' Uncle Race was juggling the books way back then and your father found out...," Cora said. "Well, he might have even more blood on his hands. Maybe ten-year-old Eddy saw or heard something back then that didn't make sense to her until she was getting ready to access her trust, and she confronted your uncle."

"Whoa, Cora," I said. "Your imagination is running rampant. We'll let Knoblett sort it out. The necklace, though, is a solid clue."

We all had a second cup of tea and sat in thoughtful silence. I heard the bustle of the shoppers passing by, and my thoughts drifted once again to my beloved. No mysterious circumstances surrounding her death. But still, bottomless grief. Maybe a solitary hike through nearby Brown County State Park would help bring closure. The thought bolstered me.

Cora reached over and patted my hand. "Excuse me for saying, young man, but you may have cured the quarry curse."

I narrowed my eyes at my dear old friend. "I suppose this will be your next installment of 'Adventures in Assisted Living'?"

Emily clapped her hands. "With the bumbling physician as the hero? Perfect!"

Cora smiled at both of us and suddenly looked twenty years younger. "You can be sure I'll give you each a signed copy."

LAST SEEN HEADING WEST
BY JOSEPH S. WALKER

Kevin knew he should be grateful for quiet kids on a drive, but there was something unnatural in the way Bryce and Lindsey sat placidly in the back for two hours, eyes glued to their screens. It didn't seem to bother Sharon, in the passenger seat, who took command of the speakers to play podcasts at 1.5 speed. Film reviews and true crime stories shifted slightly into a chipmunkish register.

Kevin looked at the road, silently noting how many trees they were passing on their way to look at trees. To Sharon, like most Hoosiers, autumn leaf peeping meant Brown County. Kevin was just thankful that Sharon didn't notice the THC gummies he took before they left. She didn't like him using them, but the roads were thronged, and he needed the little cushion of calm detachment to deal with the traffic.

A few miles outside Nashville, Sharon stopped her podcast and compared the map on her phone with her Brown County Scenic Art Drives printout. "Look for a turnoff about half a mile past this antique store," she said.

"Right or left?"

"Right."

"What?"

"*Right.* Slow down. What's so fascinating back there?"

Kevin brought his eyes back to the road and hit his blinker. "Just a car in the parking lot. Sixty-seven Mustang. My dad had one."

BRYCE WAS SHARON'S SON, and Lindsey, Kevin's daughter. Kevin thought of the melded family as something like a newborn colt, still wobbly, uncertain of how the parts worked together. He would have welcomed some light squabbling on the drive. *His feet are on my side. She's breathing weird.* Instead, the kids treated each other with the stiff, minimal courtesy of fellow passengers on a bus ride.

At least they looked up from their phones when Kevin, following Sharon's directions, turned onto a narrow road winding up a crest, the asphalt crumbling at the edges. The cabin at the top had been converted to an art studio, with a wide porch overlooking a long wooded slope exploding with yellows and reds. "Look at that, kids," Sharon said. "Isn't it worth the drive?"

"It's very pretty," Lindsey said. At twelve, she was developing a sense of what people wanted from her. Bryce, three years younger, didn't answer.

Kevin squeezed into the one open space in the tiny gravel lot between two big black SUVs. A handful of people stood around the grass lawn, taking pictures of the brilliant canopy. Two of the men made quarter turns to keep him in view as he killed the engine.

"Be careful getting out," he said over his shoulder. "Don't scratch up those other cars."

Of course, both the kids could slip out with the doors open a few inches. Kevin had to suck in his gut to shimmy through the gap, feeling the men's eyes on him.

He followed the kids and Sharon to an unoccupied picnic table, propped one foot up on the bench, and leaned forward to stretch out his leg. Lindsey pivoted slowly, taking a panoramic shot. Sharon shaded her eyes with her hand to read the sign hanging over the cabin door.

"Fabric and paper arts," she said. "Lindsey, why don't we go browse and let the boys relax for a few minutes?"

Lindsey looked at her father. Kevin gave a tiny nod. This was part of Sharon's plan for the day, finding chances to bond with each other's kids. He watched them walk toward the cabin. Sharon put her hand on Lindsey's shoulder for a moment as they went inside.

Bryce sat at the picnic table, radiating discomfort. His arms were crossed tightly across his chest, but at least he wasn't mesmerized by his phone. Kevin sat, not too close, but not as far away as he could have been. "Quite a view," he said.

Bryce nodded but didn't say anything. Kevin propped his elbows on the table behind him. The soft autumn air felt luxurious. He had a brief, vertiginous sense of the enormity of the space around him. Other than a line of turf cleared for power lines, the vista was almost unbroken by any sign of humanity.

Off to the left, a group of five or six turkey buzzards made lazy circles high in the air, spiraling in and gradually getting closer to the crowns of the trees. Kevin pointed. "Something died over there."

The boy looked. "Those birds are going to eat it?"

"Turkey buzzards. It's what they do." Was he supposed to say something wise now? "Circle of life."

"Maybe it's a dead person," Bryce said.

"More likely an animal."

"People are animals."

This was what exhausted Kevin about kids. Every statement became a possible landmine, inviting commentary, contradiction, and confusion. "Sure," he said, biting back his first response. "But it's good to focus on the positive, right? We're lucky. Not everybody gets to see things like this."

"It is good to see it now," the boy said, his words suddenly coming in a trembling rush. He kicked his legs. "While we have the chance."

"What's that mean?"

"Climate change," Bryce said, in the voice children use when adults are being morons. "I bet in a few years this will all be, like, desert or something. Or all kudzu like the woods down south. We'll have to go to Canada to see fall leaves."

"You don't have to worry about that." What the hell did the kid know about woods down south? He was looking at Kevin now from the corner of his eye, waiting for something more. "People are working on it. Things always seem worse than they are." Memory stirred, a headline he'd noted approvingly without clicking. "I just read about a new way to make concrete that traps carbon from the air."

Bryce shook his head and propped his elbows on his knees. "*I* just read that in another twenty years, Indiana will have the same climate as Arizona."

The sound of an approaching engine saved Kevin from thinking of a response. The '67 Mustang came into sight with two women in the front seat. Kevin nudged Bryce and pointed. "My dad had a car just like that," he said. The car looked pristine, candy apple red with two broad black stripes running down the middle of the body. "Same color and everything. He loved that car. Washed it every single weekend."

He didn't know the memory was there until it hit him, as real as the rough wood of the table under his hand. Clumps of suds floating lazily down the driveway to the gutter. The slick, heavy feel of the wax. The sun off the fender outshining the one in the sky. His father in a lawn chair, shirt discarded in the grass, drinking a beer, looking at his own reflection in the side of the gleaming wonder.

The cabin's small lot was still full. The woman in the Mustang's passenger seat showed something to the driver, probably the same map Sharon had. The driver nodded. The engine noise picked up as the car continued along the road, disappearing into the trees on the way to the next view, the next shop. Nebraska plates, Kevin noted. Long way to drive for leaves.

"It's a pretty cool car," Bryce said. "Do you still have your dad's?"

"No," Kevin said. "It was stolen."

For the first time that day, the boy seemed interested. "No way."

"We got up one morning, and it was just gone. Filed a police report, but nothing ever came of it."

After that, his father didn't spend weekends outside, pampering the car and the lawn, but inside, staring at the TV and building pyramids of beer cans. When the long, exhausting fight with the insurance company was finally over, he took the check and bought a cheap beater that would be in and out of the shop for years to come. He rarely spoke of the Mustang, but Kevin believed he thought about it every day, right up until the end.

Sharon was standing beside him, holding up a red and white scarf. "They were pretty picked over already," she said. "I thought this would be good for Linda for Christmas."

"Sure," Kevin said. "Where to next?"

<hr>

THEY STOPPED at a roadside rummage sale because Lindsey spotted a table with an extensive display of Magic cards. While she rifled through the albums, the other three wandered separately, each, Kevin suspected, glad for a few minutes away from the others. He bought a bag of caramel corn, something the kids could maybe share. A bonding experience. He went around a corner and found Sharon standing in the middle of an aisle, stabbing furiously at her phone. She was oblivious to the annoyed stares of people navigating around her. He took her elbow and pulled her to the side. "What's wrong?"

Before she could answer, Bryce was there, pulling urgently at her other arm. "Mom, this place sucks, and I'm hungry."

Sharon shoved her phone into her pocket and gave Kevin a brittle smile. "Lunchtime," she said. "Let's get Lindsey and head into town."

"Sure." The set of Sharon's jaw promised another landmine. Kevin had no doubt this one was going to blow, and soon.

NASHVILLE'S STREETS WERE THRONGED, cars crawling along between crowded sidewalks. For the small town's shops and galleries, these fall weeks were a second Christmas, the boom time that would keep them afloat through the lean winter months and into spring.

Kevin willed himself into long, slow breaths as they inched along the street. The few parking lots he could see had signs charging forty dollars and up for a space. They also had signs saying "FULL."

"Is this where the Grand Old Opry is?" Bryce asked.

"That's Nashville, *Tennessee*," Lindsey said. "It's much bigger. A real city."

"They used to have one here, too," Kevin said. "A concert hall where they played country music. It was called the Little Nashville Opry."

"Nuh-uh," Bryce said.

"No, it's true. It burned down, though."

"Is that for real?"

"Kids," Sharon said. "Get out and find a restaurant where you can get a table. Anyplace. Text us where you are. We'll come meet you as soon as we can park."

In the moment of hesitation following this, as the kids gauged whether Sharon was serious, Kevin saw the Mustang coming from the other direction. Every line of it, from every angle, was as familiar to him as the contours of his own hand. He was half aware of negotiations and instructions, the back doors opening as the kids got out.

The two women in the car were younger than the car itself by at least three decades. They were laughing, singing along to something.

A cacophonous few seconds of some beat Kevin didn't know as the cars passed each other.

The seats were the creamy white vinyl he remembered. Another stab of visceral memory: riding in the back, showing off his new pocketknife to a friend. A moment's clumsiness and suddenly the three-inch gash in the seat between them. It was the angriest he ever saw his father.

"They're giving it to *Janice*." The tang of venom was familiar in how Sharon said the name.

"You're kidding." The Mustang was behind them now, indistinct in the mirror's jumble of cars and people.

"Of course, it's *so easy* to travel to the Boston office when you don't have to deal with kids. That place would fall apart without me."

"Sure would." A car was coming out of a lot on the right, the attendant getting ready to flip the FULL sign over. Kevin spotted it just in time to cut off a Mini Cooper that feinted at making a move from the other side of the road. He gave the attendant two twenties and headed for the spot just vacated.

"I think I need to be able to quit," Sharon said.

He took the keys from the ignition and listened to the car settling into place.

"Kevin."

"Six months," he said. "We talked about it. Can you just do the six months?"

Sharon's phone buzzed. She glanced at it. "The kids got a table at a pizza place."

"Sounds good."

"Six months. Six. Not seven." She got out of the car.

Deep breaths. Calm breaths.

It was late afternoon, and the crowds were thinning when they got to the scenic overlook in the state park that Sharon had picked as their last stop of the day. As Kevin pulled into the parking area, he heard Bryce gasp. Four hot-air balloons were hanging in the air in front of them, drifting along above the valley, almost level with the overlook. They were close enough that Kevin could see the people in the baskets clearly and distinctly, close enough for the size of the big silk envelopes to be impressively apparent. Nobody else noticed what Kevin had, even before he saw the balloons: the Mustang, parked just a few spaces away.

He lagged behind as Sharon and the kids headed across the street to the bluff, pulling out their phones. When none of them were looking, he doubled back and ambled around the Mustang, resisting the urge to run his finger along the line where the trunk met the body. Kevin felt like he was Bryce's age, but Bryce never seemed to be as happy as the car made Kevin feel. Maybe he was. Maybe parents never really know.

Something caught his eye. He leaned forward and cupped one hand against the glass. The patch on the back seat had been expertly done. It was barely visible. It was also in the exact spot where Kevin had dropped his knife all those years ago.

He tried to get his breath under control. Thirty years? Thirty-five? The women couldn't be the ones who stole it. One of their fathers, maybe, and then the thing just sat under a tarp somewhere for decades? No. There had been a long chain of owners. At some point, he assumed, phony papers. Likely the people who owned it now had no idea it had ever been stolen.

"Is this the car Grampa had?"

Lindsey was standing next to him. He had a feeling this wasn't the first thing she'd said.

"Yeah," he managed. "This is it."

"It's nice," she said. Her voice clearly indicated that the car had claimed the smallest possible part of her attention for the smallest possible moment of time, a moment now forever lost. "Sharon sent me to get you. She wants a picture with us all in it before the balloons are gone."

"Sure," Kevin said.

Lindsey turned toward the bluff, then back. "Dad," she said. "Mom wanted me to ask you about Christmas. She wants to take me to California for two weeks."

"Sure," Kevin said. "Wait. California? You're spending Christmas with us."

His daughter looked tortured. "Can you think about it? She wants to take me to Disneyland." She put her clasped hands under her chin, a parody of a begging child. "I'll bring a present back for Bryce," she offered.

There had to be a right thing to say. He couldn't even feel the shape of it. He felt suspended, hanging in midair like the balloons. The only thing he wanted to do was look at that patch again, feel again the gut punch of the car resurrected. There had been the smallest shift in perspective, and now the path of his life was revealed as a long arc, connecting the last time he'd seen the Mustang, in a suburban Philadelphia driveway, with this hillside in Indiana.

"Sure," he said. "I'll think about it."

He watched her decide not to press her luck. "Okay," she said. "Come on. Those balloons are amazing, right?"

She dashed back toward where Sharon and Bryce stood, just at the edge of the meadow before it began dropping back toward the yellowing wood. There weren't many years of that left—Lindsey running with the flailing, unselfconscious freedom of a child.

Kevin trailed her. The women from the Mustang were standing near a picnic table. They had a camera mounted on a tripod, an enormous telephoto lens aimed at the balloons. They were huddled together closely behind it, and Kevin had a sense they were looking at the shots already taken, judging whether they had what they wanted. Purses and camera cases were stacked at one end of the table. A set of keys rested on the bench beside a phone and a small wallet.

Kevin walked twenty feet past the women before he stopped, patted his pockets, and turned, heading back toward the parking area as though he'd forgotten something. He didn't let himself think. It turned out to be easy, not thinking. Walking past the table, he picked up the keys without breaking stride, clutching them tightly in his fist to keep them from jangling against each other.

Nobody yelled. Nobody chased him.

The Mustang was unlocked. Kevin slid behind the wheel. In all probability, this was the first steering wheel he had ever touched, sitting in his father's lap. He gripped it tightly, then let his right hand fall to the shifter. How many years since he drove a manual? He closed his eyes for a moment, rehearsing the old movements, the timing of pedal and stick. The knowledge was still there. When he opened his eyes, the key was in the ignition. He turned it, and the answering rumble was like a pet welcoming him home.

One of the women looked at him and pointed, tugging at the other's arm. Twenty yards beyond that, Bryce stared, stock-still. Sharon and Lindsey were still looking at the balloons. The women began running. He couldn't make out their yells, but other people were looking now. He put the car in first gear and rolled out onto the road, leaning over to push down the lock on the passenger door. For a moment, he thought he'd killed the engine trying to shift into second, but it caught, and the beast leaped forward. *American muscle*, his father's voice said from somewhere.

The women fell back in the mirror. Kevin felt the phone in his pocket buzzing. He ignored it. The park entrance was about four miles off. From there, he could choose any direction he wanted. He didn't have a plan. He didn't need one. He had his father's car and an open road to run on.

He ran.

GUARDIANS OF THE LAND
BY ANDREA SMITH

The small meeting room at Majestic Realtors was packed, so Maeve joined the people who were standing alongside the wall. Those fortunate to have arrived early enough to grab one of the cheap metal chairs shifted uncomfortably in their seats. Their expressions pinched with worry.

Two men stood at the front of the room. The one wearing black jeans, a black tee-shirt and a scowl was Preston Hayes who refused to return her calls. The other was Lucas Foster, a real estate developer and her competition. He was round and squeezed into an expensive suit.

An older woman standing in the front row was speaking. She exuded royalty with a scarf of various hues of blue elegantly draped about her shoulders.

"Lucas, my grandchildren are uprooting their lives to return here because you promised this deal of yours was going to bring this community back. They're giving up good paying jobs for what they expect to be a slower, better way of life. But you haven't given us any details of this development of yours."

"Mrs. Collins. Nelda. You've known me since I was two." He held his arms out in an expansive gesture, putting his hand over his heart over the pristine white handkerchief of his breast suit pocket. "How long have I been working on behalf of our families? My word is my bond, Madam Council President. When I say we're close to a deal that'll rescue this community, you can trust it's done."

"You've been promising the community you're going to deliver a miracle for how long now, Lucas?" Preston asked, crossing muscular arms across his chest.

Murmurs came from some of the attendees in the room.

"And you've been strutting around the community like somebody crowned you king. Your ancestor might have founded Hayes Station but that doesn't give you the right to show up here after all these years and decide our future. Your folks might have owned the most acres, but we worked, too."

"Not how I remember it," Preston said. "My grandfather told me all the stories. When the going got rough, your folks left the community to rot."

"That's a lie!" Lucas stalked toward Preston who didn't move. Just gave Lucas a 'bring it" glare. A slender guy wearing a bow tie came up behind Preston and touched him on the arm. Preston seemed to relax.

Lucas decided he didn't want to get hit today and backed away. 'I assure you that you will be happier than you ever dreamed of with my development plan. It's going to bring more businesses, more investment."

"Our land is all we have. We can't afford to risk it," Mrs. Collins said.

"With my 20 years of experience and success, I assure you, it's not going to come to that," Lucas promised.

Maeve took this as an opening. "If you don't mind. I can speak to a possible way to earn revenue for its development."

Eyes fixated on her.

The man named Lucas swiveled to look at her. "And who are you?"

Maeve answered in the calmest voice she could muster. She didn't want to alienate the residents by coming across as the outsider, convinced she knew what was best for their community after being here a few hours.

"Maeve Evans with the Wadsworth Museum in Washington DC. We want to work with Mr. Preston Hayes on an exhibit on Hayes Station's remarkable history. It could generate some tourism for the town."

Silence. Then Lucas doubled over with laughter.

"Ha! This little thing in high heels and braids is your cavalry?" he said. "She's cute, but your ancestors would bust out of their graves before they let what they built be destroyed by crooked bureaucrats and your incompetence. Go back to that little historical center you're pretending to rebuild."

Preston, fist balled up, started to cross the space toward him but his friend held him back.

Lucas stared at Maeve and chuckled again. "Promise I'll have a proposal for you folks soon."

With a final scowl at Maeve, Preston Hayes stalked out of the meeting room, the bowtie wearing man and a petite woman trying to keep up with his long strides.

Maeve followed them. "Mr. Hayes. May I have a word, please."

Preston stopped and turned so abruptly, Maeve almost collided with his chest.

"I've heard enough from you folks. Got your e-mails. How many times do I have to say I'm not interested in helping you people make money off us?"

"Really? Submitting an application to be considered for an exhibit is certainly a poor way to show it."

"What application?"

"Our curator and the committee thought your submission was excellent. They're excited we might be able to help preserve the history of Black farmers in Indiana."

His jaw clenched. "You're crazy. I didn't submit any application."

Maeve saw the woman clutch bow tie's arm.

Preston didn't miss the gesture either. "You two know something about this?"

The man cleared his throat. "Not a thing. I've been strictly working your strategy."

Preston looked at the woman. She clearly wanted to melt into the gravel lot. Maeve resisted the urge to run to her side to shield her from the bully.

"Okay. It was me. I submitted it," the woman confessed in a small, scared voice.

Preston stared at her. "Wilma. Why?"

"Why not, Preston? It might help us save this place."

Preston blew out a breath. "These greedy folks just want to make money off our community."

He patted Wilma on the shoulder. "We can rebuild ourselves. It's what our families would have wanted."

Maeve said, "Wadsworth isn't trying to con your community. Our only goal is to preserve Black history."

"Come on, lady. You're not talking to some country hick. You're just here to cheat us like they cheated my grandfather. Every year he applied for subsidies. Subsidies he was owed just like the white farmers. That he was owed as an American farmer. But every year they came up with another reason to deny him. Destroyed hundreds of Black farms across this country."

Maeve could only purse her lips. Nothing she could say would refute the truth he'd spoken.

"As a museum, we want to build an exhibit to showcase what they achieved and give hope to—"

"Have a good trip home, Ms. Evans," he said dismissing her. "I need you two to get an early start tomorrow. Follow up on the roofing contractors and donors." He turned and stalked toward a blue SUV.

Maeve drove to the small motel in Hayes Station where she'd booked a room. She could have stayed in the largest city in the county where there were newer hotels, but she loved to absorb the feel of the places she was working on. It made the history come alive for her. That's what she hoped this exhibit on the Hayes Station community would do for those who experienced it.

Hayes Station was so quiet and peaceful. Not that she was knocking city life. Born in DC, she loved living in the heart of the nation. But something special and calming was blowing in the June breeze in this little town.

The Spring Inn had seen better days. The exterior needed painting. The furniture in the lobby was faded. Well, she hadn't expected five-star luxury. Working shower and Wi-Fi was all she needed. A young man running a buffer over the gleaming hard wood lobby floor pushed his machine aside to let Maeve get to the desk.

"Hello there. You must be Ms. Evans from the museum. I'm Noreen."

Noreen's huge smile was welcome after that contentious encounter with Preston.

"I am and I hope you can put up with me for a few days. Are you the owner, too?"

Noreen smiled proudly. "My mother opened Spring Inn twenty-five years ago with money my grandfather left her. Here's your key. Now we don't have a restaurant, but Josie's café is a short five miles down I-88. She's open until nine. Best smothered pork chops you'll ever eat."

"She serve a good breakfast, too?" Maeve asked.

"Hotcakes so delicious you have to push yourself from the table."

"I'll try her then." Maeve pulled up her map app. "Does this look like the right way to get to the Hayes Station cemetery?"

Noreen squinted at Maeve's phone. "I guess. I'm not good with all this tech stuff. Why are you headed there?"

"Our exhibit, should Preston Hayes agree to participate, will include replicas of some of the family headstones. I have to make sure the information I have is right."

"Evening, Noreen," a familiar voice said.

Maeve turned her head slightly. It was the real estate developer.

Noreen's smile evaporated just long enough for Maeve to notice. She brought it back quickly.

"Lucas."

"Missed you this evening."

"Short-handed this evening. Heard it was lively."

He flashed a look at Maeve. "I just want to make sure that as a member of the community council, you still agree with our direction. Renovations under my plan will revive this old place. Bring in more money than your folks ever dreamed."

Noreen's shoulders stiffened. "My family has been here longer than yours. Worked from sunup to sundown to keep this place going. I'm not letting it go."

Lucas flashed a just-landed-a-sale grin. "Knew we could count on you."

He turned to Maeve. "How you like our little community? We're going to be big news."

"Yes, who would have thought so much history would be tucked away in this little Indiana county? May I ask how that's going to fit into your development plan?"

"What? The history? Humph. It doesn't. Hayes Station is about the future." He gave Noreen one last glance. "Talk soon."

MAEVE'S ROOM WAS COZY. Decorated in purple and yellow with a small round table where she could work. Fresh yellow carnations on the table.

After a shower, she powered up her laptop and wrote an email to her boss summarizing her encounter with Preston Hayes. She thought about the people who were at the community meeting. How much their lives could improve through exposure of the exhibit highlighting the historic community.

She opened her tablet to the Hayes Station file and flicked

through the photos. Her heart swelled with pride every time she reviewed the story of Elias and Jonas Hayes, two brothers and former slaves who escaped from Kentucky to free Indiana and established a prosperous Black farming town in the 1850s. The exhibit would showcase farming tools they developed, handmade quilts and a tribute to the schoolhouse the community established.

She opened Preston's file. Maybe reading it for a hundredth time would give her a clue for how to negotiate with the man. She leaned back in her chair. Preston graduated from Harvard Business School with top tier grades. He'd been an investment banker at Simmons and Hughes. For how long she didn't know because all that company would tell her was that he'd worked there until two years ago. Not one mention of him on the company website. No social media accounts.

It was as if Preston's previous life had disappeared into a witness protection program.

Lucas Foster was another story. He bragged about record real estate listings and sales. He claimed to have a major development for Hayes Station in the works but offered no details. He'd said the community's history didn't matter. That made her shiver. She couldn't let this history be lost. She had to convince Preston to work with her.

THE NEXT MORNING, fortified by a breakfast of pancakes and smoked sausage at Josie's café, Maeve headed for the Hayes Station cemetery. The app gave her clear directions to the location. She didn't stop at the cemetery office building, but followed the path on her app.

The Hayes section was in the back and on a hill. Some of the family plots were well-kept and even had fresh flowers on the graves. Others hadn't been maintained or pruned for a while. Maeve was glad she'd opted for flat shoes rather than heels that would tear up the grass. As she walked, Maeve felt as if some invisible spirit was guiding her along.

Maeve got to a hill near the back of the cemetery. She gasped as she read the words on the first headstone. She felt the rush she usually felt when she had a new historical find. Wilson Hayes. 1845-1925. This was it. The Hayes Family section.

With her tablet opened to the sketch of the plot, Maeve almost tip-toed among the graves, checking them off the diagram she'd printed out.

There he was. Elias Hayes himself. His monument was shaded by a magnificent oak tree. Maeve took a moment to honor this pioneer – farming genius some would say.

Next to the tree was a small wooden cross. A make-shift grave? There was no name on it. If it was a grave, it would be too small for a human. Had someone buried their pet here?

So, there were forty-one headstones instead of the forty on the application Wilma submitted.

Maybe Wilma could tell her something about the small grave.

PRESTON'S OFFICE was a large trailer set up kitty-corner to what originally was the community school. It was established in 1865 and is now a museum. Maeve took several photos of the run-down building with her tablet.

Preston's loud angry voice reached her ears before she cleared the first step of the trailer. The guy just couldn't control himself. When she opened the door, she could see his anger was justified this time.

It looked like a tornado had roared through the place. Pictures were scattered on the floor. Desk drawers had been pulled out and the contents dumped in piles. Files had been flung everywhere.

Wilma was in tears.

Preston was yelling into his phone. "Lucas Foster is behind this. Gets questions about his plan so he tries to destroy me before we can present anything to the community. If you don't pick him up, I will, sheriff."

He punched off the call and trained his angry eyes at Maeve. "As you can see, we're a little busy right now."

"Can I help?" She directed her question to Wilma as she knew what his answer would be.

"We don't—" Preston's phone rang. "I'll be right there."

He cursed and snapped off the call. "That was Everett," he said to Wilma. "Someone broke into the warehouse where we're storing our artifacts. The Sheriff is sending a couple of deputies over here. I need you to help them."

Wilma nodded.

Preston was out the door, Maeve right behind him following his racing SUV along a winding road through woods, finally kicking up gravel and stopping before a large warehouse. She parked behind him.

Everett was leaning unsteadily at the open door of the warehouse. "Cousin, they already had a box on a truck. Clocked me before I could even get in the door. Gone before my head could stop swimming."

Preston bolted into the building.

Maeve and Everett followed.

Maeve's anxiousness at what they'd find was quickly replaced by relief from the sight of rows of crates that were untouched. It looked like Preston had done everything right to preserve the precious farm artifacts. Boxes were on pallets that were at least ten feet off the floor so they wouldn't get wet if there was a flood. Preston scurried among the crates, examining each one.

"It's okay. That one pallet they took only had a few minor tools in it and some quilts."

"You're sure, cousin?" Everett asked. "What do you think they were after?"

"It's Lucas. He just wants to eliminate his competition," Preston said. Then he noticed Maeve. "Why are you still here? Between you and that thief, Lucas, I don't need any more help. Go back to civilization."

"Now, Preston. You can't blame her for Lucas," Everett said.

"Looks like you need all the help you can get," Maeve said and spun on her heels and headed back to her car.

Maeve drove back to Hayes' office trailer. Wilma was still cleaning up the mess the vandals had made. Everett joined them a few minutes later.

"Let me help," Maeve said, bending to pick up a photo. It was fascinating. "What a handsome family."

"Oh, that's Mrs. Collins' folks. They came here shortly after the Hayes'. My, the stories she can tell."

"Yeah, her family was just as much a staple as the Hayes," Everett said. "Thought you could still use some help."

"We're making progress, but I definitely can," Wilma said.

Maeve began to fill a box. "This may sound like a strange question for me to ask, but do you know anything about a small, unmarked grave in the back of the Hayes family plots? Your application listed 40 plots in the Hayes' family area, but I counted 41."

Wilma scrunched her face up in puzzlement. "I'm sure what I submitted was right. Everett?

"First I've heard of it." he said. "Course I haven't been up there in a long, long time."

Shoot. She was going to have to go back and do one final check. They couldn't have a mistake in the exhibit and perhaps they could get a headstone for it.

The wind had stirred up when Maeve reached the cemetery. Almost as if the ancestors felt the disturbance in their community. The hike to the top of the area seemed harder than before. When she made it, her jaw dropped. The cross was cast aside, and the grave was now a hole.

"Looks like I got here just in time."

Maeve whipped around to see Preston coming toward her. He was holding a small shovel.

Lord, was he really crazy? Maybe he'd gone off the grid the last two years because he was a serial killer. Maybe...

"I don't know how you figured out something of value was buried there, but I'll take my property now," Preston said.

Maeve took a step back from him. "You're accusing me of stealing?"

Preston grabbed her tote bag and dumped its contents on the ground.

"What are you doing?"

Preston ran his hand over the items. Looked up at her. "That's all right. I'm going to have the police search you and your hotel room."

Maeve bent down to put her items back in your tote. "You do that. Nutcase."

MAEVE WAS SEETHING. She was sure steam was coming out of her ears. How dare he bully her.

"Are you okay, Ms. Evans?" Noreen said from behind the desk.

Maeve took a deep breath to calm herself. "I will be. Can I ask you a question?"

"You and Lucas Foster had a discussion yesterday when I arrived. You looked a little upset."

"Really? No, I wasn't upset."

"Actually, you seemed on the verge of tears."

Noreen looked at the floor. "He was just making sure I'm supporting his development plan."

"It seemed like more than that. Almost like an unspoken threat."

Noreen was silent.

"I'm told I'm a good listener," Maeve said.

Noreen cleared her throat. "Two years ago, the state was going to shut us down because it needed so many upgrades. I just didn't have the money. Lucas offered me a loan. I had no choice. I didn't know what strings would be attached to it."

"Like voting with him on every issue," Maeve said.

Noreen nodded. "And a ridiculous loan rate. He never lets me forget it. Said even if the deal went through, he might still take my Inn. I don't know what to do. He probably owns the mortgages on half the community. The only people he can't intimidate are Mrs. Collins and Preston. They've been wise with their land."

WHOEVER CAME up with the term curb appeal must have had Mrs. Collins in mind. Her yard was like a lush green carpet. Flower beds were resplendent with bright red roses, yellow daylilies and other exotic flowers Maeve couldn't name. The sweet fragrance of lavender followed her as she strode past the exquisite garden paradise leading to the front door of Mrs. Collins' well-kept brick home.

Mrs. Collins opened the door with a smile.

"Thank you for seeing me," Maeve said.

"As I said on the phone, I want to ask you some questions that might help me win over the community."

"I'm open to anything that gets us out of this mess."

Inside was just like Mrs. Collins. The large living room was elegantly furnished. There were glass cases along a long wall that were filled with photos. Photos on every table in the room. Photos covering the walls. Black people of all ages and shades.

"Your photos are amazing," Maeve said, thinking how she'd love to have copies for some of them for the exhibit.

"My prized possessions. Especially my tintypes. They're from the 1870s. Like this one."

She led Maeve to a glass case.

"Yes, when photos were made using a thin sheet of metal."

"You do know your history," Mrs. Collins said. "My third great grandparents. Darcy and Melinda Collins, in their Sunday best. Worked sunrise to sundown to run their farm but always made time for church."

"He worked with the Hayes family?"

"Heavens yes. He and Elias Hayes were like brothers. Shared all their ideas for growing good crops. Looked out for one another."

Maeve was mesmerized by the photos. She wanted to take photos with her tablet, but she didn't want to offend Mrs. Collins. On one the tables there was a photo of three familiar looking young guys.

"Is that Preston Hayes?"

Mrs. Collins smiled. "You have a good eye. And Preston's cousin, Everett, and Lucas. Thick as thieves in high school."

"Why did they stop being close?"

"Preston got scholarships and went away to college. The other two didn't care about getting an education. After the flood, their families' farms went under. Lucas went into real estate. Everett worked odd jobs. Preston hired him on the community project."

"Why did Preston and Lucas become such enemies?"

Mrs. Collins thought a minute. "Lucas was always chasing money. A showboat. Preston was always looking to do good. He's all bark and no bite."

TALK ABOUT A CONTRAST. Overgrown weeds. Brown grass where there was any. Sagging porch. Preston Hayes' sure didn't seem to care about his home. Is this what he wanted for the community?

When Maeve knocked on the outer door, it shook like it was going to fall off the hinges.

She walked around to the back of the house. The small porch and tiny patio were in the same bad shape as the rest of outside. There was a large greenhouse at the end of the backyard.

Maeve walked to the greenhouse and tried the side door. Locked. She looked in the window, blinked in amazement. She'd never seen corn stalks so tall they touched the ceiling. The tomatoes were big as grapefruits. Strawberries the size of golf balls. She took out her tablet and captured what she could. What was going on with this guy?

Back in her car, she called Ava.

"Hello, sis," Ava sang. "About time you checked in."

"I'm going to email you some photos. They're a little fuzzy, but you'll get the idea."

"Just what am I supposed to do them?"

Maeve gave Ava a short version of what had happened in Hayes Station.

"Send them," Ava said.

Preston was alone in his trailer office. He looked up at her through knitted eyebrows. "Lady, I had a really disgusting day. I don't need you to add to it."

"I'm not leaving until I get some answers. Maeve opened her tablet, scrolled through the photos she'd taken through the window of his greenhouse.

Hayes shot up from his seat. "You were on my property? That's trespassing."

"Why are you hiding those beautiful crops you're growing? How is that helping the community?"

"You tell me, Miss Doctor of History candidate."

Maeve blinked at him. "What's that supposed to mean? I have bad intentions because I'm working on my doctorate?"

"You said yourself this exhibit could be well received. That would certainly give your career a boost."

"Unlike you, I'm not hiding anything. My background is out there for the world to see. You know what? Maybe I'll call one of my public relations contacts and tell them how you're saving the community. Turn you over to our fair and balanced media."

"You really have no idea what you're talking about."

"Educate me."

With a sigh, Preston lifted a backpack off the floor and pulled out an oversized book.

The cover featuring a tall Black man standing among huge stalks of corn was mesmerizing.

The title was fitting. *From Hayes Fields to Your Table.*

Maeve opened to the table of contents. There were chapters on everything Hayes farming did, from its seeding to harvest to irrigation.

"My grandfather taught me everything that had been passed on to him from our ancestors. He told me the stories about the size of the crops we grew and sold throughout the county."

Maeve kept paging through the book. "This is incredible."

Preston plopped down in his chair. "I was good at what I did. Helping selfish rich people makes millions to hoard. When my grandfather decided he'd had enough and was going to sell, I just couldn't let all that he worked for be forgotten."

"You've been secretly working on this for the last two years?"

Preston nodded. "Rented a little space three counties over where no one knows me. Kept this mock-up under lock and key in my SUV. I put everything on a jump drive because I didn't want it floating on the cloud where just anybody could grab it."

Maeve just looked at him.

"Dumb, I know. And useless because I'm sure Lucas has gotten his grubby hands on it."

"How would Lucas know you were even writing a book?"

Preston hunched his shoulders. "You know I've been rolling that around in my head because I didn't tell anyone about it. If there's a dollar to be had that crook will sniff out a way to get it. I didn't think he was smart enough to figure out I'd buried the jump drive with my ancestors. Didn't think anyone would notice that little grave. But you did."

Maeve's phone buzzed.

"Honey, I have never seen crops like that before. Is the whole community like that?" Ava said. The excitement in her voice told Maeve it was okay to put her on speaker.

"It can be with a little help."

"We just got a line of funding from some new grants. I think Hayes Station is the perfect project. What else can you send me?"

"There's a manuscript—"

"Email it."

"How are you going to do that?" Preston asked after Maeve ended the call.

"We're going to get that jump drive. Ask Wilma to call an emergency meeting for this evening. Then let's stop by your greenhouse."

———

THEY WERE PACKED into Preston's trailer office like sardines. Lucas bounced in flashing his salesman grin.

"Preston, my brother, we could have used my office. Good news. We are closer to a deal than ever."

"These good people are anxious to hear the details," Mrs. Collins said.

"Umm, well, I didn't know you'd be calling this meeting so soon. I don't want to get into the weeds on this since there are still a few items to work out."

There were a few groans from the residents.

"You realize he never had a plan except to take the community's money," Preston said. "I have more than that."

He and Maeve uncovered the table they'd set up to reveal vegetables from Preston's greenhouse.

"Will you look at that," Mrs. Collins said. She picked up a tomato. "That's how we used to grow them."

"And using my family's techniques we can again. Free of chemicals. Crops we can grow to feed our families. Sell to market. Maybe you want to open a restaurant and serve farm-to-table food."

"How? Where's the money going to come from?" Mrs. Collins asked.

"I'll let our—eh—friend explain," Preston said gesturing to Maeve.

"Your Department of Agriculture provides grant money to rebuild and rejuvenate farming communities. My contact who approves the projects believes we can get a grant that will cover all that we need to do, including shoring up the water systems to prevent the kind of flooding that wiped out your farms. Since it's a grant, the community doesn't have to pay it back."

"Come on. You can't fall for this," Lucas sputtered. "When has the government helped people like us?"

"What about our mortgages?" Noreen asked. "What if we need help there?"

"Hey, haven't I taken care of you all this time?" Lucas sputters.

"Yeah, to line your own pockets," Noreen snapped back. I'm going to sue you for the mess you've made of mine."

"Me too," a man said. "Can you help us there, history lady?"

Maeve looked at Preston.

"I still have a few banker friends from my days on Wall Street." Preston said. "We'll get to the right people."

"The heck you will," Lucas blustered. "I'm in charge here."

Preston laughed. It was the first time Maeve had heard that from him. Even Wilma looked surprised.

"Sure, you are. Folks, Lucas here has been trying to sell his house and shady real estate business for over a year. He never planned to help our community."

Gasps escaped around the room.

Mrs. Collins stepped forward and gave Lucas a stare only an elder queen could give. "We take care of each other in Hayes Station. Always have. Always will."

"Now you can return the jump drive that has my family's hard work on it before the police get here," Preston said.

"I don't know anything about a jump nothing."

"Hand over my property."

"For once he may be telling the truth." Maeve said. "You might want to talk to Wilma and Everett."

Everett whipped his head around to stare at Maeve. "Talk to who?"

"You and Wilma are the only two people who knew about that extra grave after I told you. One of you must have figured out Preston had hidden something valuable there."

Wilma clutched her hands to her chest. "I would never."

"I know you wouldn't, Wilma. You cried over how the vandals destroyed this office."

"Hayes Station is my home. I want to save it," Wilma said.

"That leaves you, Everett. How did you know Preston was writing a book?"

"Right. How would I unless he told me, which he didn't."

"But you found out about it and orchestrated the break-ins here and the warehouse. That didn't turn up the book. Then I told you about the extra grave."

Preston walked over to Everett.

Everett took a step back. "C'mon, cousin. You know me better than that."

"She's right. I didn't tell anyone about the book or where I'd hidden the jump drive," Preston said.

"How'd you know about the book?" Maeve asked.

Everett tugged at his yellow bow tie. "Heard him telling his gramps on the phone about the book. How big the crops were. But he didn't trust me enough, his cousin, to let me in on the deal. Been scraping all my life. Time for that to stop."

"It wasn't about you," Preston said to Everett. "It wasn't about me. It was about saving our community."

Everett stared at Preston. Then he reached into his inside jacket pocket and produced a small plastic bag with the jump drive and handed it to Preston.

THE FOLLOWING SEPTEMBER, the Hayes Station Farming exhibit opened at the Wadsworth Museum to record attendees and acclaim. Maeve hosted the Hayes Station community, including Preston's grandfather, Elliott Hayes, and his father, Joseph Hayes.

From Hayes Fields to Your Table by Elliott and Preston Hayes, was an instant bestseller and was approved as a textbook at Historically Black Colleges and Universities and a top agricultural university. Hayes Stations farmers' crops were thriving thanks to his ancestor's methods.

No one was interested in buying Lucas' real estate company. The empty building he left behind was turned into affordable office space for rent to entrepreneurs.

THE SACRED BARN
BY RAMONA G. HENDERSON

When most people pay their respects to the dead, they go to a cemetery or chapel. When I pay my respects to Harley Williams, I go to a barn. It's the last place I saw Harley alive and where I found him dead.

The Williams' farm was adjacent to my grandfather's farm and their house was a little less than a mile from where I grew up. My dad wasn't a farmer but all our neighbors were. My family lived on a three-acre corner of my grandfather's farm. The land was a wedding gift to my parents.

Five days a week Dad drove the ten miles to town where he managed a farm equipment company. Mom took care of me, my two younger sisters, and the house.

I could have gone in a four or five-mile radius of the countryside and not found enough boys to make up a baseball team, let alone two. My sisters tended to play with their doll house and other things that didn't hold my interest. So, I spent a lot of time doing things I could do alone: riding my bike, hiking in the woods, building things with my Erector Set or Lincoln Logs, and reading everything I could get my hands on.

I also spent a lot of time helping my mother and grandmother with the gardening and helping my grandad and Harley Williams with farm chores. Harley wasn't officially my godfather but he was the closest I had to one. It got to the point I was spending more time with him than my grandad. The reason I loved being with Harley so much was because he treated me with a kind of respect that I didn't receive from other adults.

I failed an English exam when I was nine years old because I didn't read the material. Although I liked to read, I thought the assignment was a boring waste of time. My mother asked me, "How does it feel to be a failure because of pure laziness?" When I told Harley about it, he said, "Well, you must have learned something from the experience. What did you learn?"

"I learned I should not disappoint my parents and my teacher. I learned it doesn't pay to be lazy."

"Did you learn you should never do it again?"

"Yes."

"Then you're not a failure. I think you learned a great deal."

When the weather was too bad to work the fields, Harley was usually in his workshop, where he fashioned amazing wood carvings. A couple of them had won first place at the Indiana State Fair. Sometimes people hired him to do special projects for their home or business. He started teaching me how to carve farm animals and birds when I was nine and trusted me to use some of his best tools. Years later some of the carvings we made together were the first things I placed on my bookshelves when I opened my law office.

It was July 10, 1958. I'd just turned thirteen and got a new bicycle for my birthday. I rode my bicycle to Harley's, anxious to show it to him. As I was about to turn onto the long driveway, I saw two men run out of the barn. I brought my bike to an abrupt halt and skidded on the gravel. I quickly backed up a couple of feet to hide behind the cedars at the end of the lane. The men hurriedly ran around the side of the barn, crossed the pasture, and headed for the woods. I thought no one was home and the men were stealing something from the barn, but I didn't see anything in their hands. When I was certain they were far enough away so they couldn't hear me, I leaned my bike against the trees and ran to the barn. I've never been more horrified by anything I've seen in my whole life. Harley Williams was hanging by a rope attached to the hayloft. Blood covered the left side of his face. Terrified, I ran from the barn to the backdoor of the house and banged on the door. No one answered, so I banged harder, and the door opened because it wasn't locked. I froze. I couldn't make myself go inside for fear of what I might find. I ran to my bike and peddled to my grandparents' house as hard as I could.

I HURRIED into the kitchen where my grandma was making a blackberry cobbler. I felt as if my stomach had turned inside out, and I vomited in the middle of the kitchen.

My grandma quickly took hold of me by my shoulders. "What's happened? Did you fall off your bicycle?" She began checking my arms and legs. "Did you get another snake bite?"

I finally managed to say, "Sheriff."

"Sheriff, you want me to call the sheriff?"

I nodded my head frantically. "Yes, it's Mr. Williams. In his barn."

Grandma led me to a chair and sat me down. Then she grabbed the receiver from the wall phone in the kitchen and called the sheriff's department. "I need someone to come quickly. This is Mrs. Arthur Decker. Something's happened at Harley and Bess Williams' farm on rural route three. No, sir, I don't know, but something has happened in their barn. My grandson saw something there and it's scared him half to death. He ran into my kitchen, and he can barely speak. Please hurry."

Grandma walked me over to the sink and had me rinse my

mouth with cold water. Then she had me lie down on the couch with a cool cloth on my head. She telephoned my mother and told her to come. My mother and sisters must have run the whole way because they showed up in record time. My sisters kept watch at the window, and about twenty minutes later, they saw a sheriff's car pull into the Williams' place. They were all fixated on the scene up the road for the rest of the afternoon. I had no desire to look. I knew what the sheriff had found there. And when my mother told me she saw the Williams' car pull into their lane, I knew Mrs. Williams was safe because she had not been home when those men were on the farm. I found out later she had been at her oldest daughter's house all day helping decorate the nursery for the baby that was expected in a couple of months.

———

THE NEXT MORNING Grandad drove me to the sheriff's office, and Dad met us there. Grandad went to run errands and said he would be back to take me to lunch. One of the deputies took us to a large room and had us sit at a long oak table that smelled of furniture polish. There was a tray on the table with Cokes, empty glasses, and a pitcher of ice. The deputy told us to help ourselves and that the sheriff would be with us shortly. Dad poured us two Cokes and we sipped them while we waited.

I had calmed considerably and was able to give Sheriff Ed Rayburn a more detailed description of what I had seen at Harley's farm. The two men were of average height and weight. They were both white. One had very dark hair, and the other was almost blonde. They both wore jeans and leather work boots. The one with light hair ran out of the barn first. He had on a blue plaid short-sleeved shirt. The other man wore a denim shirt with the sleeves rolled up, and something was sticking out of the left back pocket of his jeans. I thought it was a pair of work gloves. They turned to the south side of the barn and then ran as fast as they could to the woods.

"Did you see their faces?" asked Sheriff Rayburn.

"They turned so quickly, I only saw them from the side, and they were too far away."

"So, you could see a pair of gloves in the one man's pocket, but you couldn't see their faces?"

"I saw the back of them. That's where the gloves were, in his back pocket."

"I see."

"You knew Harley Williams well, didn't you, Charlie?"

"Yes, sir."

"When was the last time you spoke to him?"

"The day before yesterday."

"Did you notice anything different about him? Did he seem sad?"

"No, sir. He was cleaning stalls in his barn, and when he finished, he took me to his workshop and showed me a rocking chair he bought for his grandbaby's nursery. Mrs. Williams brought us lemonade and then I helped her water her vegetable garden."

"So, he didn't seem sad or worried?"

"No, sir, not at all."

"Now, Charlie, when you found Mr. Williams in the barn, why didn't you go into the house and use the telephone there to call us? You said the door was unlocked."

"I was afraid to go into the house because I didn't know where Mrs. Williams was. I was afraid something might have happened to her, too."

"I see."

It got to the point where it seemed to me the sheriff was asking me the same questions over and over, like he was hoping for a different answer. Then he said, "A lot of young boys like to exaggerate things. Do you ever do that, Charlie? Are there times when you don't tell the truth or maybe stretch it a bit?"

I could see my dad's jaws tighten. It was becoming clear to me that he was not happy with the way the sheriff was talking to me. He interrupted us. "Excuse me, Sheriff Rayburn. My boy doesn't lie. The two times he fibbed to us were once when he was seven and he denied putting a toad in his sister's rain boot and when he was nine, he lied about reading his English assignment. Harley Williams was like another grandfather to him. He would never lie about anything that had to do with Harley's death. If Charlie says there were two men there yesterday, they were there. And I for one am grateful he was not close enough for them to see him. God knows what may have happened to him."

Sheriff Rayburn leaned toward us. "Look, Jack, I can't assume those men did anything to harm Harley. Your son here didn't see them do anything. I don't know why Harley would take his own life but that's what it looks like. Those men may have been running because they found him hanging in the barn and got frightened just like Charlie did. Besides, everybody liked Harley Williams. Nobody would want to kill him."

"If those men found Harley, why didn't they call the sheriff?" asked Dad.

"Maybe they went into the barn to steal something. It happens a lot. If they were thieves, they sure as hell wouldn't call the law."

"If they went there to steal, where was their vehicle? How were they planning to haul things away?"

Sheriff Rayburn sounded irritated. "Maybe they were looking for something small like money."

"Oh, come on, in the barn? Dammit, everybody knows Harley was looking forward to the birth of his first grandchild and his younger daughter is graduating from college next year. He wouldn't kill himself. He wouldn't do that to his family. And everybody knows he was the most outspoken farmer opposed to the oil drilling they're trying to start doing in this county. Maybe somebody involved in that is responsible for his death."

Sheriff Rayburn seemed to want to ignore the mention of the oil drilling. "Well, the horrible heat and drought this summer has really hurt the crops. Maybe he was having financial difficulties."

"Come on, you know every farmer in this county deals with the situations the weather brings. It's part of being a farmer. They don't kill themselves because of it. There wouldn't be a farmer left in the state if that was true. Now if you're done here, my father is waiting to take Charlie to lunch."

"He can go. If I think of any other questions, I'll call you."

As we left the building, I asked my dad why the Sheriff was so set on thinking that Harley killed himself.

"I don't know," said Dad. "But that's the best question I've heard this morning."

THE FOLLOWING DAY WAS A SATURDAY. Dad and Grandad decided to go and search the woods on Harley's farm. I tagged along, not sure what we were hoping to find. After spending about three hours combing the wooded area, we found it just as Sheriff Rayburn had said. The ground was so hard and dry we couldn't see any footprints, not even our own. There were so many paths left by deer and cattle in the thickets it was impossible to tell if any men had walked through there. Discouraged, hot and tired, we decided to call it quits and head back. As we turned to leave, something of light color caught my dad's eye. He walked over and picked it up between his thumb and forefinger. "Could this be one of the gloves you saw?"

"They were a light gray color like that."

Grandad looked at the glove. "It doesn't look as if it's been out in the weather long. Looks new. How the hell did the sheriff, and his men miss this?"

Our find encouraged us to search for another half hour, but we didn't find anything else. So, we went to Grandad's house, where we sat on the porch and drank tall glasses of iced tea.

"I'll take this glove to the sheriff's office," said Dad.

"What else can we do?" I asked.

"I'm not sure," said Dad. "I suppose we could ask around and see if any of the people supporting the oil drilling have said anything threatening toward Harley."

"I'll call some of the other farmers and see if we can come up with a schedule for feeding and watering Harley's animals until Bess can come up with a permanent arrangement," said Grandad. "This is going to be so hard on her."

Grandma sat the pitcher of iced tea on the wicker table next to us. "Did any of you think to feed and water her chickens?"

The three of us looked at one another. "No," I said.

"Those layin' hens won't last long in this heat without water."

"Don't worry. Charlie and I will go back and take care of them," said Dad. "Then maybe we'll go on into town and see if some of the guys have gathered at the Co-op. Someone may know who didn't like Harley and his opposition to the drilling because it would hurt the land and the wildlife."

Grandad stood from the wicker rocker he was sitting in. "Yes, and I'd like to know if there's some reason Sheriff Rayburn is so dead set on calling Harley's death a suicide."

Grandma shook her head. "I think you all need a bath before you go anywhere and a good checking over for ticks too. And I don't think it's a good idea for Charlie to be around those men today. You know they're all going to be asking him questions."

<hr>

WE PILED into Dad's 1955 Chevy Nomad and drove to town, where we dropped the glove off at the sheriff's office. One of his deputies, Deputy Yates, was sitting at the desk and took it from my dad. Dad told him the exact location where it was found. "That corner of the woods is right next to the wooded areas on the Dawson farm. It would have been easy for them to hide a vehicle in there and take that old lane to get back to the road. Sometimes hunters park there during hunting season but nobody would be going in there this time of year so they could have come and gone unseen."

The deputy looked the three of us over. "Sheriff Rayburn ain't here today."

"How about you call him," said Grandad.

The deputy called the sheriff and explained what we had found and told him the location.

"He wants to talk to you," he said, pointing to my dad.

Dad took the receiver and listened. Then I heard him say, "You missed the glove. Don't you think you should go have another look? Maybe you missed something else." Then he handed the receiver back to the deputy.

"All right Sheriff. I understand." The deputy placed the receiver back on the phone cradle. He stood and said, "I think we're done here folks. If you don't mind, it's time for my lunch."

"So, that's it. You're not going to do another search?"

"Sheriff Rayburn says it's not necessary."

"You're looking at a glove we found out there this morning. Don't you think if you missed that you may have missed something else?"

"Like the Sheriff said, that glove don't mean anything as far as a court of law is concerned. It could have been dropped there by anybody. There's no way to connect it to the Williams death."

"It's the same color as the gloves in that man's back pocket," I said loudly, almost yelling.

"Come on," said Grandad. "Let's go get some fresh air. It stinks in here."

Deputy Yates gave us a disdainful glare as we walked out.

Dad was disgusted. "I can't believe what a pitiful excuse we have for law in this county. If I had stayed in there much longer, I might have hit him."

GRANDAD HAD BEEN TAKING me to the Farm Bureau Co-op since I was a small boy. I liked going there, especially on days when it was raining and the men couldn't work the fields. On those days the place was filled with men talking loudly so they could be heard over one another. Someone would always bring up the newest information coming out of research at Purdue University. Everyone exchanged ideas about farming. It wasn't raining that day and as we stood out front, we could tell the atmosphere inside was somber. Dad and Grandad agreed with Grandma's feeling that I shouldn't go into the Co-op, so I was given a couple of bucks and told to walk down to the soda shop for a sandwich and soda. It was a good place for a thirteen-year-old to wait, and I liked watching the older kids dance to the music from the jukebox. A guy with disarrayed Brylcreamslicked-back hair pressed buttons on the jukebox and Elvis Presley's "All Shook Up" blasted the place. The girls looked pretty with their ponytails swaying and the bottoms of their cotton skirts and bright colored summer dresses swirling as they spun around. I thought by watching them I might pick up some dance moves before I started high school. I hid in a corner booth and hoped none of my friends would come in and see me. I knew they would ask me questions about Harley, and I didn't want to talk about it. I ordered a second chocolate soda and sipped it slowly as I watched the clock on the wall. I bought some candy for my sisters and returned to the Co-op in an hour and a half, just as my dad had told me. I was anxious to hear what they'd found out.

Dad told me several of the men at the Co-op were worried Harley's death had to do with his opposition to the oil drilling, but no one could come up with a specific person they suspected.

He said one of our neighbors, John Dawson, suggested Bess Williams keep a loaded gun in her house.

Grandad said he thought there might be a reason Sheriff Rayburn wasn't keen on investigating Harley's death. A farmer named Arvin Hirsh told him that the sheriff would inherit his uncle Chester Rayburn's land when he died. "Could be Rayburn has some ideas about what he plans to do with that land. Plans that Harley wouldn't have agreed with."

I SAT STOICALLY at Harley's funeral, but when we left the cemetery, I burst into tears, and I was so embarrassed for my little sisters to see me cry. Dad put his arm around my shoulders and gave me a tight hug. "Never be ashamed to cry for the loss of someone you care about," he whispered. Harley was the first person close to me that I lost and the way he died made it even more painful.

Harley wasn't in the ground six months before Bess Williams started getting letters regarding leasing her farmland for drilling. She showed the letters to my family, and my parents and grandparents all felt some of them to be threatening. They made it sound like she had no choice but to sign a lease or sell them her farm.

Dad was furious someone would send letters like that to a widow. He had no faith that Sheriff Rayburn would provide Bess any help. Then my grandad remembered a time when Harley mentioned he had an older cousin who lived in the Washington D. C. area. The cousin was an attorney who wrote tax laws and had even presented arguments to the Supreme Court. Grandad suggested she call that cousin or write to him about her situation.

Bess told us the cousin, Theodore Schmidt, was eighteen years older than Harley and she had only met him twice. He had sent a letter with his condolences when he heard of Harley's passing.

About three weeks later, Bess received a phone call from Theodore Schmidt. He told her he was making a rare trip to Indiana to visit his sister and friends still living in the area and would be glad to look at the letters. He hadn't lived in the county since graduating from college, but he had kept in touch with several of his old law school classmates and was positive he could find someone practicing law in Indiana who could help her.

The following month Theodore and his younger sister made a

visit to Bess Williams. The circumstances of Harley's death also prompted him to make inquiries. He spoke to many of us that knew Harley, and he made a visit to Sheriff Rayburn. Theodore told my dad the sheriff kept pointing out that he was so much older than Harley and had very little contact with him in the past years that he didn't know what Harley was capable of or if he was depressed. He also said that he didn't have much faith in my story about seeing those men the day I found the body. Sheriff Rayburn thought I was in denial that Harley had killed himself. Mr. Schmidt was puzzled by how uninterested the sheriff was in the case. Theodore said he had asked about the blood on the left side of Harley's head and face. Sheriff Rayburn dismissed it as an injury sustained when Harley's head struck the edge of the hayloft as he jumped. The coroner's report stated it was possible but could have also been caused by a strike with a blunt object. The sheriff also downplayed the fact Harley had become a spokesman for the other farmers opposing drilling in the county.

Mr. Schmidt introduced Bess to an attorney named Warren Barker. He was the son of one of Mr. Schmidt's old classmates and he had no problem dealing with the oil company. Bess finally had peace of mind. Bess ended up renting half the farmland to my grandad and half to the farmer on the other side of her land, John Dawson. She sold all the animals except the chickens. With help from her neighbors and members of her church, she remained on the farm for five years. Then she decided to rent the house and move to a place close to her oldest daughter. Eventually, she sold the farmland to my grandad and John Dawson.

———

Two years after Harley's death, Sheriff Ed Rayburn signed a lease to allow drilling on the farm he had finally inherited from his uncle Chester. That certainly piqued everyone's curiosity. When he was up for re-election, he was voted out. The new sheriff was Leo Davis. He seemed to be a very fair man and took the law seriously. He fired a couple of the deputies and hired new men with experience. He investigated the Williams case, but he had nothing to go on. My conversation with Sheriff Davis was much different from being questioned by Ed Rayburn. Sheriff Davis believed I had seen two men coming out of the barn that day. He thought those men didn't live in our county and may have been from another state. They were probably hired by someone to kill Harley and had made it across the state line quickly after they had done the job. After talking to him, I no longer searched crowds of people hoping to find someone resembling one of the men I'd seen that day, and I stopped having nightmares about them returning. As the years went by, it seemed the only hope was for someone to slip up, and reveal something or maybe a deathbed confession.

Eventually, pumps were rocking throughout the county and the local utility company acquired large amounts of acreage for underground natural gas storage. As more and more drilling came about in the county, I could see that Harley was right. The creeks became contaminated with crude oil spillage killing the fish and other wildlife. But there was no stopping the progression of the drilling and the big utility companies as they invaded the land. Thankfully protecting the environment came to the forefront some years later, so all was not lost.

ED RAYBURN MADE a great deal of money from the oil drilled on his uncle's farm but didn't get to enjoy it for long. His charred body was found in his burning Cadillac DeVille at the bottom of a fifty-foot ravine off Highway 66 in the winter of 1965. I heard the attendance at his funeral was sparse.

After my grandfather and my dad had both passed on, I inherited the land and became what they call a gentleman farmer. My wife thought I was crazy when I wanted to refurbish the old Williams house and have a new roof put on the barn. Convincing her it would result in getting better tenants was all it took.

My oldest son studied agriculture at Purdue. He lives in the home where I grew up and it's had so much remodeling it doesn't even look like the same house on the outside. He formed a business with two other farmers and it's a big-time operation. Nothing like the farming that surrounded me when I was a child. I suppose that's what it takes to be successful in agriculture today.

As I stand in front of this barn, it's hard to believe it's been fifty-seven years since that day in July. Now I'm a grandfather and know that my time on this earth is limited. One day I'll hand over this farm to my son. I gave up any illusion that Harley's murder would ever be solved years ago, and most of those who cared are gone. If we'd had DNA profiling and all the technology available today in the 1950s, maybe Harley's murder could have been solved. Of course, I discovered many years ago the glove, along with any records of the Williams investigation, had disappeared. But for as long as I am able, I will come here to pay my respects in this place that still seems sacred to me. And when people bring up the local legend of Harley Williams and say, 'You know they say a farmer hanged himself in that barn,' I'll reply, "that's what they say, but if you have a few minutes, I'll tell you what really happened to Harley Williams."

THE PERFECT MARTINI
BY SHARI HELD

*D*ecember 27

Big fat snowflakes fell steadily from the December sky like oversize confetti. Nate Thompson shivered. God, he hated winter. Indiana's were particularly unpredictable. One minute, it's shorts and sandals. The next, it's so frigid a guy could freeze his nuts off. But his small hometown of Charity in the boonies of rural Indiana was his best bet for scoring big money. Fast.

Every strand of Nate's hair was tucked securely under his ski cap as he ducked into a CVS to pick up a few items before checking into a Motel 6. A bottle of Clairol's Natural Instincts hair dye transformed his golden mop into a mass of pecan-colored curls. No one would take him for the scrawny kid with a broken nose and bad teeth who once lived here. But he wasn't taking any chances. He changed into a clean pair of jeans and a Henley shirt and headed out for a beer.

He was on his second one when a red-headed chick slid onto the stool next to him at the bar.

"Do you mind, hon? It looks like the only seats left are at the bar. Tonight's the big night out for singles at Harley's."

Nate straightened a little taller on his bar stool and awarded her with his best shit-eating grin. "Be my guest. I wouldn't mind some company. I'm working my way to Florida." He stuck out his hand. "Sam Coulter."

She smiled at him. "Connie Davis."

"You from here?"

She grimaced. "Born and raised here. Will probably die here. Is it that obvious?"

Nate caught the bartender's attention. "Let me buy you a drink. What's your pleasure?"

"A rum and coke."

Nate winced.

"What's the matter?"

"Nothing. I've bartended in some of the swankiest casinos and night clubs creating all kinds of fancy concoctions. Don't take this the wrong way, but ordering a rum and coke is a near insult to me." He shuddered. "I'll do it against my better judgement for you though," he said, catching the bartender's attention and placing her order.

"Well maybe you can make me one of your fancy-smancy drinks sometime," she said as the bartender delivered her drink. "Convert me."

He leaned in closer. "There's nothing more I'd like to do right now."

"So, where you staying, Cute Buns?"

Nate took this as an open invitation. "Motel 6 on Grant. But how about I come to your place?"

"Naw. I'd rather stay with you. I'm on leave from work this week. Staying at the motel will be like I'm doing one of those staycations." She pointed her finger at his chest. "And you'll be the highlight."

Nate smiled. Things were looking up.

"How long will you be in town, anyway?"

"Depends. The bartender told me a place called Joey's is hiring temporary help for its New Year's Eve bash. Thought I'd give it a shot."

She put her glass down on the bar. "It just so happens my cousin works there. I can put a good word in for you if you want." She punched a number into her phone and talked to someone about getting him an interview. She turned to him after the conversation ended. "You have an interview at ten o'clock tomorrow morning." She polished off her drink in three big gulps. "Now, let's see if you can charm my pants off with one of your concoctions."

December 28

As he lit his first smoke of the morning, Nate glanced at the buxom redhead gently snoring in his bed. Connie something. The current temperature might be colder than a witch's tit, but there was nothing frigid about her. She possessed enough pent-up sexual energy to keep the Titanic afloat. Too bad he'd soon be skipping town, but there were plenty others like her where he was headed.

A glance in the plastic-framed, cracked mirror confirmed that, at forty, Nate still possessed a sensual bad boy appeal and washboard abs that ensured he could pick and choose a partner of the opposite sex whenever the urge hit him. Which was often. What was it that Chicago bar chick had purred into his ear last week? Oh, yeah. "Your eyes are like liquid sex." He snickered. Later that night, he'd given her some of that liquid sex in the parking lot.

This girl was a keeper while he was in town. Easy-going. Direct, but didn't ask too many questions. And as uninhibited as a precocious child. He'd used one of his favorite aliases with her—Sam Coulter.

Maybe he should have used another name. Last month's heist at Minnesota's Mystic Lake Casino Hotel as Sam Coulter had been a big bust. Everything had gone wrong. He didn't even score a shot at the safe. If Lady Luck hadn't been on his side, he would have been caught. After that fiasco, he'd suffered from crippling headaches for more than a week, compliments of a blow to the head by an overzealous security guard.

Normally, Nate would be basking in the sun's warm rays in Palm Beach by now, hobnobbing with rich divorcees and widows. Making easy money. Not stuck in the Midwest in the middle of a snowstorm trying to steal enough cash to winter over in the South.

Joey's Shangri-La Supper Club and Casino was the ticket. That's the sole reason Nate was back home again in Indiana. The nightclub, an elite mansion and estate back in the day, had become an instant hot spot for Midwest high rollers after Joey transformed it into a miniature version of West Baden, complete with an onsite hotel. It was an oasis of glamour among the cornfields.

Joey's was famous for its over-the-top New Year's Eve bash. He'd heard Joey brought in big-time entertainment for the annual event, charged an extravagant advance ticket price, and sat back in his easy chair watching his till grow fat. The obnoxious old fart.

Fifteen hundred patrons would each shell out three hundred bucks to walk through Shangri-La's doors and carouse in mindless abandon while ringing in the new year. And this year, Nate would be the one to profit from it. Not Joey.

Nate's nerves didn't start talking to him until Connie was showering. Was he fooling himself that this job would be a piece of cake? He doubted if Joey would connect him with the skinny kid who'd hung around with Joey's younger brother. That was fifty pounds, a nose job, and expensive veneers ago.

Still, something nagged at him.

Connie emerged before he could figure it out.

"Hey, you're up next, Cute Buns," she said, drying herself with a thick white towel. "I should be ready to leave by the time you're done."

Nate lathered up, wishing they'd shared the shower and wondering if she'd stick around for some more fun. As he turned to leave the bathroom, he did a double take. Odd. He'd sworn he'd scrunched the hair dye box and hid it at the bottom of the bathroom wastebasket. What was it doing in plain sight?

Nate slammed his fist on the porcelain sink. He was slipping. He'd experienced several episodes of that lately. Like forgetting to change out his ID so it matched his current alias. Little mistakes. With potentially big consequences. Fortunately, hair dye wasn't any big deal. The girl would probably think he was just covering the gray.

As she predicted, Connie was dressed and ready to go when he entered the bedroom. He propositioned her, but she bussed him on the cheek, took his spare key, and told him she'd see him later.

Before heading for the audition, Nate adjusted the collar on his crisp white shirt and checked his tight black Levi's for tufts of chenille from the white bedspread. His black loafers shone. The trick was to look sophisticated, but not too classy to put off Midwest sensibilities. He had his fake story down pat. He'd bartended in Vegas but was heading to Florida to be by his sick mother's side. Hoosiers eat up those small-town values. Mom, apple pie, and all that crap. He snorted. His mother would have traded him to the gypsies for a fifth of Johnnie Walker. Only reason she didn't is they didn't want him either.

Nate grabbed his wallet and checked his ID. It said Jake Thomas. Damn. He knew he was forgetting something. He replaced it with his Sam Coulter ID and stuck his wallet in his pocket. He was set. He locked the door and headed to Joey's.

A thin, harried-looking man carrying a clipboard came into the hall where Nate waited. "Coulter?"

"Here." Nate jumped up, a Cheshire cat smile on his face.

"Follow me." The man led him through a maze of hallways to the back of the venue, entered an office, and motioned for Nate to sit. "I'm Ken. You understand this job is temporary?" The man's bushy eyebrows rose above his black glasses as he locked eyes with Nate.

"Yes. I know it's a New Year's Eve gig."

"I see you want to bartend. We have bartenders. What I need is wait staff. There'll be several days training. You'll be paid a standard rate, plus time-and-a-half on New Year's, and any tips you earn. You okay with that?"

Nate nodded. Time to spew forth the bullshit. "You may have enough bartenders to cover the event, but I'll bet you don't have one that can match my moves. I've worked at the best places. Know all the trendy drinks."

Ken pursed his lips. "Trendy isn't exactly our style."

"But tasty is. Trendy and tasty together keeps people coming back for more. And that's more money in Joey's pocket." Nate placed his elbows on the chair arms and steepled his hands. "Tell you what. I'll train as a waiter, but during that time let me make a special cocktail each night for the boss man. If he adds one to the New Year's Eve menu, I bartend. If he doesn't, I'll shut my trap and be the best damn waiter you've ever seen come New Year's Eve. Whaddaya say?"

Nate slid back in his chair and watched the emotions flit over Ken's face.

"Deal. Report to the dining room at eight this evening. We'll see how you do. Joey's no push-over. You'd better deliver."

Nate expelled a jagged breath as he left Joey's and headed back to the motel. He'd start with one of his signature drinks—a mai tai, the official cocktail of Richard Nixon's presidency. But he didn't hold Nixon's disgraced legacy against it. He trusted Joey's would have a high quality 100-percent pot still rum. Rum was the star. Mai tais should be shaken, not stirred, like James Bond's martinis. The drink was surprisingly good, but it wouldn't knock Joey's socks off.

Connie should arrive soon. She was bringing some things from her place, plus lunch, compliments of the Kentucky Colonel. After eating, they'd watch TV, canoodle, and progress on to other things before he left for work. She'd be waiting for him when he returned from Joey's, and they'd do a repeat. It was a great set up.

Nate arrived back at Joey's twenty minutes early, introduced himself to the bartender on duty, explained the situation, and checked that they had all the mai tai ingredients.

"Is this the best quality rum you have?"

The kid laughed. "Joey only splurges on brands people ask for by name. We don't have much call for rum except for rum and coke. Those people aren't picky."

"I hear you. Hey, if you're still here when I make it, you want to see how it's done?"

"Sure. Joey always comes in at ten o'clock on the dot, after the kids are in bed and he's spent some time with the wife." He winked at that. "I'd bring him the drink around midnight, after he's had a chance to do whatever it is he does in there."

"Thanks for the tip. Anything else I should know?"

"Play it cool. If Joey detects any sign of weakness, he'll eat you alive. Good luck."

The bartender's tip made Nate's day. Since Nate would make the drink at the end of his shift, no one, Joey included, would find it odd that Nate always carried his duffel bag into Joey's office.

A few minutes before midnight, Nate stood outside Joey's office door, mai tai in hand, and knocked. Everything hinged on this moment. Would Joey recognize him? If he did, he'd throw Nate out on his ass quicker than a fox can raid a hen house. Worst case scenario, he'd call the cops.

"Come in," Joey bellowed. "And shut the door behind you."

"Hello, sir. I'm Sam, the one auditioning for a bartender position at your New Year's party." *Time to lay it on thick.* "It would be an honor to say I've worked your event, sir. I've worked in several casinos and resorts, but I've heard your New Year's Eve party is spectacular."

"You got that right. Best damn bash in the entire Midwest. And that includes Chicago."

Nate didn't detect a flicker of recognition. So far, so good. He held out the cocktail glass to Joey. "Try this. A bit of nostalgia. Women love it. Men love what it does to their women. It's pricy to make if you upgrade the rum and do it up right, but you can sell it for a premium."

While Joey was evaluating the specialty drink, Nate surveyed the office. Nothing had changed. Same banker's lamp on the desk, same pictures on the walls. Same Home Depot office safe topped with a half-dead plant in the corner. Nate cracked a smile. Barring any unforeseen circumstances, this heist was going to be a breeze.

He was familiar with that safe. Intimately. He'd dipped his hands into its steel belly twenty-some years ago. His take then was a measly two thousand bucks. But Joey had witnessed his misdemeanor and had nearly nabbed him. Nate hadn't taken any chances on Joey's goodwill. He'd hitched a ride with a trucker on I-74 and embarked on a life of crime. He'd lucked out, learning skills from the masters he met along the way, leading a life filled with cash for the taking, willing women, and the thrill of the game. No snot-nosed kids. No mortgage. No strings attached.

Joey returned the glass to the cocktail napkin and pushed it toward Nate. "Not bad." He puffed his cheeks out until he looked like a chipmunk storing seeds for the winter and shook his head. "But it didn't click with me. Don't come back tomorrow unless you can do better than this." He nodded toward the door.

Nate knew when he was being dismissed. "Oh, I'll be back, all right. And I can guarantee you'll be impressed with the next one." He exited as fast as a schoolkid when the recess bell rings, not giving Joey a chance to change his mind about tomorrow.

As he was leaving, he bumped into the friendly bartender.

"How'd it go with Joey? Did he like it?"

"Enough to keep me in the running. You're right. He's a tough nut to crack."

"That's Joey. He's an original. Doesn't want anyone knowing his business. Always keeps the shades drawn in his office. One guy told me Joey turns off his computer and cellphone when he holds meetings in his office."

"Haven't seen a safe like the one he has in a long while. Does he use that old relic as a safe? Or a plant holder?"

The kid slapped his back as if Nate had asked something funny. "Use it? That's *all* he uses. Doesn't believe in banks or electronic payments. I'm told that safe usually holds one hundred fifty to two hundred thousand dollars." He inched in closer to Nate and lowered his voice. "It's rumored the band he hired for New Year's Eve requires a three hundred fifty thousand payment. Cash only." He shook his head. "Those nut cases sure know how to find one another."

Nate whistled. "Who'd have thought a place like this would have so much cash lying around? I sure hope he has good security."

"He does. And his door is always locked when he's not here. Has so many bolts and latches on it, it takes him fifteen minutes to unlock them all. Well, gotta go. See you tomorrow."

That confirmed what Nate suspected. If everything the kid said were true, robbing Joey would be a cinch. Maybe this job was stacking up to be too good to be true. What if "Loose Lips" was feeding him shit info? Nate frowned, then shook his head. This job was getting under his skin. He was overthinking. What he needed was some mind-blowing sex.

Back at the motel Connie offered him a cold beer and her warm body. Afterwards, she asked questions.

"How'd it go with Joey?"

"He didn't bite on the first drink."

She put her arm around him and gave him a soft, lingering kiss on the lips. "I'm sure he will on the second." She ran her fingers through his hair. "So, tell me about yourself. You an only child?"

"Yep. My mom took one look at me and said 'no more.'"

"And you're headed to Florida to take care of her?"

"Sure am."

"What's her name? What city does she live in?" Connie dropped one shoulder so the spaghetti strap of her black negligee slid down, exposing even more of her breast, and smiled. "Maybe I'll come see you next time I have some time off."

And maybe I'll win the lottery. "Julia. She lives in Pensacola, in the Panhandle." He crunched his empty beer can and threw it in the wastebasket. A perfect shot. He'd been a fuck-up at school in everything but basketball. "Now, I think we can find something better to do than talk about dear old mom." Nate carried Connie to the bed and turned out the light.

After Connie was sleeping, Nate eased out of bed, sat at the desk, and doodled the layout of Joey's office. Joey's penchant for privacy was a godsend. The heist was straight-forward: On the night before New Year's Eve, he'd drug Joey with the cocktail, crack the safe, stash the cash in his oversize duffle bag, close the door to Joey's office behind him as usual, and leave Indiana in the rearview mirror. By the time they discovered Joey, Nate would have a new vehicle, a new alias, and a bag full of cash.

Life was good.

December 29th

The second night at Joey's, Nate spied a guy he'd gone to school with. Benny Cox, Class of 2000, the year Y2K had everyone's panties in a twist. Benny zeroed in on Nate from across the room, a puzzled look on his face. Nate tensed, then lowered his shoulders, and plastered a smart-ass look on his face.

Now we'll see how good my disguise is.

Benny sauntered over and stopped in front of him. "I thought you were someone I used to go to school with. But now I see I'm wrong. Sorry. Must be the lighting in here. But for a minute there I'd swear you were Nathan Thompson."

Nate laughed. "Just one of those faces, I guess." He stuck his hand out. "I'm Sam. Sam Coulter, temporary wait staff."

"Benny Cox, security. Good thing you're not Thompson. I catch him sniffing around here and he'll be in the slammer quicker than you can say scat."

As Benny turned to leave, Connie approached. Nate gave her the once over and whistled. "Hey, Babe. Looking good. You didn't tell me you were coming to Joey's tonight."

Connie twirled, playing the flirt. "I thought I'd surprise you. How's it going? Did Joey like tonight's drink?"

"Haven't given it to him yet. I'll do that right before I leave." Nate went back to work but kept his eye on her. In her knee-high leather boots and short silver dress, she attracted attention. She was friendly with several guys, including Benny Cox and some of Joey's management team. But why shouldn't she be? This was her town.

Nate rubbed his temples. His paranoia was getting out of hand. He'd fooled Joey. And now, Benny. And after tonight. there would be only one more night left before he hit the jackpot. He could do this.

After adding jalapeno juice and a dash of peppermint for a surprise twist in his special margarita concoction, he went to Joey's office and handed it to him.

Joey held eye contact over the rim of the glass while he took a sip. "This one has promise." He took another sip. "But it's not upscale enough for New Year's Eve. Sorry, kid. Better luck next time."

Nate smiled. *It will be better next time. But not the way you think.*

Connie was in the hallway when Nate walked out.

"You want a ride back to the motel? Nate asked. "Or did you drive?"

"I drove. I'm going to say a quick hello to my cousin and a few other folks, then I'll meet you back at the motel." She planted a big one on him.

After she arrived, they engaged in a little foreplay, some drinking, and a lot of hot sex. Nate's muscles relaxed and his mind was anywhere but on the job.

Connie kissed his cheek. "You know, I heard through the grapevine that Joey's impressed with your attitude. You make another great drink tomorrow and the bartending job's all yours."

Nate smiled and gave her a peck on the cheek before turning on his side to go to sleep.

I'll be long gone by then, Babycakes. Long gone.

DECEMBER 30TH

This was it. The big day. Nate's blood raced. His fingertips tingled. He was itching to make the heist, grab the money, and hit the road. He wished he hadn't told Connie his destination was Florida. Another slip. Even though she thought he was headed toward the Panhandle, in retrospect he should have told her he was headed to Georgia or Louisiana. He sighed. Too late to do anything about it now.

Tonight, all he had to do was slip his special ingredient—chloral hydrate—into Joey's cocktail. It would be a perfect martini for a perfect heist. One sip and Joey would be out for hours. Cracking Joey's safe years before was beginner's luck. He had tons of practice under his belt now. Tonight's job should go down as easy as Dom Perignon on New Year's Eve.

Nate kissed Connie goodbye and left for work. The poor girl didn't have a clue that this was her last kiss. That her staycation had ended.

He parked close to the back door to make for a quicker getaway. Never hurts to play it safe. Plus, it was snowing again. Snow mixed with icy pellets that stung when they hit his face.

On the job, he went through the motions like a robot. In his mind, he was already basking in the warmth of Palm Beach, ringing in the New Year with the Atlantic Ocean as a backdrop. At last, it was time to make Joey's final drink.

He knocked on Joey's door around midnight, as usual, duffel bag over his shoulder, martini in hand. But before he could go inside, one of the staff burst in.

"Joey, you're needed in the kitchen. There's a problem with one of the deliveries. A *big* problem."

Joey pulled himself out of his over-sized leather chair, then nodded at Nate. "Have a seat. I should be back in fifteen minutes."

Nate couldn't believe his luck. He set the martini on Joey's desk, then took a stab at the safe. He cracked it in five minutes, crammed as much cash as he could in his bag, and headed for the back door.

Only to run into Connie.

He put his arm around her and tried to edge forward toward the back door. "Hey, Babe, let's hightail it out of here. I'll meet you back at the motel." *Not.*

Connie wasn't buying it. Her face was stormy. She leaned into him until his back was against the wall.

"Not so fast, Sam. Or should I say Jake? Jake Thomas. That was what your ID said when I checked it while you were in the shower our first morning together."

"You checked my ID?"

"Sure did. I brushed off the hair dye at first. It's not unusual for men to dye their hair nowadays. But it was enough for me to start snooping. When I found you were using an alias, my suspicion-odometer took off in full gear."

Son of a gun. I did it again. The details keep messing me up.

"Connie, this isn't the time or place. Let's go back to the motel. I'll explain everything there." Nate rushed past her and took off around the corner, not giving her a chance to respond.

Only to run into Benny who lay in wait.

Benny stepped forward. "Nathan Thompson, you're under arrest for theft. Put your bag on the floor, then raise your hands, and turn around."

Nate was stunned. This wasn't the way things were supposed to go. He had to get away fast before they called the cops. He charged past Benny, who grabbed his arm and attempted to wrestle him to the floor, but Nate escaped and hightailed it down the hall, headed for the exit. Benny was no match for Nate who was in top-notch shape.

But Nate was no match for Joey who was standing about ten feet from the back exit, gun in hand. Nate dropped his duffel bag as Connie and Benny approached from behind.

Nate managed to blurt out, "What gave me away?"

Connie snickered. "Your rolling into town and applying for a job at Joey's right when the place was flush with cash was highly suspicious. You said the bartender at Harley's told you about Joey's, but I questioned him later and found out that wasn't the case. Your ploy of creating drinks for Joey to gain access to his office cinched it."

Joey took over the narrative. "Cousin Connie, here, told me the whole story. I can't believe you were stupid enough to return. And by the way, you talk a better drink than you produce."

Nate's brain was spinning. "Cousin? Joey's your cousin?"

"Damn straight," Connie said. "I'm the one who figured out who you really are. You never noticed me in school, did you? I was five years younger and had a terrible crush on you. You changed several features over the years, but not your eyes. They sucked me in back then and they still do now." Her eyes narrowed. "Too bad you're a lying scumbag."

Benny cleared his throat. "I confirmed your identity. Once we knew who you really were, it all fell together. You thought you'd rob Joey again. But this time we were ready for you. We switched the money in the safe with counterfeit cash. Thanks to Connie we knew the scam you were running with the cocktails and when you planned to execute it. We weren't sure what you were planning to put in Joey's last drink, so I instructed him to make an excuse to leave you alone in his office. Keep him safe while giving you the chance to incriminate yourself.

"The 'perfect martini' you made for Joey is on its way to the lab to analyze the ingredients. I'm sure they won't find anything lethal. You may be an idiot but you're not a murderer."

Nate's shoulders sagged as he nodded toward his duffel bag. "Well, I almost pulled it off." He kicked the duffel bag at Joey and sprinted toward the back door at full speed. Connie and Benny followed in pursuit.

If I can make it to the car, I'll have a chance.

The parking lot was covered with a blanket of snow. Nate skidded to a stop as he scrambled for his keys. His feet slid out from under him. He slammed onto the ground.

At Benny's feet.

Benny cuffed him and pulled him upright. "The only trip you'll be taking tonight is to jail."

Nate's head began to throb. "I guess you really can't go home again."

"God, I hate snow!"

WHEN YA COMIN' HOME, REUBEN T, REUBEN T?
BY J. PAUL BURROUGHS

I love a good murder. That is, *solving* a good murder. However, living in a small Indiana town in the late 1940's, that doesn't happen very often, until recently.

My name is Evangeline Taylor. I work for Sheriff Brooker. No, I'm not a law enforcement officer. Despite the fact that I was a WAC during the war and participated in investigations of several military crimes in the Burma Theater, when I came home, I was considered a "mere woman" worthy only as a secretary in Brooker's office. Any aspirations to become a detective were quickly quelled.

I grew up with two older brothers, and I learned to stand up for myself. At the age of twelve, I could punch as well or even better than my brother, Butchy. Once, I knocked out Jimmy Cherry's front tooth after he taunted me in the schoolyard. At age eleven, I discovered the Sherlock Holmes series of stories. I was in my teens when the Nancy Drew books began coming out, and I longed to be her. I was certain I'd turn out to be a master detective.

"A woman's place is in the home," Brooker insisted.

I'd have given him a piece of my mind to feast upon, but I needed a position in this post-war period when men returned to their old jobs. However, I secretly decided I would solve a murder in town.

The victim was easily identified as Martin Chambers. He was the town librarian and something of an expert on the local poet, Reuben Turlough. Possessing modest acting ability, Martin gained some fame portraying the poet at county fairs, founder's day programs and similar events. Like the writer, he donned the bright red vest that Reuben wore at formal gatherings (however, he always referred to such a trapping as a "waistcoat") and sported a flashy bowtie. He'd dressed the previous day for the town's celebration of the late Reuben Turlough's birthday.

WHO WAS THIS TURLOUGH, you ask? He was born in Greenborough, Indiana, in 1883. A farmer's son, he surprised his parents and neighbors by becoming a writer. His writings were tales for children about talking animals, and delightful poems about fairy people and spirits that haunted old barns. He gained some amount of distinction among the literary circles in this country during the late 19th and early 20th century.

To the general dismay of his family and friends, he'd enlisted in the service in World War I. However, his writing didn't end when he became a doughboy. He continued to crank out stories and poems, which he sent stateside even after arriving on the battlefields of France. In August 1918, homesick for Greenborough, he wrote these lines.

> *When ya comin' home, Reuben T, Reuben T?*
> *From far away in France, cross the sea, cross the sea?*
> *Yer ma and pa, they miss you,*
> *Sweet Eloise wants to kiss you.*
> *Won't you hurry home to all, Reuben T, Reuben T.*

Three days later, an enemy sniper took the life of the writer and poet.

I was raised with the town considering him some sort of hometown hero. He and what he wrote were celebrated with festivals, parades, storytellings and the like. I actually marched with other kids to put flowers on his statue in the town square.

Although his body lay in a forgotten grave in Europe, a small mausoleum was erected in the town cemetery in his honor.

When America again went to war in 1941, I read in the newspaper that Martin, like his hero, enlisted in the army. Martin, however, *did* return home in 1946. He resumed his position at the library and dressed as Reuben to do public readings at the birthday celebration.

Matt Greenan at the Turlough birthplace museum found him dead, dressed as Reuben, behind the home. For a Hoosier burg whose only significant crimes since the turn of the century had been two sets of bootleggers and an unsuccessful state police chase after John Dillinger through the heart of town, this event shocked the locals. The county coroner ruled that Martin had died from several blunt blows to the head.

For several weeks, the newspapers and radio carried the story. Law enforcement figures and locals pretending to be detectives speculated on the cause for the murder, but nothing definite was concluded.

When I heard of Martin's murder, I saw my chance to finally be a detective. Aside from the occasional paperwork, business at the office was slow. Thinking a woman's mind centered on going shopping, Brooker often gave me "breaks" to satisfy my female desires. These I could use to investigate the murder.

I made my first stop the home of Adelaide Reasoner, who was

Martin's fiancé. I found her home at a small cottage on North Street. Addie and I had attended grammar school together when we were kids, so I knew there'd be no problem speaking with her.

She wiped her tear-filled eyes with a hanky. "You want to know if Marty had any enemies? No, everyone in this town loved him."

"Well, someone certainly didn't," I suggested.

"It would have to be one of the newcomers. Since the war ended, at least two dozen strangers have moved into Greenborough."

While she made sense, I decided to still check with others who had been close with Martin about possible enemies. While most believe women gossip at beauty parlors, men do much the same at barber shops. I went to Leroy's barber shop at mid-afternoon when I knew I'd not encounter any of his male customers. I found Leroy seated, reading the latest edition of Big Crime Magazine.

"You looking for someone with a beef against Martin? Look no further than Howie Knapp, the milkman."

"Why him?"

"You know how Howie wobbles about after he got kicked in the leg by a cow? Well, just after coming back from the war, Martin performed as old Reuben and imitated Howie's walk when he read the poem, *The Wobbly Fella.* Of course, everyone in the audience recognized that and laughed. Howie swore he'd get even. Howie owns a shotgun, y'know."

Well, Martin wasn't shot, but I decided to talk with Howie anyway.

"Yeah, that sorry sonnava..." Howie barked. "He made me a laughingstock, but I didn't kill him."

"Where were you at the time of the murder?"

"When was that?"

"Coroner estimates it was between nine and eleven that night."

"I was playing cards in the back of Miller's tavern until eleven-thirty. Got three other fellas to prove it. You looking for someone with a grudge, try old man Applegate. Young Chambers went sparkin' with Applegate's daughter, Weezie, and then dropped her to get engaged to that Reasoner girl. Heard her pa say, that librarian shoulda died in the war."

I put off my talk with Joseph Applegate because I needed to get back to work at the office. However, that evening I showed up at his home on Noble Drive.

"Course, I hated the little snot," he admitted. "He fooled 'round with my Weezie when I wasn't home, and then up and gets engaged to someone else. I swear this younger generation is going to hell."

I asked him where he was at the time of the murder.

"I was home with my wife and kids. They'll swear it. Why all the questions? Think you're one of those radio detectives, or something?"

Fearing he'd go to my boss, I made a hasty retreat. I got very little sleep that night thinking over the case. If someone had a grudge against Martin, why did the killer dress him up like Reuben? Was the town poet somehow connected?

On my break the following day, I visited the birthplace museum and spoke to Phyllis, the docent.

"If I were you, I'd have a nice chat with old Eloise," she commented. "She's got all those letters he wrote while away in France. Maybe there's some sorta connection."

After work, I walked over to the lady's home. I found Eloise seated in front of the radio listening to Benny Goodman's orchestra. In her fifties, she still possessed the sweet smile I'd seen in a photo of her and Reuben.

"If you think looking at my letters might help you learn who killed dear Martin, I'll be more than happy to oblige," she told me. "However, I should warn you. Some of the things he said in them might shock you. Men away at war miss a woman's presence."

"I was a WAC," I told her. "I'm well aware of that."

She told me to come by the following evening. By then, she'd have them collected for me.

The following morning, I discovered a "bump in the road" for me when I arrived at work.

"Miz Taylor, we gotta have a talk," Sheriff Brooker greeted me. "Come into my office."

Uh-oh, the fat was in the fire. To use the expression from the movies, someone had *squealed* on me.

Brooker flopped into his chair and pointed me to take a seat opposite. "Care to guess who I've been talking to?"

I shrugged. "I haven't the foggiest."

"Had coffee down at the café with Joe Applegate. Told me you were asking questions about the Chambers murder. Said you were talkin' like you was Dick Tracy or something. You know how I feel about women trying to butt into cases..."

"Sorry. I was talking to one of my friends who mentioned Mr. Applegate's grudge against Martin, and out of curiosity, I just dropped by to see if it were true."

Brooker uttered a "humph" and let the matter pass, but the rest of the day I could feel his gaze, probably wondering if I was overstepping my bounds. I did *not* take a break all day to investigate further.

I WAITED until after dark to revisit Eloise for fear of being spotted by the sheriff on his rounds. She had prepared some tea for us, and we talked.

"You know that poem just before his death people quote all the time?"

"About wondering when he'd come home?"

She nodded. "I didn't turn over all of it for publication, you know. I think you'll find the missing lines interesting."

She handed the letter over to me, and I began to read.

When ya comin' home, Reuben T, Reuben T?
From far away in France, cross the sea, cross the sea?
Yer ma and pa, they miss you,
Sweet Eloise wants to kiss you.

Won't you hurry home to all, Reuben T, Reuben T.
Oh, I'm coming back quite soon, to my home, to my home
And from there, I'll ever stay, never roam, never roam.
For I've found a holy treasure,
A king's ransom without measure,
And we'll live like kings and queens, Missus T, Missus T!

"ANY IDEA WHAT HE WROTE ABOUT?" I asked.

"I haven't a clue. I told Mr. Chambers that when he asked me before going off to war. All I know was that he got all excited."

The following day was Saturday, my day off, and I made a beeline to the library. The library was located close to downtown and had been a gift from Andrew Carnegie years ago. Laurie Pickett, who had been a librarian prior to Martin's death, now was in charge of the place.

"Miss Taylor, you'll be delighted to know that the latest book by that Agatha Christie lady just arrived. I've held it for you."

I crossed my fingers behind me. "Actually, I'm here on an errand for the sheriff."

"Oh! What sort of errand?"

"He wanted me to look for some things in Martin's office."

"It's my office now, but I suppose it wouldn't hurt to let you look. Just don't mess up the paperwork on my desk. All of Mr. Chambers's things are stacked on shelves by the window. You're lucky. I was about to toss the lot into the trash."

I promised I wouldn't. Laurie unlocked the door to the office and then returned to her post up front where she reigned supreme over the books.

There were all sorts of books and maps, as well as hand-written notes. One such note caught my eye and got my blood pumping.

The Maltese Cross of Juvinoue

I examined the maps labeled "The Marne" and found a location bearing the name "Juvinoue." I looked through a book on *The War to End All Wars* and discovered that American troops had fought there in 1918. I looked up the specific date from when Reuben's letter had been written.

There had been action in Juvinoue!

After searching through over a dozen books, I found one from 1909, with a page corner turned inward to mark a place. I opened the book and began to read.

"The church of St. Pierre was known for its famous Maltese Cross that was designed by Francois DuPresin 1439. The cross was decorated with various gems and was originally designed to be a gift to Pope Callixtus III. However, before it could be delivered to Rome in the spring of 1457, it had mysteriously disappeared."

Had Reuben found the cross but died before he could bring it back to America? Had Martin traced his steps, found the cross and brought it back in secret to Greenborough? These questions demanded a return visit with Addie.

"Did Martin ever discuss how the two of you might live on a librarian's salary?" I asked her.

"He told me not to worry about money. Said he was about to come into a fortune when some far off relative died," she replied.

"Did Martin ever fight in the area called The Marne?"

"Not certain. However, before being shipped home, he visited places where World War 1 took place – places where Reuben Turlough had been."

I now was certain I knew the motive behind Martin's murder. Had he told someone here about the cross? Or had there been someone else in cahoots about finding the cross and coming home to America? Suddenly, Addie's earlier suggestion about newcomers made more sense.

But which newcomer? How could I get a list of their names to continue my search? Better still, how could I do so without the sheriff learning?

Harry Newsome.

Harry worked in voter registration, and possibly newcomers to Greenborough would want to vote in the upcoming presidential election next year. Plus, Harry had been sweet on me since the seventh grade. I could ask him and make him promise not to turn me in to Brooker.

I slipped away to the courthouse the following Monday and looked Harry up. He was pleasantly surprised to see me.

"Evie, what a nice surprise! What brings you here? I know you're already registered to vote."

"I need some information, but no one else must ever know that."

He flashed some pearly white teeth. "Count on me."

I filled him in on my mission and went through voter records. We found seven men who had listed their previous occupation as military service. I wrote down their addresses, determined to speak with each over the next few days. As newcomers, it was doubtful they knew I worked in the sheriff's office.

"This could be real dangerous, Evie," Harry cautioned. "If the guy killed once, he wouldn't be concerned about committing a second to protect his hide."

"I'll be careful. I have a story already planned to use when I'm speaking to each."

Harry's "uh-huh" revealed he had strong doubts about that.

"...and I'm working on a paper for college on battles that took place in the Marne region of France in the last war. I was hoping you might be able to help me?"

Lorne Weaver, my third to be interviewed, shook his head. "If you want to know about the march through Germany, I could help you. Not the Marne. Sorry."

Over the next two days, the following two men gave me the same response. With two names left, I drove out to a new housing development miles away down on Main Street, to speak to Edward Cooke, 29.

Cooke turned out to be a tall, trim man who looked as though his time in the war had left him pale and somewhat world-weary.

His dark-set eyes reflected some of the horrors he must have witnessed.

"What d'ya want. Lady?" he grumbled. "I got no time for small talk."

I pitched him the same line I'd done with the others. I expected him to send me packing, but I was wrong.

"Yeah, I was there. What of it?"

I took a pencil and pad from my purse. "Could I trouble you to relate what it was like?"

He gave me a hard look and then his expression softened. "Yeah, I spoze so. If you're writing some paper, I can help. Me? I'm no good at writing. Can't put two words together, if'n I tried."

He let me inside. To my surprise, the place looked neat and relatively clean. His voter registration listed him as single. I wondered if he had hired a girl to come and clean. Over the next thirty minutes, he related the various conflicts with the enemy, occasionally mentioning other GIs in his company.

Since he seemed at ease, I decided to bring up the town where the cross had disappeared.

"Were you ever in a place called Juvinoue?"

His body slightly jerked, and an eye twitched. Immediately his relaxed body tensed up.

"Why you mentioning that?" he demanded.

"Oh, it came up in another interview. That's all."

He rose to his feet. "I think you'd better leave, lady."

I stood up. "I'm sorry I upset you. I meant no harm."

He crossed the room to a desk. "You're here about *him,* ain't cha?"

"Him? I don't understand."

He yanked a drawer open, snatched out a pistol and waved it at me. "You wanna know about Chambers!"

"Chambers? Who's that?"

"You know about the cross. You musta been in on it with ole Marty-boy."

I stupidly responded. "You have the cross?"

"Yeah, and I aim to keep it. No dame is gonna see me go the chair either. You and I are gonna take a little trip into the country, and only one of us is coming back."

My heart was pounding. "People know I came here. I work for the sheriff's office. If anything happens to me, he'll be knocking at your door."

He reached across the desk and picked up some car keys. "You're lying through your teeth! Move!"

He edged me to the door, but momentarily peered outside to see if anyone was watching.

"Go on!"

I stepped out into the night air. While there were lights on inside some of the homes, no one would probably hear me if I screamed. He pointed to a Plymouth with the barrel of his gun. I slowly walked towards it.

"Hey, you!" a voice called from the darkness. Cooke swung back in the direction from which it had come.

Remember how I said that when I was a kid, I had a mean punch that could take out Jimmy Cherry? Well, I spun around and connected my fist with Cooke's chin. I heard a crack as contact was made, and the guy went down, his pistol slipping from his grasp.

I dropped down and snatched it up. To my surprise, Harry Newsome came running up.

"That...that was incredible!" he gasped.

"What are you doing here?" I asked.

"You know what the police call following a guy?"

I shrugged. "Tailing."

"That's what I've been doing each evening when you've gone about talking to these guys. Wanted to be there if you were ever in trouble. Guess I was right."

Despite my best efforts otherwise, a smile slipped across my lips. "Guess you were."

The long and the short of it, we took Cooke to the sheriff, explained what I'd been up to, and suggested he get a search warrant to search Cooke's place. Brooker's face turned so red, I thought he'd have an apoplexy, but in the end, he got the warrant. Under the bed mattress, he found the Maltese Cross.

Cooke eventually confessed. He and Martin had been buddies in their company, fighting the enemy, getting drunk, and carousing with women. After VE Day, Martin foolishly revealed what he'd learned about Reuben and the cross. A note I hadn't discovered revealed that the cross had been concealed in a church decimated by an artillery attack in early 1917. They planned to sneak it out, bring it home to the States and sell it to some rich collector.

However, Cooke had gotten drunk out of his mind days before leaving for home and been injured when he'd wrecked the jeep he'd driven. While recovering in a military hospital, Martin left the country with it, hoping to keep the money for himself.

But Cooke hunted him down, faced off with Martin at his home after his earlier performance and accompanied him to the poet's birthplace after sunset. There, he pounded the butt of his gun against Martin's head repeatedly until he was dead and strung him up on the trellis.

The people of Juvinoue were contacted and eventually the cross was returned home.

The story hit the newspapers, and you'd think I'd be the heroine of this story.

Wrong. Brooker threatened to have me arrested for disobeying his direct orders, and he took the credit. Darn business was responsible for him being kept in office at the next election. However, he swore that if another case like this turned up, he'd let me work on it with him.

Let me?

Well, one good thing came of this. When Harry asked me out after the whole shebang, I agreed to go on a date. Several dates, actually.

A girl's gotta find some happiness in a small burg like Greenborough!

HIGH ROLLER
BY P.K. RICHARD

Cora sneezed again. The funeral director called her that morning to see if she could transport flowers for the Cooper funeral. The funeral home was triple-booked, and two of their staff were out sick. She had jumped at the chance to bring some extra cash to the coffers of the florist shop she had inherited from her grandmother. Finances had been tight ever since the pandemic. She and Ralph loaded up the van with the flowers from the Peaceful Pines Funeral Home and left the property at a respectful pace. At the same time, the funeral director organized the mourners into a procession.

"Could you hand me that box of tissues?" she asked Ralph. She hadn't taken her allergy medicine the night before and was paying the price in the close confines of the delivery van.

"Why did you want to be a florist again?" Ralph teased her. He moved his seat back, stretched his long legs, and settled into the worn leather passenger seat. He was semi-retired and took up odd jobs to stay busy, including helping at Blossom Boutique during holidays or when their small town had the inevitable cluster of local deaths.

Cora ignored his teasing. She wasn't sure she ever really wanted to be a florist, but she had a certain amount of skill and had promised her grandmother she would keep the shop going after she passed. It wasn't a terrible job, allergies aside.

The cemetery was just outside town, surrounded by trees and tiny ranch-style homes that lined the rural highway. Cora drove the delivery van up one of the narrow lanes that wound through the cemetery and stopped close to the open grave. Arnie Cooper's eternal view would be facing east, with a sliver of the Ohio River visible through the winter-bare trees to the right of his family plot. It looked like spring would come late this year.

Cora got out of the van and promptly sunk into the wet sod. If she hadn't remembered her boots, the mud would have filled the flat dress shoes she had left in the van. Ralph hauled the flowers while Cora arranged them around the far side of the grave. She quickly filled the center with the standing sprays sent by the large extended family and framed the grouping on each end with matching wreaths, their ribbons embellished with *father* and *husband*. When the pall-bearers set the custom mahogany casket on the bars of the service stand, Arnie Cooper, Sr., would get a sendoff that would comfort his grieving widow and greedy children. She had already observed the frosty exchanges between Arnie, Jr., and his sister, Marilee. *No love lost there*, she thought. There had been time for a custom casket because the police took a few days to investigate the unusual circumstances of Arnie's death. There had been a need for a custom casket because of Arnie's seven-foot length, which was extraordinary even for the large—in both number and size—Cooper family, of which even Ralph was an outlying twig.

Ralph was a distant enough relative that no one noticed when he headed back to the van to quietly listen to the game while they waited for the end of the graveside service. Cora knew he was a big sports fan. He had the radio going at the shop if there was a game on. The Hoosiers were a number four seed this year, with a chance to make it to the Final Four. Cora was immune to the call of Indiana sports teams—basketball or otherwise. She just shook her head and walked to the cluster of mourners.

Arnie, Sr., had a respectable turnout, even outside of family. Cora stopped behind the group and leaned against a tree while the funeral directors herded people into the rows of white wooden folding chairs. Two tall men stood directly in front of Cora. One was Arnie, Jr. *He should be up front with the family*, she thought. She couldn't help but notice that they were in the midst of a disagreement.

"I already told you that the estate has to be settled before you get your money," whispered Arnie. His long scraggly hair didn't hide the thin scar on his left cheek.

"And I already told you that our friends won't wait for their money," said the other man—short hair and mustache. He turned to leave, but Arnie grabbed his arm.

"Wait," said Arnie. "I've got a sure thing. It will make everything right."

Arnie lowered his voice then, and Cora couldn't hear the rest of the conversation. But Mr. Short Hair pushed a finger into Arnie, Jr.'s chest before hissing, "This is your last chance."

He turned and almost ran straight into Cora. He paused, his eyes narrowing as he made note of the Blossom Boutique logo on her polo shirt. "Mind your own business," he said as he brushed past her and left behind a cloud of aftershave. He walked past her van, saw the logo, and looked back at Cora again.

Meanwhile, Cora had immediately succumbed to a coughing and sneezing fit that was enough for the minister to pause, everyone else to turn to find the source of the commotion, and for the mourners in her immediate vicinity to fumble in pockets and purses for masks. Once she could get her breath, she whispered an apology and backed toward the van.

"I think there's something going on," she told Ralph once she shut the van door. She watched Mr. Short Hair enter a dark red sedan parked toward the main road. She took a quick photo of his license plate with her phone.

"There's a funeral going on." Ralph seemed a little put out to have his game interrupted.

"No. I mean, I overheard a conversation about the Cooper estate that sounded suspicious." Cora grabbed another wad of tissues and started blowing her nose. "How did Arnie, Sr., die, anyway? Maybe we should call the police."

"Word at the barber shop is that Arnie Jr.'s brakes failed," he said. "Right at the top of their driveway. Arnie Sr. was walking his Labrador retriever back from the mailbox. He got tangled up in the leash and fell under the wheels of Junior's dually."

"Didn't the police find that suspicious?"

"Well, they made a show of investigating," he said. "But you know, Arnie Jr. has two cousins on the force. Probably, nobody wants any family drama. Last year, Arnie Jr.'s sister got arrested for OWI after she drove through a stoplight and hit a tree. Charges were dropped for no evidence. Seems like there was plenty of evidence on that tree after it fell on the Anderson's roof."

"We live in a small town," said Cora. "That doesn't sound shocking to me, but you'd think they would take it seriously when somebody dies. I heard that Arnie, Jr., and his sister Marilee were already pestering the funeral director about the death certificate. They want to get the papers filed right away to get probate started. I'm going to call Sheila Perkins when we get back to the shop to see who owns that car."

"Won't she get in trouble?"

"Nobody will know."

The shop was busy when they returned, so it was late after-noon the next day before Cora could call Sheila. As soon as Cora had his name and birth date, she signed up for a free two-week subscription to one of those services that tell you anything you want to know about a person, more than they probably know about themselves. In fact, this wasn't the first time she had signed up for a free trial. But her mouth dropped open once she looked up Mr. Short Hair's name. William Carter's criminal record was three pages long. This guy was not somebody they needed to mess with.

"Ralph," she called to the back of the shop. Ralph was in a depressed state since the Hoosiers lost to Purdue. He had been moping in the back while sorting through a flower shipment.

"Yeah?" He walked back with a basket for the cooler.

"Does the name William Carter mean anything to you?" Cora sneezed and walked to the window away from the cooler.

"Sure," he said. "If it's the one I'm thinking about, he runs one of the riverboat casinos. My sister was in school with his brother. Bad news all around. He barely made it out of high school."

"That's who I overheard at the cemetery. I think he might be involved in Arnie, Sr.'s death." She put the day's cash in the deposit bag so she could drop it by the bank. It wasn't much since most people paid with credit cards or ordered online these days.

"Well, I wouldn't be making any unfounded accusations," he said, leaning on the counter. "You don't want to become a target."

Just then, the phone rang again. Cora was surprised to see the number on the caller ID. Sheila rarely called, probably due to the need to keep her job.

"Cora," said Sheila. "You didn't hear it from me, but the Arnie, Sr. probate case has been filed. You might want to take a look at the will. It's public record."

"Wow, that was fast."

"The family got the death certificate expedited, and the Widow Cooper's lawyer has already filed the papers."

"Wow, again," said Cora. "What's in the will?"

"I've said more than I should. I've gotta go."

Cora was left staring at her phone. "She hung up on me."

"Who?" asked Ralph.

"Oh, it doesn't matter," she said as she grabbed her purse. "Could you close the shop for me? I need to run a couple of errands."

"You mean you need to go snoop at the courthouse. I assume that was Sheila on the phone."

"I mean, if anyone asks, I am running errands."

Ralph laughed. "Sure. I don't have any deliveries until tomorrow morning."

"Perfect. I'll see you tomorrow."

After making the bank deposit, Cora went straight to the courthouse. The will was a shock. Arnie, Jr., was getting absolutely nothing from the estate. Arnie, Sr., left everything to a trust with a monthly living allowance for his wife and daughter and a college fund for his grandchildren, Marilee's girls. Arnie, Jr. was explicitly excluded from the will due to "extensive funding provided to him previously." When the wife passes, the daughter will be awarded a small annuity, and the remainder of the estate will go to charity.

It was after five when Cora got the copy of the will, said goodbye to Sheila, and walked to her car.

She called Ralph and told him what she had found. "I just want to know what really happened. I might talk to Ted if he's at the diner tonight." Cora did not inherit her grandmother's skill in the kitchen. Heating up a can of soup without burning it was the extent of her culinary abilities. Most nights, she could be found at one of the local diners. Tonight, it was Gino's. She ordered the Tuesday special—meatloaf and roasted sweet potatoes.

She was almost finished with her meal when Ted Sinclair, a local policeman, stopped by when he got off shift. They had been frenemies growing up. Ted had tormented her more than once, but they had finally settled into a friendship of sorts after high school.

"What's up?" he said as he settled on the stool next to hers.

"I need to talk to you," said Cora. "About the Cooper death."

Ted shook his head. "Cora, the chief made it clear that he didn't want you meddling in our investigations. You almost got locked up for obstruction last time."

"No, this is different," she protested. "I have a piece of information that you might find interesting."

"It's been a long day," he said, running his hand over his forehead. "I just want to drink a beer and go home."

"Have your beer," she said. "It won't hurt to talk while I finish my meal."

"Talk about what?"

"Was there anything suspicious about Arnie, Sr.'s death?" She leaned in so he could hear without having to shout. "I overheard a conversation at the graveside service."

"What did you hear?"

"A man called William Carter was trying to get money from Arnie, Jr. Sounded like he didn't want to wait for Arnie, Sr.'s estate to be settled."

Ted looked at Cora for a minute like he was trying to decide something. "Tell me exactly what you overheard," he said.

Cora told him about the conversation and William Carter leaving in a red sedan.

"How did you know his name?"

Cora hesitated a minute. "Well, I'm not sure exactly. Maybe Arnie, Jr. mentioned it." She was a terrible liar. The flush started at the base of her neck and ran up her cheeks.

"Or did you call Shelia?"

Cora's eyes widened. "I'm not comfortable talking about that," she said. "Besides, there's more. Arnie, Jr. isn't going to inherit anything from the estate."

Ted focused his full attention on Cora. "And how do you know that?"

"They've filed for probate, and I got a copy of the will."

Ted waved away the bartender with his anticipated cold beer. "Well, it looks like I'm going to have to go back to the station, and you're coming with me."

"Why?" Cora forgot to whisper, and the other bar patrons looked interested.

"Arnie, Jr. was found dead this afternoon. He'd been roughed up a bit, and then his throat was slit. And until now, we didn't have any suspects," he added.

Ted told her to meet him at the station. Cora drove her car carefully, keeping an eye on her rear-view mirror, but she didn't see any red sedans. At the station, Cora parked in the very back of the parking lot. She was glad it was already dark, so maybe no one would see her walk to the front entrance.

Once they got in the station, Ted put her in an interview room and went to find Chief Benson. They didn't look happy when they entered the room and sat at the table. The chief put a cardboard box on the floor beside them.

"I thought I made myself clear last time," said the chief.

"This was totally accidental," said Cora. "I was doing my job and happened to overhear a conversation. I felt it was my duty to come forward. I can't believe there's another death in the Cooper family."

"What was Arnie Cooper, Jr., wearing when you saw him?" asked the chief.

Cora thought for a minute. "An overcoat and a suit," she said. "And a hat."

"What kind of hat?"

"A black fedora, old-fashioned," she said. "That's why I noticed it."

"Is this the hat?" the chief pulled a plastic bag out of the box.

"No, that's a gray tweed," she said. "That looks like the hat William Carter had on. Where did you find it?"

"That is not information you need to know," said the chief. "We are asking the questions here. Now we need you to repeat everything you overheard between Arnie, Jr., and William Carter."

"I already told Ted everything."

"Cora, can you just follow instructions for once?"

Cora straightened up in her seat. "I beg your pardon?"

"Sometimes you remember details when you repeat a thing," said the chief. "That's all I'm asking. Did they say anything about Arnie, Sr.'s will?"

Cora paused, looking up at the ceiling. "No, nothing about a will, just probate and going to court. But you need to see what's in the will. Turns out Arnie, Jr., didn't inherit after all."

The room grew quiet. "You have a copy of the will?" The chief waited for her response.

"Um, yeah," she stammered. "I got a copy at the courthouse this afternoon."

The chief let out a sigh. "We are done here," he said. "Officer Sinclair will write up your statement. Read it and sign, and I'd better not see you back in here unless we call you to come in." He stood up and nodded to Ted.

"Wait," said Cora. "Can I smell the hat?"

"Smell the hat?"

"Yes, William Carter was wearing a strong cologne. A cologne I'm apparently allergic to." She sat and looked steadily at the chief's scowling face, willing herself not to look away.

"Ted, open the bag, but don't let her touch it and contaminate the evidence," said the chief.

Ted unsealed the bag, took a small sniff, and gestured toward Cora. She took one breath and stumbled away from the table, sneezing and coughing.

"That's it," she gasped. "That's the cologne William Carter was wearing."

"Okay, Cora," said the chief. "Thanks for the info, but the investigation will continue without you. We can't convict based on a sneeze. Now out you go."

Cora was sorry she had parked in the back when she had to walk by herself to her car, but she made it without incident. She was on Main Street headed home when she realized there was a car behind her. Cora took several turns, but the car was still there, maybe three car lengths away. She turned at the next intersection and headed back to the station. She already keyed 9-1-1 on her cell phone when the car pulled into the parking lot of the only karate school in town. Two small boys walked from the front door and got in the car. *Just a dad picking up his kids*, she thought. *I need to chill*. She turned at the next light and headed for home.

When she parked in her driveway, the motion lights came on at the front door, and everything looked okay. She opened her car door, grabbed her bag and cell phone, and was getting out of her car when a hand grabbed her by the shoulder. She screamed and tried to shut the door.

"What did you tell the cops?" William Carter's face was red as he started dragging her from the car.

Cora knew she was no match for the big man. She screeched, hit the call button on her phone, and grabbed a handful of leftover corsage pins she had in the console of her car. She stopped resisting, and he was taken off guard when they both fell to the ground. Cora took a breath and rammed all five corsage pins into his right hand. She jumped up while he was otherwise engaged and ran around the car. It was his turn to scream as he staggered toward her. She kept the car between them and shouted her address to the 911 operator when she passed by the open car door. He still chased her, cursing as he paused to pull out the corsage pins one by one. One had even gone all the way through the skin between his thumb and forefinger.

Two patrolmen on night duty weren't far away, and they had Carter handcuffed and in the back of the cruiser before Ted got there to tell her once again to stop getting in the middle of police investigations. Cora sneezed.

It was a couple of days before news of the arrest hit the paper. Ted even brought a copy by the shop. "Riverboat manager charged with two murders," read the headline.

Ted leaned on the counter. "The chief wanted me to tell you we appreciate the info you gave us. We were able to get a warrant and gather enough evidence to back up your sneeze. It didn't hurt that we already had him in custody after he pulled that trick at your house."

Cora beamed. It wasn't often that her help was appreciated at the local station. She skimmed the article. It seemed Arnie, Jr. had made one last bet on the Hoosier game to recoup his losses, putting up his share of the estate as collateral. "Oh, my goodness, William

Carter must have flipped when Purdue won. Ralph was in a funk for a week."

"Well, Carter did more than flip," said Ted. "He cut his losses, literally."

Cora laughed. "I'm just glad you got him."

Ted's radio crackled. "I've got to go, but I wanted to tell you before you saw the paper," he said. "But the chief says this doesn't change anything. Don't meddle in police business."

"Oh, absolutely," said Cora. "I learned my lesson the last time."

She watched Ted head out the door, climb into his cruiser, and drive off with lights blazing. Just then, some activity across the street caught her attention. She leaned toward the window to get a better look, smiled, then grabbed the phone and hit speed dial.

Cora dabbed her nose with a tissue. "Sheila, are you busy right now? I need you to look something up." She tucked the newspaper under the counter.

A NOT-SO-QUIET RESTING PLACE

BY MARY BISCHOFF

"Well, I'm back." Lettie King crossed the overgrown front yard, shading her eyes from the setting August sun, and stepped up onto the porch of the neglected old Queen Anne house. Built in 1901, the three-story five-bedroom home in the tiny southern Indiana town of Campbellsburg had been home for the first eighteen years of her life. She had fond memories of hours spent reading in the third-floor turret, gazing out over cornfields and cow pastures, daydreaming of escaping small-town life.

After graduating high school, she had wasted no time in moving north to Indianapolis to get her degree in nursing. After her parents had been killed in a car accident, the family home passed to her only brother Ricky. They had never been close, and his involvement with drugs and alcohol drove them further apart. She hadn't seen him or returned home since he showed up drunk at their parents' funeral.

The call yesterday from the Washington County Coroner had come out of the blue. A neighbor had noticed the front door ajar for several days and finally had called the police. The responding officer had found Ricky's body on his bedroom floor, hypodermic needle still in his arm.

Estimated time of death was probably three days to a week earlier, the coroner had said. Both methamphetamine and marijuana were found in the toxicology results. No big surprise there, she thought. With Ricky's history of addiction -- he had been treated for overdoses several times in the past few years -- and no evidence of foul play, the probable cause of death was accidental overdose.

Lettie's experience as an emergency room trauma nurse had given her very little sympathy for patients who repeatedly overdosed, and she wasn't really surprised that Ricky's years of substance abuse had finally done him in. What a waste of a life, she thought somewhat sadly. So here she was, just a month into retirement, unexpectedly back in C-Burg to arrange her brother's funeral and finalize his estate.

"It is good to be home, I guess, considering the circumstances. I've always loved this house." Lettie unlocked the door and stepped into the dim, only slightly cooler interior. She looked around. Rays from the setting sun streamed through the worn curtains and dirty window panes of the parlor, illuminating thick swathes of dust motes floating in the air and drifting over the shabby furnishings.

She wrestled the nearest window open and leaned against the sill. The heavy smell of roses wafted in on the gentle breeze, and she inhaled appreciatively. Taking a minute to enjoy the quiet evening sounds, Lettie felt her tight shoulders relax. She had worked night shift for years, and the coroner's call had woken her earlier than her normal 2 pm wake-up time. After hastily packing essentials, the long drive from Indianapolis and meeting with the mortician in Salem, the county seat, she was exhausted.

A plaintive meow drew her attention to the ornate wooden stairway leading up to the second floor. A plump orange cat sat on the bottom step, tail neatly curled around his feet, and turned a commanding green gaze on her. "Hello, cat," she greeted it politely. Something else to add to her to-do list, find the cat a home. She really did need to start a list.

The cat turned and wound his way purposefully down the hall

and into the dingy kitchen, where it took up position by an empty water bowl. At least there was still some dry food in the accompanying dish. The coroner had said that the cat had been hanging around the house when the police and forensics team arrived. The chained back door was propped open about six inches by a rusty metal flat iron, evidently so the cat could come and go at its leisure. She didn't see a litter box anywhere. Although, it could be upstairs.

Upstairs, where her dead brother had lain for several days.

Fortunately, the coroner had reassured her that the bedroom door had been closed, and the cat hadn't been in the room when the body was discovered. I can deal with a lot of things, Lettie thought with a sigh, but not a cat that ate its owner.

After some groaning and shaking, the kitchen faucet finally yielded some water and Lettie refilled the empty bowl. She placed it on the floor, managing to get a look at the cat's hindquarters as he drank greedily. Yes, he was very definitely a male. "I don't know your name, so what shall I call you? Frodo? Bucky? Solo? You kind of look like a Solo to me," she addressed the cat, who ignored her completely. Spying a yellowed notepad emblazoned "Stevens Memorial Museum" on the edge of the kitchen counter, she picked it up and began making a to-do list.

"I guess I'll be staying here a few days, at least until I get things sorted. What do we need? Food for me. Food for you. Do you have a preference?" She politely addressed the cat, who lifted his head sharply from the water. "No? Okay, then. Definitely cleaning supplies." She tapped the pen on her lip as she gazed around the kitchen.

A loud thump from overhead froze her hand. Lickety-split, the cat dashed past her and disappeared through the cracked outer door. Her grip tightened on the pen as she stared up at the tin ceiling. It's nothing, she told herself resolutely. It's an old house, not in the best of shape. They make sounds. Slow footsteps sounded above her, followed by a dragging noise. Definitely that was not a normal old-house sound!

Digging her cell phone out of her pocket, she ran back through the house and fumbled open the front door. She skidded across the porch's uneven floorboards, pushed through the weeds and stopped on the far side of her parked car.

"9-1-1, what's your emergency?"

"I think there's an intruder upstairs in my house." Lettie gave her name and the address. The reassuring voice of the dispatcher asked her to stay on the line until the police arrived. She anxiously scanned the yard and the woods across the road in the growing twilight, but saw nothing. Climbing into her Prius, she locked the doors. Although it seemed longer, it was only a few minutes before she heard a siren approaching and a police car pulled into the driveway. Thanking the dispatcher, she disconnected the call, unlocked the door and got out to greet the officer.

"Evening, Ma'am. What's going on?" The tall, slightly graying policeman approached her car, hand resting casually on his weapon.

"I heard someone walking around upstairs in the house. There shouldn't be anyone here but me." Lettie peered at his name tag. "N. Chastain," it read. "Nick? Is that you?"

"Lettie? It's been a long time. I guess you heard about Ricky. Why don't you wait in your car while I go inside and have a look around?"

"Of course." She climbed back into the car and locked the doors. She turned on the air conditioning and was rewarded with cool air on her flushed face. Nicholas Chastain, the responding officer, had been in her same class at West Washington High School, where she graduated almost forty years ago. He had matured into one fine-looking man.

Lettie watched as, one by one, lights appeared in each window of the old house, illuminating Nick's progress through the rooms. Every window glowed briefly, then went black, with the exception of the circular window in the turret on the third floor. That stayed stubbornly dark.

Expecting him to walk out the front door, a tap on her window glass brought a shriek to her lips and her hand to her chest. Gathering herself together, she unlocked the door and stepped out of the car to join him. "Jesus, Nick! You scared the hell out of me. Where'd you come from?"

"I looked around but I didn't find anyone inside. I couldn't get into the attic. That door is padlocked shut, but I checked all the other rooms. The basement door was open, so I locked it as I came out. It would be a good idea to change your locks, in case someone else has another set of keys."

"I don't know what anyone would want in there. I doubt Ricky had anything of value." She tried not to notice the way his steady brown eyes inspected her from head to toe.

Nick said, "It could have been one of his drug buddies looking to see if he left any drugs laying around." He paused. "You did know Ricky used, right? He'd overdosed before but I guess there was nobody around to Narcan him this time."

"You think they'll come back looking for drugs?" Lettie glanced around apprehensively.

Nick shook his head. "We went through the house pretty thoroughly after we got the call. We confiscated all the drugs we found, so I don't think there was anything left behind." He rocked back on his heels and grinned. "Maybe it was the ghost. You know we always said that your house was haunted. What was it? The lady in black, the one that got hit by a train? Back around the Civil War, maybe?"

She self-consciously wiped a trickle of sweat off her forehead, then shook her head. "The house was built at the turn of the century, so it's not that old. I lived here for eighteen years and never heard or saw a thing. I really doubt it was a ghost, unless it's Ricky's. I can't imagine him hanging around to haunt the place. But thanks for putting that idea into my head."

"Sure. Anyway," Nick fished around inside his bulletproof vest and handed her a business card. "I live in my mom's old place over on Sycamore Street. That's got my cell number on it. Just give me a call if you need anything else."

"Thanks," she said. "Hopefully it was just a one-time thing, but I think I'll get a motel room in Salem for tonight and have the locks changed tomorrow." She waited for him to climb back in his car, anxious to be on her way to a hotel room with air conditioning and a nice cool shower.

"You know, Lettie," he said slowly, "maybe we can get together for a meal and catch up on old times. The town café is open again. I usually work nights, but I'd like it if we could find a time to do that." The fine lines around his warm brown eyes crinkled as he smiled.

Oh, my goodness, he was asking her out. Flustered but flattered, Lettie managed a smile while surreptitiously checking his hand for a wedding ring. Nope! "I used to work nights, too. You know what, I would really like that. I'll give you a call tomorrow and we'll set it up."

Lettie waved goodbye as Nick reversed the patrol car and headed down the gravel road back towards town. "Oh, my stars and garters, as Grandma Etta used to say. It has been a day, for sure. And now I'm talking to myself."

She needed to add getting a locksmith to her list, absently patting her pockets but then realizing she had dropped the notepad in her haste to escape the house. Oh, well, she would get it in the morning. Not that she was scared of going back into the isolated old house, all by herself with the full moon rising over the trees. It's not like the house was haunted. Of course not!

Climbing back into the Prius, she carefully reversed out of the driveway and headed off to find a hotel room. Behind her, high in the darkness amid the surrounding trees, a small flickering light appeared in the turret window, but there was no one there to see, not even the newly-christened Solo.

GET OUT!

Lettie stared at the words heavily scrawled across her to-do list. When she'd arrived at the house at noon, the crack of dawn in her "normal" schedule, she had been determined to treat the events of last night as just one more thing to deal with, simply resolved by changing all the locks. Everything in the house seemed just the same as last night. Until she had retrieved the fallen notepad from the kitchen floor, that is. Had the intruder come back after she left last night? Was he or they possibly still here?

Lettie hated to call 911 again so soon after making the call last night. She pulled her cell phone from her pocket, scrolled through the entries and called Nick.

He picked up on the second ring. "Chastain," he said gruffly.

"Hey, Nick, it's Lettie King. I'm really sorry to bother you but I'm out at the house and came across something strange."

"Shoot," he said.

"I had started a to-do list yesterday and left it in the house. When I got here today, someone has written "Get out" on it."

"Huh," he said, sounding more alert. "That's not good."

"It had to have happened after I left yesterday. So either it happened after you cleared the house last night..." She hesitated. "...or this morning and they might still be here."

"Why don't you wait outside? I'm off-duty now, but I'll send Willa, one of the day shift officers, over to make sure no one is there."

"I really appreciate it," she said sincerely. "And I'm sorry to have woken you up. It's probably nothing."

"Could have been the ghost," Nick remarked, entirely too cheerfully in Lettie's view. "Maybe she just wants the house to herself."

"Oh, my God, Nick," she stifled a chuckle. "Jeez. Get some sleep. Bye." She hit the End button and contemplated the kitchen. No sign of anything out of place that she could tell, but it was hard to tell in the mess. Housekeeping had never been one of Ricky's strong suits. The house was silent, and there was no sign of the cat. Resignedly, she went outside to wait for the police to arrive.

Lettie was fishing in the cooler in her trunk for a soda when the police car pulled up and parked. A petite policewoman in her 20s, layered brown hair clinging to her head, exited the cruiser and approached her.

"Good afternoon, Miz King," she said cheerfully, her duty belt jingling merrily as she jogged over to the car. "I'm Officer Spears. I hear you might have another prowler. Please wait out here while I have a look, okay?"

Lettie waved a hand towards the door. "Thanks. It's open."

Hand on her weapon, Officer Spears disappeared inside.

"Caffeine. I need caffeine. It is way too early." Retrieving an ice-cold can of soda, Lettie took a deep swallow. She had hoped to get some cleaning done in the house before the temperature reached the expected high in the upper nineties, though it was getting close to that now. She hoped somewhere inside there was a working fan. She could put that on her to-do list.

She stared down at the heavy black printing on her original list. It might be evidence. Although it wasn't likely much evidence could be gleaned from a scant two words. Did ghosts leave fingerprints? Probably not. But illiterate rural meth heads? Possibly so.

She dug through her cavernous purse and fished out another notebook and a pen. "Let's try this again," she muttered to herself. "Check about a fan. Locksmith coming today. I can't do anything about the bank until I get the death certificate so that's for later." She chewed the cap of her pen and made a few more entries.

The screen door creaked open, then closed with a bang behind Officer Spears. "Well, ma'am, there's no one there now. We don't get too much crime down here in the 'Burg besides drugs and domestic violence. It's not like the big city, where people who want your stuff will shoot you as soon as look at you."

"Thank you for checking the house for me." Lettie proffered the original notepad. "I don't know if you need it, but this was what I found when I came back this morning."

Willa bent over to inspect the paper. Competently, she whipped some nitrile gloves out of her back pocket, produced a paper evidence bag and sealed the notepad inside, carefully initialing the tape. "We don't have much of a budget for forensics, but we'll just keep this in case it becomes important in the future. Probably not, but you never know," she said brightly. "If there's anything else, you just give us a holler. Somebody will be out right quick." She declined a soda, strode back to her car and drove off.

Lettie heaved a sigh. She was sure she would hear about this from Nick the next time they met. She closed her trunk, locked the car and went inside. She made a quick circuit of the parlor, living room, and dining room, making notes for her to-do list as she went. The bones of the house were wonderful; it only needed a good cleaning and some redecorating to set it to rights.

The sun cast red and blue shadows through the stained glass windows on the landing as she climbed the front stairs. At the top, to her right were the front two bedrooms. To her left, a short hall led to the other three bedrooms, bathroom, rear stairs and attic door. First stop, her old bedroom in the front of the house.

Opening the door, she saw her childhood cherrywood bed still sat beneath the window. An unfamiliar white IKEA desk and bookcase were new. The dresser drawers had been pulled out, emptied onto the floor and the contents of the closet and bookshelves dumped on top of them.

Lettie frowned. Surely the police hadn't left this mess when they searched the house. Making a mental note to ask Nick, she wondered whose belongings these were. Maybe one of Ricky's three ex-wives? Other than the mess, though, the room seemed quite habitable. Thank God, Lettie thought, I can clean this up and stay here. She didn't know how long it would take to get all of Ricky's affairs in order, but it would probably take at least a week. She didn't have room in her budget for a lengthy hotel stay.

The guest room next door was in much the same condition. The contents of both dresser and closet were strewn across the floor, and the mattress sat askew on the box frame. Down the hall, what used to be their mom and dad's room had been used for storage, old furniture and boxes spilling out into the hallway. Thankfully, the bathroom was functional, although Lettie planned to clean and disinfect every single surface before putting it to use.

The fourth bedroom had been turned into a game room of sorts. A big-screen TV hung on one wall, flanked by this year's Indiana University basketball calendar, along with some of its older editions. Facing the TV, the faded plaid couch was surrounded with empty chip bags, to-go boxes and beer cans. It was a wonder the place wasn't full of mice, she thought. At least Solo the cat seemed to be earning his keep.

Bracing herself, Lettie poked her head through the door of her brother's bedroom. What a mess. Scattered cigarette butts, discarded syringes and dirty dishes littered the stained carpet, and the reek of death and cigarette smoke still hung in the air. Wincing in reluctant sympathy, she wondered about his final moments. Had Ricky tried to call for help and no one came? A pity he should die so completely alone, even if he had brought it on himself. Retreating into the hallway, Lettie shut the door firmly behind her.

Continuing on, at the end of the hall, a padlock secured the door to the attic. Frowning, she wondered when that was added. This end of the house was noticeably cooler than the rest. She thought of tales of cold spots in haunted houses and jumped as someone pounded on the front door.

Hurrying down the stairs, Lettie nearly stumbled over Solo. "Where have you been?" she scolded. Scooping him up, she carried him with her to answer the front door. It was Clarence, the local handyman she had hired to change the locks. It was fortunate that she had seen his ad for odd job work at the local market where she'd stopped for ice and sodas and that he'd been able to come out today, especially being Sunday. Thrusting off her chest with powerful hind legs, Solo yowled and leapt out the door, leaving stinging claw marks in his wake.

"Sorry to have to knock so hard, Miz King," Clarence apologized. "The doorbell don't work. Sorry I startled Garfield."

"Garfield? Ah, so that's the name of the cat. I wondered." Lettie backed up to let the skinny man enter, gingerly rubbing the smarting welts. She automatically noted his long sleeves despite the August heat, and the scabbed back of his hands as he twisted the brim of his baseball cap nervously. Great, another drug user, she thought. "Thanks for coming out so quickly," she said. "I'd like you to change all the locks, and there's a padlock on the attic door. Can you take that off?"

"Sure thing, ma'am. Sorry to hear about Ricky. We used to shoot hoops together, back in the day." He shifted his weight anxiously from one foot to the other. "So are you putting the house up for sale? I hope you're not too nervous out here, all by your lonesome. You know, Ricky always said this place was haunted."

"I haven't really decided yet," she said stiffly. Why did everyone think the house was haunted? "There's a lot I need to do before I decide if I'm keeping it or not."

"I work at the factory during the week but I'll be glad to come do any jobs you might need before you go back north. Well, ma'am, let me get my tools out of the truck, and I'll get started."

Lettie half-wondered if Clarence's politeness came from a long-ago stint in the military. More likely prison, she thought wryly. Both certainly taught you to mind your manners. She left him to his work, gathered some cleaning supplies and went upstairs. Her middle-aged bladder made the first order of business to get the toilet clean enough to use.

By the time the bathroom was as spick-and-span as possible, it was late afternoon. The air was hot and thick, despite the high ceilings and open windows. She hadn't seen a fan anywhere, so she added that to her list of things to get. Carrying two full trash bags, she descended the narrow back steps to the kitchen where Clarence had finished replacing the door lock.

"All done, ma'am. This here's the key to the front door lock, this one is the basement and this is the back door. I took that padlock off the attic door. I'll mail you the invoice in the morning. And if you need any help moving stuff out or anything else, just let me know."

"That's great," Lettie said, adding the keys he handed her to her key chain.

She followed Clarence's rusty blue pickup truck back across the railroad tracks, through Campbellsburg's tiny downtown, then turned onto State Road 60 and headed towards Salem. She stopped at the ubiquitous Walmart and bought some miscellaneous supplies, including two fans and a litter box and all the accoutrements for Solo. Or should she call him Garfield? Time would tell which name was more appropriate. The cat might be used to doing his business outside but he was going to have to learn to use a litter box.

When she returned to the house after her errands, the big orange cat contritely padded his way through the tall grass to meet her at the front door. "You look more like a Solo to me," she said. "I think we'll stick with that, if you don't mind." He purred as she stroked the soft fur behind his ears.

Peace and quiet, she thought contentedly, straightening up and looking around the serene countryside. No city noise, no nosy next-door neighbors. This was the life. Or rather, this could be her new life, if she wanted, she realized. It wouldn't be so bad to move back here into her old home, Lettie thought. After working so many years, dealing with the Covid pandemic and the increasing number of patients with mental health problems, she had jumped at the chance for early retirement from the chaotic, stressful emergency department environment.

Once probate was done, Lettie would own this house and property free and clear. She had no special someone up in Indianapolis. There was no reason she couldn't let her small apartment there go, then put some money into improving the house here. Maybe she could even afford to travel a little bit. The house would look quite lovely with a new paint job, she thought wistfully, maybe even like one of those beautiful Painted Ladies houses in San Francisco. Bringing herself back to reality, first she needed to pay for Ricky's funeral, and that would take a chunk out of her savings. Certainly the idea of moving here was something to think about.

Unlocking the front door, she deposited Solo's things in the kitchen and carried a fan, her new sheets and towels up to her bedroom, the project she intended to tackle next. Turning down the hall, a flicker of movement caught her eye. Frowning, she turned her head to see nothing there, but the attic door now stood open.

Nothing happened when Lettie flicked the light switch just inside the staircase. One more thing for her to-do list, she thought, now multiple pages long. Keeping one hand on the wall for balance, she climbed the stairs and emerged into the attic proper. Cheap Venetian blinds covered all but one of the tall windows of the turret. Fumbling for the strings, she managed to get two of them to retract, letting plenty of blinding light in and raising clouds of dust.

In the light from the windows, she could see a broken rocking horse, stacks of phonograph records, a couple of cedar chests and piles and piles of boxes, the accumulated discards of generations of Kings, reaching back into the depths of the attic. Her dad's old Army footlocker stood open off to the side of her mother's vintage treadle Singer sewing machine. It could take a year or two just to go through everything here, Lettie thought. The air was definitely colder up here, which was kind of strange. Heat usually rose, right? Maybe there was a leak in the roof somewhere. She sighed. Great, just another thing for the list.

***

LETTIE SPENT the next few days going back and forth to Salem for meetings with the family attorney, the mortuary and the bank, making all the arrangements necessary after an unexpected death. She met Nick for a meal at the town café and enjoyed his company. Soon they were texting late into the night as his duties allowed. Clarence dropped by once or twice in the evenings asking for work, but she politely declined to hire him to do any more odd jobs. She'd have to see if Nick could recommend someone reliable.

Lettie was starting to wonder if the house was haunted after all.

Every now and then, the attic door would slam itself open and shut, and Solo seemed to materialize at will inside or outside the house, even when she was certain everything was locked up tight. Several times she'd gone to the attic to look for old dishes or lamps they used to have and found items had been rearranged. "Cut it out, Ricky," she muttered under her breath, as she closed the Army footlocker yet again.

Ricky's funeral took place one cloudy Saturday afternoon not quite a week later. Located about a mile north of Campbellsburg, Hop Cemetery carved out a narrow piece of grass among the emerald soybean fields and scattered dense patches of woods. Since the late 1800s, most of Lettie's kinfolk were buried here, including her name-sake, Letitia Bryan King. Her brother's cremains were to be buried adjacent to their parents, in the shadow of the tallest monument in the graveyard.

There were more people at Ricky's graveside service than Lettie had expected. Several members of a local church showed up to pay their respects, as did Clarence and several of Ricky's high school buddies. After the brief memorial, she dutifully shook hands with each person under the lowering sky, hoping that the coming rain would hold off until they all got back to town. Nick's presence would have been welcome, but he'd texted her that he was testifying at the courthouse in Salem and probably wouldn't make it.

Lettie took a few minutes to bow her head over her parents' graves, the wind pressing the skirt of her black suit against her legs, hearing the slamming of car doors as people left, eager to escape the coming storm. The temperature dropped appreciably. Thunder rolled across the hills. Any minute now, it would start to pour.

"Miz King," called a familiar voice.

Opening her eyes, she saw Clarence standing a few feet away. Puzzled, she glanced around, seeing there was no one else left in the cemetery.

"Before he died, Ricky told me about a gun your dad brought

home from World War II. It's a Luger. He said I could have it and I need to get it now," the handyman said belligerently.

"Sorry, Clarence, I'm just beginning to clear the house out. When I come across it, I'll let you know." She started to turn away when Clarence surprised her by grabbing her arm and pulling a pistol from under his jacket.

"You don't understand," he shouted above the thunder, gesturing threateningly with the weapon. "I've looked and looked all over that stupid house but I can't find it. My dealer won't give me any more meth until I catch him up. Ricky said that gun was worth some money and I need to have it now! I took all the cash he had in his wallet."

Lettie swallowed hard. "You and Ricky did drugs together, didn't you? And you were there when he died?" she managed to say, playing for time. With a sick feeling, she realized it hadn't been a ghost moving things around the house. Of course Clarence could get in anytime he liked, having installed the new locks himself.

"You should have left when I told you to!" Clarence raged at her, shaking her angrily and gesturing at her brother's final resting place. "It was all Ricky's fault!" The rising wind whipped the words from his lips. "We got high together, just like we always did. He bragged about selling that gun to get rich, but he wasn't going to share. I just gave him some extra dope so he'd sleep while I searched the house. It wasn't my fault he died!"

Lettie slowly edged her foot backwards on the uneven cemetery ground. "Calm down, Clarence. I understand, it was an accident." Overhead, the dark gray clouds hung lower, and the air was heavy with the scent of rain. Lightning flashed off to the west, and thunder rumbled closer.

When the rain started pounding down, Lettie took it as a sign. She slammed her free hand down into the middle of Clarence's arm, twisted free of his hold and ran for her car.

Lettie's heart leapt as she saw Nick running towards her, weapon in hand. He swept her around behind the cover of his body and yelled at Clarence. "Police! Drop the gun, Clarence, you're under arrest!"

Lightning flashed again and Lettie squinted into the pouring rain. It was so hard to see clearly. Was there someone else there, a black-clad figure struggling with Clarence, raking at his eyes?

Screaming thinly, Clarence dropped to the ground, clutching his face. Nick moved quickly to secure the gun. After handcuffing the crying Clarence's wrists together, he spoke into his lapel radio. "You okay?" he shouted to Lettie, who nodded dumbly. Soon, the wail of sirens cut through the storm as EMTs and additional police arrived on the scene to take Clarence away.

THE FOLLOWING DAY, Lettie and Nick sat comfortably across from each other at her kitchen table. "I've been meaning to ask you, although you may think I'm crazy. Did you see something there in the cemetery? Or someone, rather?" Lettie said hesitantly, gently urging Solo off the tabletop. "I could have sworn there was someone there with Clarence."

Nick dropped two lumps of sugar into his coffee, stirred and took a cautious sip. "What, like a shadowy woman in a long old-fashioned black dress?" He put a lemon pastry from the local bakery on her plate and helped himself to two blueberry donuts. "Something or someone put those scratches on his face, and it wasn't you and it wasn't me. I certainly didn't put anything into my official report."

"If it was a woman, it certainly couldn't have been Ricky, come to take his vengeance from the grave," Lettie said thoughtfully, nibbling her pastry in careful bites. "What does Clarence say happened?"

"He claims it was your cat, even though no one else saw a cat there. Like a cat would be out in the rain, right?" Nick snorted. "And don't worry, he won't be getting out of jail any time soon. We've got him on multiple felonies, maybe even drug-induced homicide, among other things. That's up to the prosecutor's office."

"Well, whoever she is, I thank her very much for saving my life. Evidently Casper isn't the only friendly ghost." Lettie smiled at Nick.

"So, have you decided to sell this place and move back to Indy?" Nick asked, in a carefully casual tone. "You probably won't need the money now."

"No," Lettie acknowledged. Once she knew what Clarence had been searching for, she'd had a good idea where to look, her grandmother Lona's cedar chest next to the window seat in the attic. Covered by a hideous orange crocheted afghan and piled high with old issues of *National Geographic*, her dad's Army papers and souvenirs lay buried under layers of hand-pieced quilts, reeking of mothballs. It was no wonder Clarence hadn't found them.

Her father had rarely spoken of his time as a soldier in the 42nd Infantry Division and his participation in the liberation of Dachau, the oldest concentration camp in Nazi Germany. Skimming through her dad's wartime journals, it was clear to Lettie that he had taken the Luger, among other things, from the camp commandant. Possibly, guilt over the theft and the remembered horror of the Nazi atrocities led him to hide the reminders of his Army days away, out of sight and out of mind.

Funnily enough, when Lettie had done some research online last night, the Luger proved to be relatively common and was only worth around $1,000. However, the dusty volume of *Mein Kampf*, personally dedicated to the camp commandant and autographed by Adolf Hitler -- that was likely to be worth quite a bit more.

"No, I've decided to stay here. I should have enough money to fix this place up and make it comfortable, and I can always work part-time if I need to. There's plenty of room here for me and Solo. I think I'll make this home again." She smiled at him across the gingham tablecloth.

Nick reached over and took her hand. "It sounds like a good plan to me," he said gruffly.

Above their heads, the attic door slammed with satisfaction.

THE SECRET OF BONES
BY C.A. PADDOCK

I look across the fallow field, dead corn stalks the only reminder of its once fertile soil. Tears fill my eyes. I tell my mother, long gone from this world, "I know that this land fed and supported our family for many generations. I know that the money you received from leasing this farm paid for our rent and groceries many times, and that you left it to me so I too would always have something to fall back on. But I can't keep it any longer, this dark soil of secrets, because I remember everything, Mom. I remember the day we found the bones."

<hr>

"I think I found one, Mike!" I yelled to my cousin as I dropped to my knees on the raw earth.

"Let me see, Karen!"

It was a warm Easter day in 1976. As soon as Sunday dinner was over, my cousin Mike and I changed out of our Easter outfits and barreled out of the house to play on our grandmother's farm. We hadn't seen each other since Thanksgiving as my mother didn't like spending too much time with her family. The day she turned 18, she left that "god-forsaken, life-draining place" to move to the big city of Indianapolis, where she could be who she wanted to be without someone telling her she "wouldn't 'mount to nothin'." This was one of those rare holidays that my mother decided we could visit my grandmother, aunt and uncle, and cousins. Mike's sister was away at college, and so it was just Mike and me on this day.

We explored the meadows and the vegetable patch near the creek where we looked for expelled mounds of mud surrounding crawdad holes. We would bend down close to them and drop pebbles into the hole to listen for the splash of water at the end. We found abandoned bright orange pinchers, pulling on the white tendon to make the claws open and close. I screamed as my cousin chased me with them, trying to latch hold of my pink plastic barrettes clasping the ends of my pigtails. We ran over to the small creek that cut the farm in half and carefully stepped across smooth, flat rocks. They had been spaced perfectly to match a footstep, even ones as small as ours, by our grandfather or perhaps his father to go between the fields. A tractor crossing was next to the stones. Once on the other side, we scurried up the plowed hill to a green island inhabited by a lone sycamore tree that shared its shade with a large stone, wide and flat, that served as a respite for a weary farmer or 9- and 10-year-old kids on a Sunday afternoon adventure.

Mike came running to where I had started to unearth the dingy, yellowish white object I had spotted near the edge of the grassy border. I pushed my fingers deeper into the moist soil.

"I can't get it. It's not as small as the arrowheads we used to find. Maybe it's something else. Help me dig it out."

Mike sank to his knees next to me. We both grabbed hands full of dirt and threw them to the side until we could see the stone-like mass more clearly.

"That's not an arrowhead or even an ax head," I whispered, realizing what it might be, but wanting my cousin to confirm my suspicions. "What is it, Mike?"

"It looks like a bone." Mike pulled out a long, pale stick, brushing away the dirt. He used the hem of his white and blue Spirit of '76 t-shirt to remove the last bits of soil.

"Is it from a rabbit? Or a cat?"

"Maybe...Or maybe this is an old Miami Indian burial ground, like Grandpa used to say."

"Do you really think so? Let me see it." Mike handed me the bone after I wiped my mud-covered hands on my red "Love is...never having to say you're sorry" t-shirt. "It just looks like the remains of the chicken leg we ate for dinner."

Mike began to scoop out more dirt. "Let's see if there's more."

Like dogs excited to find their rewards, we dug further down to see what else we could find. Before long we uncovered a skull, and it was obvious this was not a rabbit, cat, or any other animal that roamed the countryside. We stopped and looked at each other and knew what we had to do. Mike pocketed the chicken leg bone, and we ran back down the hill, across the rocks and back to the house as fast as our Keds could take us.

***

"Grandma Ida, Uncle Jim, Aunt Mabel, Mom, Dad, look what we found!" Mike and I shouted at our respective family members as we ran into the house through the back door, our voices in a syncopated chorus.

"Shut the door! Do you think we live in a barn or something?" Grandma yelled. I turned back and pulled the door closed. Mike ran into the dining room where my aunt, uncle, and grandma were sitting around the dinner table. Mom was nowhere to be found.

"Look at this! And there are more." Mike held out the object for the adults to inspect.

"Oh, it's just an animal bone. Where did you find it?" Grandma Ida asked us.

"We were up on the hill by the sycamore tree and big rock

looking for arrowheads," I began. Suddenly, Grandma grabbed the bone out of Mike's hand and held it up to her face.

"I thought it was an arrowhead and so we started digging it out," I said. "When we pulled it out, we thought it was from a rabbit or a cat, but when we dug down more, we found—"

"—a human skull!" Mike shouted. "You've got to come see! Maybe it's a Miami Indian who used to live here that Grandpa used to talk about."

Uncle Jim had a funny look on his face and glanced at my grandmother. She returned his look, but quickly turned her attention back to Mike and me. At the time it seemed odd, but I was so excited I didn't realize what that look meant.

I jumped up and down, thrilled to think about our find. Just as I wondered where my mother was so I could tell her, she came in the front door, her eyes red and moist.

"What's all the yelling about?" Mother asked, wiping her eyes.

"We found bones! Mike thinks that it could be Indian bones!"

"Now hold on, sister. We don't know anything about them yet," Grandma said, stopping me from speculating any further. "And if they are Indian bones, we need to pay them respect and leave them alone."

"But what else could they be?" Mike asked.

Mom looked at her brother. "You don't really think they could be Indian bones, do you, Jim?"

"What else could they be, Maxine? You know dad always thought there were Miami Indians that lived here at one time. Besides no one goes to that back field except us."

Uncle Jim turned to Mike and me, "You two needn't worry about them. I can go find them and cover them back up to leave them in peace."

"But we want to show you where we found them, Dad!"

"Don't you think we need to go look at them first, Jimmy, before you decide if they are Indian bones?" Mom asked.

In a flash the normally pink color of Jim's face deepened ever so slightly and just as fast it returned to normal. Uncle Jim turned to Mike, "Okay, we can go take a look at them first." Then to me he said, "Can you two show us exactly where you found them?"

Grandma Ida stood. "I think I better come with you," she said, slipping the bone into her violet print apron pocket.

Uncle Jim also got up from the table and said to Aunt Mabel, "Do you want to come with us?"

"I think I will stay here and finish cleaning up. This is between you and your family," she replied.

Mother's eyes and mouth opened wide. "Well, I'm not sitting around here. I'm going with you."

Since it was farther than Grandma could walk, we got into Uncle Jim's brand-new gold and white Ford pickup truck. Mike and I climbed into its bed.

"I think I will sit back here with you two," Mother told us, stepping up on the shiny bumper, her blue-checked dress billowing up, showing her stockinged legs.

Uncle Jim handed us a large, rusty shovel. "Can you two grab a hold of this and keep it from sliding around?" When he turned to open the truck door, I noticed he had an old feed sack in his hands and a pair of leather work gloves stuffed in the back pocket of his blue jeans. He threw the cloth bag into the cab before he got in. I wondered what he needed the sack for.

Uncle Jim slowly drove the truck down the lane as we bumped along. He paused at the creek crossing, like a horse unsure whether to take the next step into the water, before guiding our ride through the shallow stream. Once on the other side, the truck lurched forward when he pushed on the gas to make it up the hill and through the field.

He stopped about halfway and opened the back sliding window of the truck. "This's as far as we can go. You said it is up by that sycamore tree and rock? We will need to walk the rest of the way." Mike and I jumped out of the truck and started running towards the location where we found the bones before the rest of them got out.

"It's here!" Mike and I pointed to the hole we had made, our bodies quivering with excitement.

When the adults got there, they stared at the skeletal remains in the open ground. Uncle Jim and Grandma Ida looked at each other again but did not say anything. Mother eyed them with suspicion.

"Did you already know about these bones? I saw you looking at each other." Mother's voice betrayed her earlier recovered demeanor. "Do you think it is an Indian burial ground? Dad always said that he thought this area was just a small Indian settlement. And not a place they would bury their dead."

Mom squinted her eyes and wrinkles formed across her forehead the more questions she asked. When no one answered her, she yelled, "Is this another one of the secrets you have kept from me?"

"Now, hold your horses, Maxine! This ain't the time or place to talk about these things." Grandma looked over at Mike and me. My mother crossed her arms and turned her back to all of us.

Grandma Ida continued. "You know what? I think these bones have been here for a very long time, and it's not our place to disturb them. We need to cover them back up and let them lie in peace."

"But don't you think we need to tell someone, Grandma?" I asked.

"No, we don't. Do you know what they would do? They would come and dig up the bones and probably destroy this whole field looking for more. We couldn't get the crops in this year, and we would lose a lot of money. Besides, if this is a burial ground, how would you feel if someone dug up your grandfather and all the rest of your relatives and took them away to study them? It's best that we cover them back up and leave them alone." And with that, she reached into her apron pocket, retrieved the bone we had found, and returned it to its resting place. She nodded at my uncle, who picked up the shovel.

"Now you both know why we can't tell anyone else about what you found here today, right? It would be bad for us and much worse to disturb the bones just so some high and mighty professor types could pick them apart. Do you both promise not to say a word about these bones?"

Mike and I both nodded.

"I need to hear you say it."

"We won't tell anyone, Grandma," Mike and I answered in unison.

"Good. Now why don't you both go on back up to the house and play while your uncle covers the bones. We will be up shortly."

I looked at Mike, and then over at my mother, who still had her back to everyone. She turned her head slightly towards us and nodded.

"I'll race you back to the house. First one there gets to eat the other's Easter candy," Mike said, taking off. I followed quickly behind him.

MIKE WAS RUMMAGING through my candy on the front porch when we heard the truck return and doors slam, first the truck doors, then the back door of the house. When Mike stopped to listen to what was going on, I grabbed my basket of treats from his lap before he could eat any more. He picked up his basket from the cement floor and began to unwrap a chocolate rabbit. A few minutes later, we could hear loud voices coming from inside.

"I wonder what they're shouting about. Do you think it could be about the bones?" I asked.

"I don't know, but let's find out."

We quietly set down our baskets and crept to the front door. Mike pulled on the handle and opened the glass storm door enough for us to slide behind the burnt orange- and gold- flowered velvet couch where we could hear better and see into the dining room.

"You've always left me out of everything, Ida. Like today when you told me you were leaving the farm to Jim. The farm should be split between both of us! You have all your little secrets with each other. You've never treated me as part of this family!" Tears streamed down Mother's face as she tried to speak.

"As I told you earlier, your brother has been farming this land ever since your dad died and it should go to him. You don't know a thing about running a farm. You're the one who didn't want anything to do with us, taking off to the big city like you did," Grandma replied.

Mike looked at me. We knew we shouldn't be spying on them, but we couldn't stop.

"Because you treated me like a farm hand and not your daughter! Jimmy always got what he wanted. He got a new sports car when he turned 16. But when I was old enough to drive I was told there wasn't enough money to even buy me a used car!"

"Stop being so dramatic, Maxine! You always make everything about you. You decided to leave us, and I stayed to take care of mom and dad and the farm. I deserve everything I have gotten," Uncle Jim said, jumping into the shouting match.

Before anyone could continue, there was a knock on the front door. I glanced at Mike and he nodded. We stood up from behind the couch. A surprised look crossed the adults' faces as we scurried into the next room.

Grandmother Ida waited a moment before she went to answer the door.

"Hello, Fred. This is not a good time. You know it's Easter and we have family visiting."

"Yes, that's why I've come. I thought Maxine might be here, and I haven't seen her in many years. I wanted to stop in to say hello. I also need to talk to Jim for minute," the man at the door replied.

Mom leapt across the room when she heard who it was.

"Mr. Burkhart, please come in! It is so good to see you!" Mr. Burkhart carefully stepped into the living room using a cane to guide his way. What little white hair he had stuck out like the bristles on a hairbrush and a blue and white handkerchief peeked out from the front pocket of his bib overalls.

"Karen, come meet Mr. Burkhart who lives down the road. He's lived there ever since I can remember."

Uncle Jim cut me off before I could greet the neighbor. "What do you want, Fred? As Mom said, this is not a good time."

"This is the perfect time to visit, Jim. I've got news to share, and it gives me a chance to tell everyone what's been going on all these years."

"Now listen, old man, get out of our house or you'll be sorry!"

"Be sorry? What more could you do to me? I am not leaving until I've said what I came here to say, you little weasel!"

"I haven't done anything to you that you didn't deserve!"

"I was only trying to be a good friend and help your dad. I didn't deserve you blackmailing me all these years just so you could have your big house!"

"Shut up! You don't know what you're talking about!" Uncle Jim grabbed the elderly neighbor's arm.

"Let go of me!" With his other arm, the neighbor raised his cane and hit Jim's side. Jim pushed back on the arm he held, causing the old man to fall against the velveteen couch.

"Jimmy, how dare you!" Mom yelled, rushing to Mr. Burkhart and helping him sit up. "Are you okay?"

"I'm fine, Maxine. Let me have my say and I will be on my way."

Glowering at the two on the couch, Uncle Jim didn't move until Grandma pulled him away and whispered, "Jim, what did he mean by blackmail?"

"It's time you all told me what's going on." Mom's eye narrowed as she looked at Grandma Ida and her brother. She turned her head. "And how are you involved, Mr. Burkhart?"

The neighbor leaned forward and exhaled. "I did something years ago that I regret to this day. I was only trying to be a good friend to your father, and at the time it seemed to be the only option. Your brother here found out about it and started blackmailing me after your father died."

Grandma's chin dropped and glared at her son. "What? You've

been blackmailing Fred at the same time you've been blackmailing me to get what you want?"

"Would someone just tell me what the hell this is about!" Mom screamed.

"Years ago, your dad came to me one night asking for help…"

"Let me tell her, Fred." Grandma walked over to the couch and sat down by my mom. "Do you remember when you were little there was a man who came and slept in the barn while he helped your dad plant corn?" She paused. When Mother didn't answer, she continued.

"One day your brother, who was about the same age as Karen is now, and I went to the barn to feed the cows. Your brother was in the back stables dropping hay into the troughs and I was filling a bucket from the corn bin when the man—Mr. Fields he called himself—came down from the hay mow and asked if he could help. He came up to me and said that he knew a good-looking woman when he saw one. One who knew how to help a man. He rubbed the back of his hand across my face and leaned in. I could smell the whiskey. I told him he better back away because my son was in the barn. That's when he pushed me up against the wood post and said that was good because he could learn what kind of woman his mother really was." My grandmother paused and then continued.

"I didn't want your brother to see what was happening, but I couldn't keep quiet when he lifted my dress. Your brother heard my scream and came running, just as your dad opened the barn door and came in. Your dad saw what was happening and grabbed a shovel, all the while yelling, "Get off my wife!" In one fell swoop, he swung the shovel down on the man's head. Mr. Fields collapsed to the floor. Dad told us to get back up to the house and stay there. When we got back to the house, you were still upstairs in your room playing with your baby doll and carriage."

Mother whispered, "I don't remember that day."

Grandma Ida sighed again before she continued with the story.

"Later that night when your dad came back to the house, he told your brother and me to forget about Mr. Fields and that he wouldn't bother us no more. He told your brother there was nothing to worry about and to forget what he saw. Everyone was ok now."

"But that's not the real story, is it, Fred?" Uncle Jim said. "Yes, it's true that Mr. Fields attacked Mom and Dad hit him with a shovel. But I know what happened after that. I snuck out of the house and ran back to the barn to see what Dad was going to do. That's when I saw Fred here stab that drunk bastard and made Dad help clean up his mess."

"My mess?? I saved your dad from his mess! Your dad came to me to help him get rid of that vagrant, not knowing if he was dead or alive. When we got back to the barn, he was hiding behind the door and jumped out with a knife. Your dad knocked the knife out of his hand and pushed him to the floor. I grabbed the knife and stabbed him before he could hurt anyone else. I didn't mean to kill him." Fred's eyes began to water before he continued.

"Your dad and I didn't know what to do, but we knew we couldn't call the police. We loaded him in the back of the truck and took him to the back field and buried him. We figured no one knew where he came from, and he said he didn't have any family, so we thought our secret was safe. That is until Jim started threatening me."

"It's that man's bones the kids found today, aren't they? They're not from some Indian. I knew you both knew something about them!" Mom looked over at Grandma and up to Jim.

"You found the bones today?" Fred started to shake, shrugged his shoulders, and stopped.

I started to leap out of my chair in the dining room from where Mike, Aunt Mabel and I had been watching the fight to tell him about our find. Aunt Mabel touched my arm and shook her head. I sat back down.

"When did you find out about all this, Ida?" Mom asked.

"I didn't know what happened that night until your dad told me just before he died. I don't know if it was his conscience bothering him or if he was afraid of what was going to happen to him after he died, but he told me what he and Fred had done, and that Jim had been extorting him since he turned 16. Once Jim found out that your dad told me everything, he made me continue to give him money and let him run the farm like he wanted, or he would go to the police and tell them what had happened, and that Fred had killed the man. I didn't know that he was also getting money from him." Grandma leaned over and looked at her neighbor. "I now understand why you've avoided us all these years."

Fred sighed. "And that's why I came today. I wanted to see you one last time. I have cancer and I don't have much time left to live. You can't take from me anymore, Jim. It just doesn't matter to me if you call the authorities, especially now that you have found the bones."

Uncle Jim, defeated, finally sat down in the stuffed chair behind him.

No one said a word for a few moments. Scowling, Mom stood up from the couch and walked a few steps. She turned around to face her friend and family, words exploding from her mouth.

"How could you keep something like this from me all these years? You made me believe there was something wrong with me, that I was not good enough to be part of this family." She stopped yelling and directed her gaze to the elderly man.

"I'm so glad you came by, Mr. Burkhart, and I'm sorry about your cancer, but I think it's time for you to leave. Karen and I will stop by the house later on our way home. And don't worry, I'll make sure Jim doesn't bother you again."

"I'm sorry you had to find out this way, Maxine. I'll go now." Fred struggled to stand up. On the third try and with the help of Grandma Ida, he stood up, paused to steady himself, and left. Grandma uttered a "goodbye" and sat back down.

Mom resumed her outburst. "I still don't understand why you didn't tell me what was going on, Ida. And, Jimmy, I always knew you were rotten, but to find out you blackmailed your own parents and Mr. Burkhart for years is despicable. I should call the police on you for what you've done!"

"Be quiet, Maxine!" Grandma shouted back. "You weren't here, and your dad and I didn't think you needed to know. You had moved to the big city and were making a life for yourself. You had a good job. You even had a good man until he left you and Karen. So why burden you with long forgotten memories that didn't make a difference to anyone anymore?"

"Didn't make a difference, huh? You don't know what difference it would have made to me! I had a right to know why you treated me the way you did. I needed to know. And it sure doesn't sound like they were long forgotten memories with Jimmy reminding you all the time. The only reason I know now is because Mr. Burkhart came by. You wouldn't have told me even earlier when the kids found the bones because you've let your son control your life.

"You've let me believe all these years I was the problem. YOU were the problem, thinking you knew what was best for me. Well, now I'm telling you what's best for me. Ida, you're going to sign the farm over to me. Jim, you will let me have the farm and everything that goes with it, or I WILL call the police and tell them about your blackmail. Do you hear me?"

Uncle Jim raised his head up and down once.

"I don't want anything to do with either of you for the rest of my life. I don't want you to call me ever again to say you're sorry or invite me to Sunday dinner. I want you to stay away from me and my daughter. Karen, get your things. We're leaving."

Mother and I left. I never saw Grandma Ida again, but I know Mom saw her a few more times to transfer the farm. Mom allowed her to live at the house until she died. Mike wrote me once to tell me that he was moving to Michigan with his mom since his mom had divorced Uncle Jim.

———

I TAKE a deep breath in and fill my body with the earthy smell of the land. I hear the whispers of that day, the whispers of the bones and the secrets of our family's story.

"That's why selling the farm is so important to me, Mom, to throw off those cloaks of secrets and lies that weighed on you for so long. I've signed over the deed to the new owners. It is theirs now to add to their family history and create new stories—stories I hope will be void of the secrets and lies that tear families apart."

It begins to rain. I turn and walk away.

WOULD YOU RATHER?
BY ELIZABETH A. SAN MIGUEL

I gotta tell you, it drives me nuts when some adult goes on and on about always having a choice. I mean sure, you might sort of have a choice, but all the options are so bad it's the same as not having any choice at all.

Had it been my decision, I wouldn't live in a small rural town in the middle of Indiana. I certainly would not have let my father name me, I kid you not, Sierra Nevada Olmstead. I'm named after the place and not the beer by the way. Nor would I have decided to have my father disappear when I was only four. I have no idea where he went, and Mom and Granny won't talk about it. I could also do without the gnawing fear in my stomach when I think about him. Finally, I would never ever have chosen to have a brain tumor. Yes, a brain tumor.

Sometimes at school I would play this dumb game with my friends called "Would You Rather?" Someone asks two horrible things and you have to say which one you would choose. Would you rather lick an ashtray or eat a worm? Would you rather be blind or crippled?

Would you rather have a brain tumor and have your Dad in your life or no brain tumor and have him be gone?

Nope, no choice for me. I had a brain tumor and every day I wondered where he had gone. Was he alive and didn't want me, or had he wanted me and died? I can't remember a time when that question was not my first thought upon waking in the morning and last thought as I fell asleep at night. It's sort of like an ache in your muscles after you ran too fast and far the day before. In this case, my brain is the muscle and rampant curiosity is the activity. Not just about my dad but everything.

"Sierra, sometimes you should just let sleeping dogs lie," my Granny would sigh after answering a barrage of questions I have been asking since I started talking. I've been told many times my first word wasn't Ma or Da but why? Granny's reply caused me to ask a bunch more questions. I mean if a dog can't speak and it's sleeping, how's it supposed to lie? Give me a break, I was six during that particular exchange.

Anyway, back to the brain tumor. I woke up with a hella bad headache on my twelfth birthday. My friends and I planned to get together to celebrate my birthday at the ice-skating rink and then go to Mom and Granny's café afterwards for a meal and cake. Instead of enjoying time with my friends, Mom took me to the doctor, who diagnosed migraines and prescribed Tylenol. I was so angry my party was cancelled I yelled at my mom. I wasn't angry at her, but I couldn't exactly yell at my head.

"Sierra, do you think it's a picnic for me? I had to cancel bidding on a job," Mom yelled back. Besides owning the café with my Granny, Mom was also a building contractor. She crossed her arms over her chest and took a few deep breaths. "What's gotten into you? You used to be such a pleasant child. Now you're moody and angry all the time. I hope this isn't what your teenage years will be like."

I tried not to, but I started crying and had the worst time stopping. I hoped this wasn't my future as well. Yelling at people I love, anger, tears, and waking up scared out of my mind at I don't know what. Happy freaking birthday to me.

A few weeks later I was outside my school, sitting on a swing talking to my best friend Maya, when I fell off and started shaking. Maya's smart. She put me on my side and called 911. Turns out I had had a seizure. This led to fun medical tests where I was put into a tube with loud knocking sounds while a machine looked at my brain function. Oh, another thing I would have chosen was to *not* have a fear of enclosed spaces.

"Always such a troublemaker this one," my Uncle Ryan said before we drove down to Indy for some specialized tests. He did one of those quick side hugs and leaned down to give me a quick peck on the top of my head and patted me on the back. Uncle Ryan was always good about letting people know he cared, but there was a strain behind his smile. A few years ago, when I was a kid, if you had asked me what my Uncle Ryan feared, I would have said nothing. Now I'm not so sure.

I don't suppose both he and my mom needed to be there, but it was kind of nice. Uncle Ryan is my Dad's older brother. He is also an FBI agent. When I'm scared or sad, he's the best at cheering me up.

He loves my dad and I know he still misses him. I think he and Dad argued about something dumb before my dad disappeared and Uncle Ryan always regretted it. My uncle was one of the few people who would tell me about my dad. Ryan adopted me so that I could benefit from his excellent medical insurance. I love my uncle and I loved that he adopted me. I don't remember much about my dad and what I do remember is jumbled. In my memories I am not always sure if I'm remembering my dad or if it's my uncle. I live a few houses down from him with Mom and Granny. Even though legally he is my dad, I have always called him Uncle.

A week after those tests, I had an appointment with a pediatric oncology neurologist. Mom just called him a specialist doctor. Mom, Granny, and Uncle were all with me for this first visit to go over the tests. Looking back, I should've been able to figure out something bad was happening. Otherwise, having all three of them there was overkill. The doctor was located an hour's drive one way from Littleton in a city north and east of Indianapolis.

All I can say is, I'm glad I didn't know what 'oncologist' meant beforehand. Once you get there and find out this specialty means you have brain cancer, all you want to do is find a dog, a blanket, some chocolate, and a closet to hide in.

As the doctor explained my condition, I wondered if oncologists went through training to be so boring you inevitably calmed down even though what they are telling you is as serious as a heart attack... or, you know, brain cancer. Nothing the doctor said upset me. It was the reactions of my family that scared me. Or rather their non-reactions. We're all talkers. They just sat there silent.

Dr. Ulam was an old guy. Probably in his forties. He mainly talked to my uncle, but he tried to keep me, Mom, and Granny in the discussion. I have an excellent vocabulary, but not an excellent medical vocabulary. I was totally lost when Dr. Ulam started throwing out words like meningioma, seizure, neurofibromatosis type 2, et cetera. On the upside, so were my Mom, Granny, and Uncle Ryan.

"Sorry," Dr. Ulam said when he saw our confusion. "I try to not be that doctor. What I was trying to say is that usually the type of cancer she has is genetic. Did anyone else in your family develop brain tumors?" Dr. Ulam asked.

Mom and Granny looked at one another. "Not that we been told," Granny said.

"Well, do you have any stories of people in your family going a bit odd, usually in their late teens or 20s?"

Mom and Granny didn't say anything but they both stiffened a bit and looked at one another again. My uncle Ryan must have noticed too.

"What? Was there someone?"

Granny shrugged, "We had at least five generations who all were born, lived, and died in Littleton. Some are bound to be odd."

"Right, but is there someone specific?" Dr. Ulam asked.

Both Mom and Granny shook their heads while my uncle tilted his head in such a way I knew he was in deep thought.

The doc picked up on it too. "Mr. Olmstead?"

"Uh, sorry, my brother, Sierra's father, disappeared when she was what 3 or 4, right?" He looked at Granny, his mom. She nodded. "It was bizarre. I mean he was just gone. Completely unlike him. And, I haven't been able to find him...and I looked."

I leaned against my uncle. He and my father had been close growing up, just over a year apart in age. Uncle Ryan had been away learning how to be an FBI agent when my dad disappeared.

"You...you looked for him?" Granny asked him. Of her three children, Uncle Ryan was the only one still around. Sherry, my Granny's only daughter, had died when she was maybe six.

"Well, yeah. It's not like him...he would never have left Sierra without a word. Ever since Sherry died, he wanted to be a dad." He frowned.

My uncle continued, "No way Baz would intentionally leave Sierra. Plus, there's nothing to suggest he was still walking around past the time you last saw him. I wonder if he had a tumor and it caused him to wander off and maybe killed him...and we just never found him?"

"Perhaps, but who's Sherry?" Dr. Ulam asked.

"My only daughter," said Granny.

According to my uncle, my dad had doted on her. He was, wow, my age now, 12 when Sherry died.

"And she died?" Dr. Ulam said. "From what, if you don't mind my asking."

"Stupidity. Not hers," Granny said under her breath and crossed her arms in front of her. We were all quiet for a minute.

My mother cleared her throat and quietly asked, "Doctor, what might be symptoms of a brain tumor?"

"Well, it mainly depends on where the tumor is located in the brain. But the seizures Sierra is experiencing are fairly common. Sometimes, it can change an individual's personality."

"Change their personality?" Granny said.

"Well, yes, a kind or passive person might become aggressive or violent and sometimes the opposite is true."

"Well, I guess we don't have to worry about that with Sierra. You haven't ever been sweet so any change is gotta be an improvement," Uncle Ryan said and then winked at me.

But there was an ever so slight tremor in his voice. I punched him in the arm, and then leaned up against him. Thinking about the lost siblings he loved on a day he also was thinking about me and my predicament was hard for him. My heart sped up a bit. He was worried about losing me. I felt a heat on my ears. I was glad they were covered by my hair.

"If there's a personality change, is that permanent?" Granny asked.

"Oh no, well, I mean, if she were to have a personality change, after the surgery, she would most likely return to, uh, normal."

Granny nodded, put her hand to her mouth, and then a tear ran down her cheek. She wiped it away quickly, but it was too late. I saw.

Please don't cry. Please, please don't cry, I thought. I wasn't sure if this was thinking to Granny or myself.

"Ms. Olmsted, considering the nature of the tumor, we caught it early. Her prognosis is good."

"Yes, yes, thank you," she said.

Mom looked upset. And now, I hoped she wouldn't cry too.

"Will she need the surgery then?" Mom said.

"Yes, I think that would be best. It's not a simple surgery, but it could be so much worse."

"When?" Mom asked.

"As soon as possible. She'll need to see the surgeon first. But as soon as they can get Sierra on the schedule. If all goes well, maybe next week."

"How long...how long will I be in the hospital?" I asked.

"Well, that's difficult to say. I would expect at least a week, but maybe less. It depends on how well things go. You will have to have follow-up treatment as well. Possibly radiation. We'll see."

Radiation? "Uh, does this mean I'll lose my hair?" I asked.

"I'm sorry, Sierra, but a good chunk of your hair will need to be shaved off for the surgery. Your hair will grow back though. Afterwards the radiation will cause the hair on the affected side to be thinner. Eventually, it will get back to normal."

If I lived.

"Oh Sierra, you can just start wearing hats. I still have some of my mother's hats," Granny said.

I smiled at her. "That'd be so cool," I said and then I looked down and got super worried.

Some of my Granny's most cherished items were her mother's clothes. I must be dying. There's no other reason I could think of why Granny would let me wear one of Granny V's hats. It must have upset me way more than I realized because the next thing I remember, I was on the floor, looking up into Dr. Ulam's face. I had had another seizure.

"Well that sucked," I said.

"Yes. I think next week," Dr. Ulam said to my family who were all down on the ground with me.

It was a quiet drive home. Everyone, including myself, lost in their own thoughts. My Uncle Ryan dropped my mom off at her and Granny's café.

Uncle Ryan dropped us off at our house. "Carmen said dinner should be ready in about 30 minutes."

My Aunt Carmen's cooking is almost as good as Mom's and Granny's. And I enjoyed going over to their house because she and Uncle Ryan talked to me like I had a brain. Not that Granny or Mom made me feel stupid, it's just they wouldn't always answer my questions. Or they would try to candy coat the answer to make the world not seem so scary. The thing is, the world's scary. I'd rather be prepared.

"How are you doing?" Aunt Carmen asked as we finished clearing. Granny had gone for a walk and Uncle Ryan was taking care of my little cousins.

"Oh, well, did Uncle Ryan mention the incident earlier?"

"Incident?"

"The seizure?"

She just looked at me.

I sat down hard in the kitchen chair. "I was ok...except, Granny is out of sorts, and they're all being so nice to me."

"And?" Aunt Carmen said gently.

"And...it's freaking me out. Am I going to die?"

"Eventually, we all do...but while a brain tumor will never be minor...my understanding is they caught yours early and it's operable. You're young and otherwise healthy. There's no reason to believe you won't survive for the foreseeable future."

As far as I know Aunt Carmen has never lied to me. Her statement seemed factual, and I suddenly felt lighter. Then I felt irritated. "Why are Mom and Granny acting so weird then? Even Uncle Ryan's been strange too."

She was quiet for a moment while she pulled her thoughts together. "You remember when your Great Granny V was sick before she died."

I nodded. It had only been a couple of years ago. I loved her and still missed her. "For about a year before she died, Granny V kept getting sick and ending up in the hospital. Whenever she took a turn, how did you feel?"

"I was scared she would die...and then she did."

"You kept asking if you could do anything for her, right?"

"Well yeah...of course."

"Why?"

"Why what?"

"Why did you keep asking her? I know you did, even when she was doing a lot better."

I thought about it. Wasn't that what you were supposed to do? "It's polite, right?"

Aunt Carmen smiled at me. "It is, to a point, but you kept asking, and she would occasionally get annoyed."

I remembered Granny V's regal look as she would shoo me away and in her still thick French accent say, "I am well. Stop hovering."

"Why did you keep asking?"

I remember spending a lot of afternoons with Granny V. She taught me to knit and sew and was the type of person who would let you know if they didn't want you around. I felt loved and safe when I was around her. She kept getting sick and I wanted to fix her and couldn't. I felt helpless.

"I wanted to be able to fix the situation and I couldn't. That's why they're being so nice? They can't fix the situation?"

"Maybe," she smiled. "Don't take advantage but let them help. We all love you."

I MOVED into the family room where Uncle Ryan was playing with my two little cousins. Jenny was two and baby Baz was one. His name is actually Sebastian, named after my Dad. My uncle was sprawled on the floor with them. They were all coloring. Uncle Ryan looked up at me as I came in.

"Join us." He held out the coloring book. I shook my head and sat down next to him with my back against the couch. I looked at Jenny and Baz and smiled.

"Do you think they'll be as close as you and Dad?" I asked.

"I hope so," he said. "I wish..."

"What? You wish what?"

He sighed and quietly grunted. "Lots of things. I wish you had a sibling."

"Well, technically I do," I said and looked at my cousins. "You realize my favorite part of you adopting me is that I can tell people you're my dad and my uncle." I snorted a bit at this and so did Ryan.

"You're so like him," he said. "Same silly sense of humor. Same sass. Same...," he looked at my head on the side where my tumor was. "I never could understand, he would *never* have left you. All I can think was, he must be somewhere nearby. Maybe he had a seizure like you did, but no one was there to help him. If he fell in the lake or he was in the middle of the woods and he die..., uh, nevermind."

"Sheesh, Uncle Ryan, you think I can't add the D to the end and get died. Do you know what happened? Mom and Granny won't ever talk about it."

"I was in Virginia at the time. Got a call from Mom a couple of days after he went missing. She wondered if he had come out for a visit with me. Your mom said he had walked to the store to get some milk or something like that and he never returned. They told the sheriff the next day, but he just figured Baz had gone off to be alone for a day or two and would be back. Your Mom said they had some stupid argument, but she said it wasn't like him to just disappear. But Baz was an adult so the police didn't bother to start looking for him right away."

"An argument?"

"Yeah, your mom said she was feeling cranky and was mad Baz hadn't stopped at the store and gotten milk."

"Did they argue a lot?"

Uncle Ryan shook his head. "Not that I ever noticed, but remember I was away a lot at that time. I looked for him for years... and nothing."

"Um, did he get the milk?"

Uncle Ryan smiled. "Nope."

So, he never made it to the store.

Baz came over and sat on my lap. I softly kissed the top of his noggin. "Where could he have walked between here and the store, had a seizure, and no one would have found him?" I asked.

"Yeah, my thought exactly. Maybe, if he had an argument with Grace, he took a walk. He could walk fast and far. At first, I thought maybe something had happened where he fell and got hurt or drowned. I even tried checking for people showing up with amnesia. Then for a long time I thought he'd been murdered."

"Murder?"

"Yes, and as horrible him getting hurt and dying alone would be, it's what I would prefer. Well, actually, I would prefer he was still alive and would come back to us. Barring that, I would prefer him dying alone."

"Why?" I was stunned.

"If I knew who did it but didn't have enough evidence to convict them...I don't think I could forgive them. I'd have to kill them."

At this point, feeling baby Baz squirm happily, I learned holding a child while talking about death is a major comfort.

I STAYED another 30 minutes and then headed home. The house was empty. Granny had left a note. "Gone to see Claude and Sherry."

I decided I wanted to talk to Granny and headed out of the house and walked two blocks to the cemetery where my grandfather and aunt were buried.

The light was getting low and fog seemed to rise from the ground. Granny was looking down at their graves.

"Granny?" I said quietly.

Granny gave a start. "Sierra, you trying to give me a heart attack? Shouldn't you be resting?"

"No and no. I just...it's just, you've been down ever since the doctor's appointment."

She looked up from staring at the gravestones. "Sierra...," she said, and her voice trailed off. She closed her eyes and looked away again.

"I'm sorry," I said.

Granny tilted her head a bit to the left, "Why? What'd you do?"

"Getting cancer. I'm sorry I got cancer." I was on the verge of tears when Granny rolled her eyes.

"It's hardly your fault, Sierra. That doctor says the outlook is good."

"Well then...why're you so upset?"

She gathered her thoughts. Granny looked up at me and I could tell she had decided to tell me something but just as quickly she changed her mind back. She sighed.

"When your Gramps and Aunt Sherry died, I was in my early 40s. I was so angry at Claude after it happened. She was only six. He should have protected her better." Granny's voice cracked. "She should have been in the back seat and buckled up in a car with some safety features. Instead, she was in the front and unbuckled in his 'classic' car. I will never know what he was thinking."

"You were angry at Gramps? But he died in the accident too."

"Someday, if you ever have children...it's hard and wonderful all at the same time. Sherry was a surprise. I loved my boys, but I always wanted a girl." Her voice cracked. "He should have been more careful. When you were born, I swore to protect you."

"You can't exactly protect me from cancer."

"No, I can't." She shook her head then looked back at the graves. "But, compared to what Claude did, what I..." she sighed. "Sierra, let's go home. You have school tomorrow."

We walked back to the house and found Mom home. She was standing on the driveway looking down at something.

"Something wrong?" I asked.

She seemed kind of out of it but after a moment she pointed. "There's a crack in the driveway."

I looked down and sure enough there was a crack running through the upper right-hand side. "I hear that happens sometimes," I said. Mom works as a contractor. She often does driveways and I think she did this one. Mom looked at me and put her hand on my shoulder. She kissed my forehead gently and then embraced me.

"Grace, we'll worry about it some other time. Nothing can be done now," Granny said.

Mom nodded and we all went inside. I went up to my room. I had a book I needed to finish in time for English class tomorrow. It was Jane Austen's *Northanger Abbey*. The only Gothic novel she ever wrote. An odd one to be sure but I didn't think it should cause me the strange dreams I had that night.

YOU WOULD THINK GIVEN my health issues my nightmares would have been, well, I don't know, maybe hospital or doctor related. Instead, they seemed construction related. Maybe it was Mom's weird reaction to a crack in the driveway, but I could see it before it was constructed. Dark and windy out, I could hear crying. A child was crying. I was looking into a deep pit where our driveway was. Someone had dug it up. Gravel was rolling into the pit. I could hear a scraping sound.

My heart sped up and I felt a pounding in my ears. I looked down and my feet were bare and dirty. The crying intensified. It was so dark, but I could see a beam of light. Flashlight? It moved around some more. Yes, flashlight.

As the light flicked about, I could see further into the pit. I tried to make sense of the shapes and was irritated by the crying child. I wanted very much to slap the child. Make it shut up. And then the light stopped and shone down for a moment. At the bottom of the pit and under a layer of dirt and stone was my Uncle Ryan. He wasn't moving. I started screaming.

"Sierra! What's wrong with you. Stop that screaming!" Then someone slapped me across the face and I woke up. I was outside. We were on the driveway. It was Mom who had slapped me. Granny was on my other side.

"Uncle Ryan!" I yelled. Both of them looked around.

"Where?" Granny said.

"He's dead. I know it. He's dead."

"What? How?" Granny said.

"I saw him. In the pit. He was being covered up with rocks and dirt and...," I said.

"What pit? Where?" Mom said.

"Everything ok? You need something?" Our next-door neighbor had come around the fence dividing our yards. He was holding a gun.

"Carl, put that thing away. Sierra has a brain tumor. Doctor said she might act different," Granny said. "Just a bad dream is all."

"Sorry, when I heard the screaming, I just thought I should come prepared. Brain tumor? I'm sorry to hear about it. Can it be fixed?"

"Yes, she'll be operated on next week sometime," Mom said. "They expect her to be ok."

"Good to hear. You let us know if you need anything, ok," he said.

"We will and thank you," Granny replied.

Carl turned around and went back to his house. The early spring nights were cold. I started to shiver. My feet were bare and all I had on were my pajamas.

"Sierra, let's go inside," Granny said.

"But, Uncle Ryan...he's...I saw him," I said.

"You must have been dreaming and sleepwalking. Ryan's probably in bed sleeping, which is what we all should be doing," Mom said.

Granny and Mom took either side of me and we walked back into the house. I looked over to where the crack Mom saw earlier was located and was afraid all over again.

"You lie down on the couch. You want some hot chocolate? Or maybe some of that sleepy tea?" Mom said.

I lay down on the couch and she covered me up.

"Uh, hot chocolate would be nice. Or, anything warm," I said.

She nodded and both Granny and Mom went into the kitchen.

Great, I was sleepwalking now? And that had been a dream? My brain started hurting and I knew I wouldn't be able to keep down anything they gave me. I got up and headed to the kitchen to tell them.

I know I shouldn't have but, well, it was difficult to stop myself. I heard Granny and Mom talking.

"I think she must remember," Mom said.

"It was just a nightmare. We promised never to talk about it," Granny's voice broke.

"Look, she must remember. She was so young though. And now we know why, probably why, anyway." Mom went to the tap to fill the kettle and put it on the stove. She pulled down the canister with the hot cocoa mix and a mug for me. Mom looked at the canister and her shoulders began to shake. Her hand went to her face as she shook.

"I can't think about it," Granny said. She paused in thought, "Grace, what did we do?"

I moved into the kitchen, "What did you two do? What am I remembering?"

They stood up straight and looked like they had been caught with their hand in the cookie jar.

Mom wiped the tears off her face and opened her mouth to say something but Granny replied, "Sierra, go lay down."

"Granny, please just tell me the truth for once. Please."

"Sierra, you don't want to know," Granny said.

Sometimes I didn't want to know. But, well, I *always* want to know.

"Please, please tell me. I might die next week. I need to know."

Mom's hand went to her mouth and she shook her head and tears started flowing down her cheeks again. Mom and Granny looked at each other and seemed to have an entire conversation with a single glance. Mom may not have been related to Granny by blood, but they were as close as any mother and daughter could be.

"Sit down Sierra. Get warm and we'll tell you."

I sat and then waited. Granny was not someone who could ever be described as being lost for words. The pause was unnerving.

"Granny?"

She scrunched up her face and blurted out, "Sierra, I was just trying to protect you. I...," she fell silent again.

"Protect me? From what?"

Granny's face crumpled and she started breathing hard. "Baz," she whispered.

"Huh? Dad?" That statement made no sense based on everything I knew about him.

"You were crying, and he was so angry. I killed him. I didn't want to, I..." She trailed off. I had never heard or seen Granny in as much pain. After a moment she breathed in hard, "Grace and I buried him where the driveway is now."

I guess there was no way to sugarcoat what she'd done. Direct was the best way to go. Still, there was a pounding in my ears.

"But...why...why did you do it?"

"She was protecting you," Mom said.

I was stunned. "Uncle Ryan always said how much Dad loved me."

"Yes, that's true," Mom said.

"Well, then?"

"Sierra, your dad and I were friends from 4th grade on. We started dating in high school and got married after we finished college. The one thing I would say about him was that he was kind and gentle...until he wasn't."

"Huh?"

"If it had happened suddenly, we would have seen something was wrong. But I don't know when it started. At first, he became cranky and tetchy. And little by little, I was afraid of him. In fact, I decided to leave him. But that night, the one you're remembering he became violent. He hit me and your Granny. We tried to get away and leave, but he wouldn't let us take you with us and we couldn't leave you with him. And then when he hit you...we had to protect you."

"He was screaming at Grace and that set you off crying," Granny said. "And that just made him angrier. I thought he was going to hurt you and I couldn't let him do it. I had a kitchen knife in my hand and I...Oh, God, I killed my baby boy." Her voice trailed off.

They were both crying now but worked hard to pull themselves together.

Mom continued the story. "After he was dead, we weren't sure anyone would believe we had done it in self-defense. We were in the process of having a driveway put in and there was a fairly large pit where his body could go."

"We, we managed to get him down there, and covered him with rock and dirt. Your mom was the one who was building it, so she put down the rebar and the next day they came and poured the concrete," Granny said.

"We came up with the story that he walked away. By the time anyone started looking, he seemed long gone. Didn't have to act like we were upset since we were." Mom placed her hand gently on my arm.

"You think he had a brain tumor too?" I asked.

They both nodded their heads.

"But we didn't know that then. Neither of us wanted him to die. We just acted on instinct," Mom said.

"Instinct," I said. My instinct was to tell Uncle Ryan, but I thought he would be more hurt than relieved at knowing.

"Sierra, whatever you decide to do with this, we'll understand. Please remember though, he's been gone a long time now and nothing can be fixed by letting people know," Mom said.

I wished I didn't know, but too late.

Would you rather turn your Mom and Granny in for protecting you all those years ago and perhaps cause your uncle to murder his own mom leaving his children without a father or do you keep it to yourself even though knowing makes you feel sick. I chose a third option.

I'm writing this all down in case I die during the surgery tomorrow. I will put it in an envelope, tape it up, and give it to Maya. I talked to her and made her swear she wouldn't look at it. Maya's the best person I know for keeping secrets and her word. If I die, I want her to wait until Granny and Mom are gone and then read it. She can decide what to do with it later. I wish I could tell Uncle Ryan.

If he knew what had happened, given his job, he would have to make some hard choices of his own. I want someone to know what happened to my dad, that he probably died because he had a tumor in his brain in a worse spot than I have in mine. Mom and Granny were trying to protect me. I hope I recover and writing this will have been all for nothing.

SINCERELY,

Sierra Nevada Olmstead

PURPLE MURDER

BY ROSS CARLEY

The State of Indiana crime lab said that Aunt Tillie didn't die of no heart attack. She was poisoned. The question was, whodunnit?

I was determined to find out.

It was 1973, and I was visiting her like I do every year in July at Mulberry County Fair time. My name's Mandy. That's short for Amanda. I live in Oakport in southern Indiana near the Ohio River, where Tillie was born and grew up.

Tillie was killed the evening before the very first day of the county fair at a shindig put on by the Organizing Committee of the Mulberry County Fair Baking Competition. Those invited to the reception had entered the baking contests happening on the next to last day of the fair. Refreshments included iced sugar cookies in the shape of Indiana and hot spiced apple cider.

The winner of each category in the county competition would qualify for the bakeoff at the Indiana State Fair. I hadn't entered the contest, so I was just hanging around Tillie's house, waiting for her to come home. Which she never did.

According to those at her table, Tillie had been listening to the conversations going on around her when her eyes glazed over. She grabbed her neck, let out a choked scream, and pitched forward nose down into her mug of cider.

Aunt Tillie and Uncle Hector – we all called him Heck – had been married for over twenty years. Aunt Tillie taught home economics at Clancy High School, where Uncle Heck was the principal. Clancy, by the way, is the county seat of Mulberry County.

Aunt Tillie was best known for her pies. She could put any fruit filling or even a cream filling in her pies, and as long as she used her secret pie crust recipe, they won blue ribbons.

Growing up, I had to put up with two brothers, Benny and Jeb, but didn't have a sister. Tillie was Ma's youngest sister. Just fifteen years older than me.

I went to her for advice – including things I was too embarrassed to ask Ma about. So Tillie was like my sister. Folks even said we looked like sisters.

BUT BACK TO THE STORY. Since it was a Wednesday, Heck was out bowling with his team at the Sycamore Lanes when Tillie died. Officer Johnny Dudeck was dispatched to tell him and bring him home. He came into the house bawling like a baby. Tillie's doctor, Doc Garrett, came right soon after that.

I did what I could to comfort Heck.

"Had to been her heart," he sniffed. "She's had heart problems for a while."

"I don't know, Heck," said the doc. "She had minor heart murmurs, nothing really serious, and she's had them for several years."

"What're you saying, Doc?"

"If it was me, I'd get an autopsy."

Heck slowly shook his head. "I don't know. I don't think I want to put her through that."

"Come on, Heck. You owe it to her, and it won't cost you anything."

Heck blew his nose and looked down at his shoes. "Well...well... okay, I guess."

When I heard the word autopsy, I knew the doc suspected foul play. I decided to call my brother Benny in Oakport soon as I could. He had recently solved a murder there with a little help from me.

I took Heck to the hospital to get Tillie's personal stuff. They had her clothes and shoes and purse in a box waiting for us. When I saw her purse, I remembered that she kept a copy of her pie recipe in her address book, so I looked for it. The hospital lady told me the ambulance guys had put all her belongings together in the box, but I looked through it and there was no address book. She *always* carried that dang address book. I was sure that someone had swiped her recipe.

There was no telling when it'd been stolen. Would've been too obvious for someone to be messing with her purse at the shindig where she died. The ambulance folks swore that they were the only people who'd collected her things.

I knew that Tillie'd kept her prize-winning recipe to herself. She'd shown me the copy in her purse, in the back of her address book. She'd hidden the only other copy in the bottom of her silverware drawer. She may have let it slip that she kept the recipe in her address book, or someone may have seen it there, but the way she'd sworn me to secrecy, I was sure that nobody but me knew about the other copy.

When Heck and I got back to the house I made a beeline for the kitchen, scared of what I might not find. I dumped the silverware on the counter and peeled up the drawer's lining paper.

I let out a whoop – Heck must've thought I'd gone crazy. The recipe was there, safe and sound. First thing I did was get a ballpoint pen and paper and make two copies. Heck promised to put the original from the drawer into their—now his—safety deposit box at Farmers and Merchants Bank as soon as they opened next morning.

One of the copies went back under the liner and silverware. I put the other one in my purse.

I made coffee and got Heck settled in the kitchen with a cup, then went into the living room and called Benny. I told him everything I could remember, including Tillie's recipe being missing from her purse.

"I'm glad to help," Benny said, "I'd like to do it in person, but work is real busy. You'll have to be my boots on the ground. Okay, sis?"

"Sure," I said. "I'll call you again when we get the autopsy. Then we'll know what killed her. We'll know what, when and where. All that'll be left to figure out will be who and why."

"Sounds good. Then we can work out a plan," he said. "Who d'ya think coulda done it?"

"Most likely somebody entered in the apple pie bakeoff. All together there were nine of 'em."

"So we have nine suspects?"

"Not really. Three had day jobs and couldn't make it to the four o'clock event. So five besides Tillie was there – Maxine Wright, Esther Duckworth, Vivian Schumann, Dorothy Robbins, and Eunice Clark. Well, actually, Maxine works as a court reporter, but was off that afternoon."

"Nobody else?"

"There were other folks at the reception, but I figure one of them five probably did Tillie in. She's won first place for her apple pies three years in a row, and there ain't nothing more important every year to the womenfolk in Clancy than that bakeoff."

"Find out what you can about each one of 'em at the reception," he said. "Also, set up a meeting with the coroner."

Soon as we said goodbye, I called Doc Garrett and asked him to schedule a meeting with the coroner first thing next morning. He agreed to ask the questions I had.

The doorbell rang as I hung up, and Heck was answering it as I walked into the living room. A woman came in carrying a box with food. She seemed surprised to see me.

"I didn't realize Heck had company," she said.

Heck set the box on the dining table.

"Mandy, this is Vivian Schumann," he said. We nodded at each other with polite smiles.

She was all dolled up, probably from going to the shindig. Her black hair was permed into curls so tight they squeaked.

"I threw a chicken casserole and mess of green beans together. I knew that Heck wouldn't feel like cooking or going out. I'm sorry to intrude."

She turned on her heel and left before Heck or I could say anything.

Doctor Samantha Collier, the local coroner who ordered the autopsy, seemed right on top of things. The newspaper mentioned that she'd gotten some fancy degree in Indianapolis at the university. The morgue was all stainless steel and concrete and smelled so strong of disinfectant that I almost gagged, and I saw silver and black flashes through watery eyes.

Doc Collier's office was cold and plain, but the smell of coffee let me to breathe easier. She didn't offer us any. She was skinny as a rail and looked real official in her white lab coat and glasses hanging from a chain around her neck.

It was obvious that she agreed to meet because of Doc Garrett, and I was just along for the ride. Since he knew what I wanted to know, I let him ask the questions.

"What are your observations, and do you think an autopsy is indicated?" Doc Garrett asked.

After some hemming and hawing around, she answered. "Yes," she said. "I would have recommended an autopsy even if the husband hadn't asked for one."

It bothered me that she didn't even know Heck's name.

Then she said, "The EMTs who responded reported that she had frothy blood coming out of her mouth which is a possible indication of poisoning. So, I sent samples of her blood and the contents of her stomach to the State Toxicology Lab. It'll probably be a couple of days before we receive results."

She looked right straight at me as she said, "The information I've just given you is confidential. It's for Doctor Garrett and the family only."

It hadn't been declared a homicide yet, leastways not officially, but I knew in my bones it wasn't a heart attack. So I decided to learn what I could about each of the five women most likely to have murdered Tilley.

I was especially interested in gossip and rumors. In a small town like Clancy, the best places to hear them are beauty parlors and barber shops.

Heck told me Tillie got her hair done at Liz's Beauty Shop, in the middle of town. He told me that a woman named Charlene always did her hair. I got right over there as soon as Heck's brother arrived to keep him company.

Charlene was just sweeping up from trimming someone's hair. With her salt and pepper hair pulled back in a bun, she reminded me of Aunt Bee on *The Andy Griffith Show*. I told her who I was. She put her broom down and gave me a hug.

"God, I miss Tillie," she said with tears starting to flow.

"I know. So do I. I'd like to talk to you. You got a minute?"

"I just had a cancellation, so you bet. I got the next hour. Come with me. I live just a coupla blocks from here."

We settled into the porch swing of her little white bungalow after she'd gotten iced tea for both of us.

"Whatcha want to know?"

"Well, for starters, we need to keep this confidential. Can you do that?" I asked.

She nodded, and we were off to the races.

I explained that I was sure Tillie's pie recipe had been stolen and that she'd been murdered, but nothing had been made public yet. Then I asked her about the five women entered in the contest who were at the shindig where Tillie died.

"Well, well," she said. "Y'all came to the right person.

"Maxine Wright works as a court reporter in the County Attorney's office. Her husband Jim is a World War II vet. Medal of Honor on Guadalcanal. Not quite right in the head. Some say he had battle fatigue – some call it shellshock. He works construction. Rumors are that he knocks Maxine around some when they argue. Tillie said she has urged her to get help."

Charlene choked back tears, then calmed herself and took a sip of tea.

"Esther Duckworth's an even bigger gossip than me, and that's saying something. Lives out in the country on a small farm. She has a herd of goats and loves to talk on her CB radio. Her husband Ernie's a truck driver. He's put up a fancy CB antenna so they can talk while he's at work. He's out of town two or three days each week. Folks say that she talks to other truck drivers, too – rumor is that she does more than talk with some of 'em."

She took another sip.

"Let's see, where was I? Vivian Schumann. In addition to teaching at Heck's school, Vivian and her husband Doug palled around with Tillie and Heck before Doug died. They belonged to the same square-dancing club. Vivian took over managing Doug's business, Schumann's Feed and Seed. Folks were kinda surprised she didn't quit teaching, but she said she couldn't leave her kids. She hasn't had children, people say, because Doug didn't want any. After Doug died Tillie felt sorry for her, so she invited Vivian to hang around with her and Heck.

"Then there's Dorothy Robbins," Charlene continued. "She's the wild woman of the group. Lives on the edge of town. She raises pigs and chickens, and her kids raise hell. Supposedly, in addition to using foul language, even around young folks, Dorothy throws things when she gets in a snit. Maybe that's why she's divorced. Folks say she openly chases men, married or single, but can't seem to hold onto one longer than a night or two.

"Who's left?" Charlene asked.

"Just Eunice Clark," I said.

Charlene nodded and snickered.

"Eunice is easy to forget – she's the quietest and most private of the group. She lives out a mile or so on County Road 100 with her husband Stanley. He's a postal carrier during the week and preaches hell fire and brimstone at the Pilgrim Holiness Church on Sundays. They have three kids, all quiet, well behaved, and always dressed in clean clothes. Nobody has a bad word to say about her."

I thanked Charlene for the tea and the information and headed back to be with Heck. I hoped the gossip about Clancy folks would come in handy when I knew more about how Tillie died.

BENNY CALLED THE NEXT DAY, and we put our plan together. The day after that the coroner gave us the autopsy results. Tillie'd been poisoned by something called sodium cyanide. Again, the information was confidential. All that would be released to the public was that her death was now being investigated as a homicide. No cause of death would be mentioned.

Our plan used some of the stuff that we'd learned when we helped solve the earlier murder. I called Doc Holly down in Oakport, explained what was going on, and said we'd appreciate his help.

"What would you like me to do?" he asked.

"The main thing is for you to put in a good word for me with the Clancy Police Department and Mulberry County Sherriff's Office when I ask you to. Also, could you call Tillie's doc and the coroner and fill them in?"

"I'd be pleased to do all that. Just let me know when you want me to make the calls," he said.

Our plan depended on something that me, Benny, and Tillie had in common with several of the folks on Ma's side of the family. Something that Doc Holly knew lots about – a brain condition called synesthesia.

Most folks don't know anything about it, but Doc Holly says that two out of every one hundred folks in the U.S. have some version of it. Parts of our brains are wired together in ways that aren't in most people.

I have two types of synesthesia. For one thing, I see shapes whenever I hear sounds. Some sounds look like figures that are all jaggedy. Others are smooth like eggs with bunches of bumps. The other type is that I see colors with combinations of taste and smell. Doc says that taste and smell are tied so close that he isn't surprised that it's the two together that get colors going for me.

Benny sees colors with sounds. For instance, different people's voices have different color combinations. Our ma, God rest her soul, saw colors whenever she read words or numbers. For example, the word Wednesday and the number two both looked red to her. Doc Holly said that synesthesia is often inherited.

The business with my taste and smell makes trouble for me. I walk right out of a restaurant if the smell inside has ugly colors. And if I'm not sure, I may only take one bite of food with colors that don't quite look right.

THE FIRST FOLKS interviewed by law enforcement in a murder investigation are usually the next of kin. I'd warned Heck to be ready to talk with the police as soon as we knew Tillie'd been murdered. The question was, who was gonna be doing the investigating.

There hadn't been a murder in Clancy since Harry Truman was president, and only a few in the county. They didn't even have a homicide unit. So, murders were investigated by the Mulberry County Sheriff's Violent Crimes Division, which consisted of a sergeant and two deputies who spent most of their time writing speeding tickets.

When the knock came at the door, Heck and I welcomed Officer Dudeck and Deputy Sheriff Wade Radford into the kitchen for coffee. We introduced ourselves all around.

Officer Dudeck was real friendly. He asked Heck how he was doing and did he need anything. He looked right spiffy in his summer uniform, and he looked me in the eyes long enough I felt my cheeks getting red.

Then the deputy cleared his throat and looked at Heck.

"We want to talk with you alone," the deputy said.

"That'll be fine, but Mandy would like a word with you first."

The deputy took a deep breath and let it out with his lips shaped like the letter O.

"I'll give her a few minutes but remember that I'm in charge."

Heck nodded at me. That was my cue.

I looked back and forth between the officer and the deputy. I tried not to let my nervousness into my voice.

"I might be able to help you with the case."

"Just how could *you* possibly be helpful?" asked the deputy with a sneer.

I told them about my synesthesia.

"By tasting the pies entered in the bakeoff, I might be able to identify the one who stole Tillie's recipe according to the way the flavor mixed with the smell look to me."

Officer Dudeck's eyes sorta rolled back in his head, but that wasn't anything compared with Deputy Radford's reaction. He snorted, shoved his chair back, and said "Go on. Get outta here. You're crazier than a bedbug."

Bennie'd told me to expect something like that. Same kinda thing had happened to him during the murder case in Oakport, so I was ready with two copies of the name and phone number of Doc Holly.

As I handed each one a copy, I said, "Please check with Doc Garrett, too."

"In your dreams," Deputy Radford said as he crumpled up the paper and dropped it on the table.

Officer Dudeck nodded, then carefully folded it and put it in his pocket.

The police in Oakport had treated Benny like a lunatic at first. They even hauled him down to the police station for questioning. I'd gotten involved then, supporting Benny.

I was really scared, but I owed it to Tillie to do what I could. I'd eaten her pie and those baked by others bunches of times. And I was right sure I could tell the special color combination of her pie from anyone else's.

I headed over to the Hoosier Diner for coffee. I'd gotten one ball rolling, but there was another ball. The cyanide poison that killed Tillie. I figured that the best place to start finding out about it was the coroner, so I called Doc Collier from the pay phone at the diner. She said to come right over. I took my own coffee.

Soon as I walked in her office, she said, "You understand that you must keep the autopsy results confidential, correct?"

"Yes, Doctor. I promise to keep my lips zipped." I figured she had agreed to see me just so she could hit me with that.

"So why did you want to see me?" she asked.

"Well, I'm trying to learn more about cyanide. I have no idea what it is except a nasty poison. I've seen a coupla episodes of the TV show *Columbo* where somebody was killed with poison. That's about it."

She sat up and laced her fingers together on her desk. "It's quite easy to get, especially in rural areas," she said. "There's a device used on farms to control coyotes and wild dogs who stalk and kill cows, sheep and other animals. Including chickens. It's called an M-44."

"Some kind of military contraption?" I asked.

"No. And I've no idea what M-44 stands for," she said. "But a capsule full of sodium cyanide is loaded into a capsule holder that's coated with an odor especially formulated to attract coyotes and wild dogs. When one of them tugs at the capsule holder, a spring-driven plunger shoots the sodium cyanide capsule into its mouth."

"How many of these capsules does it take to get enough cyanide to kill someone?"

"An M-44 capsule has just under a gram of sodium cyanide, which is more than ten times as much needed to kill someone Tillie's size," Doc Collier said.

"How much does a gram weigh?" I asked.

"There are twenty-eight grams in one ounce," she answered. "It's odorless and tasteless, and very fast-acting. Someone who swallows it is dead in a few minutes."

You could have knocked me over with a feather. One gram of sodium cyanide powder was a teensy, tiny amount. I figured it was probably put in Tillie's hot spiced cider. It would only have taken a few sips to kill her.

Doc Collier let me use her phone to call Heck. The officer and deputy had gone, and he was by himself, so I thanked the doc and went back to the house.

Wasn't more than an hour or so, Officer Dudeck called. He'd given the slip of paper to Chief Morton, and the chief had called Doc Holly.

"The chief told me to ask if you can come right down to the station," he said.

"You bet. I'm on my way, and I'm bringing Heck with me."

The Police Department was in the same building as the Volunteer Fire Department. A mousy receptionist named Margie sat just as we walked in, and the chief's office was right past her. There was one other office with desks, a small conference table, and a single jail cell.

There wasn't room for more than one chair in the chief's office, so we sat at the table. Margie brought coffee to us. I sniffed it. Smelled like burned toast. Colors were a downright horrible mish-mash of red and chartreuse with black flashes. I didn't even taste it.

Chief Morton was a large man with bushy eyebrows, black hair and Elvis Presley sideburns. He acted gruff, but Heck'd told me he was a big teddy bear.

"Glad y'all could come by," he said. "What's this about your being able to help us?"

I started to tell him about my synesthesia.

He waved a meaty hand like he was shooing a fly and said, "Doc Holly's filled me in on that there synes – whatcha call it?"

"Synesthesia," I said.

"Yeah, synesthesia. What I want to know is what you would suggest. Be as specific as you can."

He picked up a pen, listened real hard, and took notes while I answered.

"Well, bottom line is that I should be able to tell if one of the women who entered the bakeoff contest used my Aunt Tillie's recipe, and if so, which one," I said.

His eyebrows raised and his eyes got wide.

"Well, well. Tell me how you'd do that."

"It's pretty simple. I just have to smell and taste a bite of each pie and compare how it looks with one made with Tillie's recipe."

"You do this with just one taste?"

"Well, probably it'd be a good idea for you to mix 'em all up and have me do it again. Maybe two or three times, until you're satisfied."

"That sounds good. I'll need a little time to set it up. The county prosecutor needs to okay it and be there as a witness. How about you do the tasting on the morning after the judging?"

"Suits me," I said.

The way he smiled at me I figured I could trust him.

He called Margie into the room.

"Notify the county fair baking contest folks that the pies will be held as evidence after the judging," he told her. "And tell them that the results of the judging are to be kept secret until the next day."

Chief Morton looked at me. "That way you won't possibly be influenced by which pie is the winner."

"Where are we going to store them?" asked Margie. "We don't have any refrigerated space where we can keep them here in the department."

The chief thought for a few seconds. "Well, I guess we're gonna have to borrow the refrigerator from the Fire Department and lock it in the jail cell overnight. We'll wrap yellow evidence tape around the cell. And don't none of you tell anyone about this."

Looking at me, the chief said, "One more thing. What are we gonna do if someone, somewhere down the line, accuses us of putting together a set-up? Tillie didn't get a chance to bake a pie for the contest. How will we know if the pie or pies you identify actually are from her recipe?"

Heck spoke up. "Tillie always baked what she called a 'dress rehearsal' pie before every contest. I have the one she baked for this contest at home in the freezer. We were going to eat it while Mandy was here. I can testify she baked it from her recipe."

The chief nodded. "That ought to do it. Bring it in and we'll put it in the refrigerator."

He took a deep breath, looked at Heck and me, and said, "Well, that's taken care of. Moving along to another subject, what do you know about the poison used on Tillie? I know what Doc Collier told you."

"I don't know diddly squat about the poison itself," I said. "The coroner told me that it's used to control predators on farms. So I've looked at the five women at the shindig competing with Tillie, and only two of them live in a rural area with livestock. Esther Duckworth's got a goat herd and Dorothy Robbins raises chickens and pigs."

"I've been thinking along the same lines," the chief said. "Those two seem like the prime suspects to me, too. I'll tell Officer Dudeck to follow up. Interview them. See if either of them is familiar with the M-44 device, or, more important, has ever used it."

THE DAY of the pie judging, I made myself scarce. Partly because I was missing Tillie so much, and partly because it looked likely that one of the contestants had poisoned her. Heck and I had Vivian Schumann's chicken casserole and green beans for lunch, then watched soap operas the rest of the day.

The morning after, we gathered at the police station for me to do my tasting. Margie and the chief had set up a table out in the reception area. Chief Morton, Officer Dudeck, and the county prosecutor, Bart Hickock, were sitting around the edges of the room. Deputy Radford pushed a chair into a corner, tilted it back and pulled his Stetson down over his eyes. He obviously thought it was a waste of his time.

Hickock was a big man with gray eyes, sandy hair and a drooping handlebar mustache. Cowboy boots reinforced his Wild Bill image.

"I know how random numbers work," Hickock drawled, "so the chief put me in charge of arranging the pie samples into a different order for each tasting round. Margie and I set the samples up so Mandy couldn't see what was what."

While we were waiting to start my taste testing, Chief Morton asked me, "Is your synesthesia always around and has it changed since you first noticed it?"

"Yep and nope," I said. "I've had it long as I can remember. Sometimes I pay more attention to it than other times. It's kinda like standing in my living room looking out the window. The scenery outside and the lace curtains on the window are there together. I can always see both, but at any particular time I may notice one more than the other, and I'm able to flip my attention back and forth whenever I want to."

The room got really quiet when they put the first group of five samples in front of me. The first time I sampled them, one of them stood out. It was definitely from Tillie's recipe. The same for the next two tasting rounds, only it was a different place in the order each time.

"Tell us what you're seeing," Chief Morton said.

"Well, the taste of each pie sample flashes color combinations different enough that I'm able to group the samples from each of the five pies. All of the pies taste great, and each one has a different combination of real pretty colors. Vivid reds and golds twirled with muted greens, pinks, blues and lavenders."

"So how did you pick out Tillie's recipe?" Hickock asked.

"It was easy as pie," I said.

Folks laughed before I realized what I'd said.

"Anyway," I continued, "The color combination from Tillie's recipe was the only one with a swirl of deep purple."

I could hardly wait to hear whether the pie baked with Tillie's recipe took first place, and whether it was entered by Esther Duckworth or Dorothy Robbins.

Chief Morton consulted the sheet of paper with the judging results and cleared his throat.

"Yep," he said. "The winner was baked with Tillie's recipe."

No surprise there.

But I nearly fell off my chair when he said, "It was entered by Vivian Schumann, and I'm issuing a warrant for her arrest."

He turned to me and said gently, "Sometimes things aren't what they seem. Officer Dudeck's interviews of Esther Duckworth and Dorothy Robbins had surprising results. Seems that Esther had heard of the M-44 device but had never even thought about using it since she herds her goats into a barn every night. Dorothy, on the other hand, used M-44s about a year ago to get rid of two coyotes that'd been killing her chickens."

"So, what wasn't as it seemed?" I asked.

"Well, of course Schumann's Feed and Seed stocks a variety of feeds and seeds. But they also carry fertilizer, tools, and among other things, pest control products. Dorothy bought the M-44s she used there."

I called Benny that night.

"Mandy, you done great," he said.

"Thanks, but I've learned not to jump to conclusions, especially where murder is involved."

Officer Dudeck called the next morning.

"I'd like to thank you for your help by buying your dinner at the Hoosier Diner."

I muffled the phone and asked Heck what he thought. He got this crooked grin on his face and said, "Sure, that sounds fine."

So I went.

At dinner, Johnny asked, "Would you give me your address in Oakport so I can keep in touch with you?"

I blushed big time as I said, "Sure." Then he gave me his. I think that Aunt Tillie would have approved.

A couple days later, a real embarrassed Heck handed me a letter, saying, "I was mortified when I got this. Figure Chief Morton ought to see it."

I took a look and agreed. It was from Vivian and was of a very personal nature and mentioned just how profoundly she was attracted to him. It said things that would even make a dog in heat blush.

Vivian pleaded guilty to avoid risking execution.

The last I heard they were fixing to exhume Doug Schumann's body.

FEEL THE HEAT
BY N. W. CAMPBELL

I can feel the heat. My bones ache. A powerful cramp grips my stomach. Lying in the summer sun, I struggle to shake off the fog. My hip is tender to the touch. I sense I'm naked, and I react, startled. How did I wind up like this? I roll over and look around. To my left, I see her lying naked, breasts splayed, arms and legs spread awkwardly. A wisp of her blonde-streaked hair wafts slightly in the morning breeze. She is not moving. Overhead, turkey buzzards circle in the early morning sun.

"Ariel," I say weakly, "can you hear me? Are you OK?"

Ariel and I share the same cubicle and have for the past five years, working within arm's length of each other. We settle property claims for Corn Belt Independent Life and Property Indemnity Company. Ariel knows this business and fills me in on the latest repair estimate rates. She connects me to the contractors who keep the claimants appeased and will toss a little under the table into the adjuster's lap just to keep work headed their way. I'm good with the client end and sometimes step in as a "senior claims specialist" whenever she deals with a hostile claimant who thinks he can bully her. She could handle things herself, but I offered to help one day when a claimant got rough over the phone. She let me take it from there.

I was raised to respect women and to be on hand whenever there's heavy lifting to do. It's a kind of chivalry that may have grown out-of-date, I suppose. My wife Carol thinks I'm a cornball, but Ariel tells me I'm sweet.

Occasionally, we stop by the Tool Factory, a former wrench plant that's now a grill and bar, where we have a few cocktails after work with our fellow adjusters. Ariel has a husband, and there's a daughter in college, neither of whom I've met.

About a month ago, she caught my eye as I was leaving the cubicle.

"How about a drink? I'm buying."

She smiles seductively and flicks her index finger under my chin. I follow her out the door.

Twenty minutes later, drink in hand, she settles on the bar stool and looks into my eyes. "Ever think about fooling around?"

I stop mid-sip and look into her eyes. Under a layer of foundation, the left eye appears slightly discolored. She turns her head a bit to the right so her left eye is away from me. I say nothing, and she continues.

"How long's it been for you? I've got a kid in college whom I see during semester breaks, and that's it. My ex-old man never did anything but retreat to his six-packs and NFL on the big screen in the den. It's been a year at least since I last had sex with *anybody*. And I want no part of him, especially after this," she says, gesturing toward her eye.

"How often did he hit you?" I ask.

"Just the once. I called the cops over and told him right in front of them that I wanted his ass out, and if he didn't leave, I was having him arrested for domestic battery. He left, and he knows damn well not to come back. He knows he's licked. He agreed to file jointly for a no-fault divorce, then left town to God knows where. He hasn't worked in two years, and my name is on everything. The divorce is pending. It's taken longer for this eye to heal than it did to get rid of him."

"This is all moving pretty quickly," I say, "Is this a good idea, getting into an affair right now? With me, I mean?"

I'm intrigued by her offer, risky as it sounds, but I am nervous. My wife Carol ignores me most of the time, even though I've tried to live the domestic life, with a house in the country and a mortgage with payments I can barely reach. There are no kids, but we have a cocker terrier that gets way more attention from Carol than I do. Carol works but leaves the mortgage up to me. Her salary, she says, is being saved up to "pay for the kids" – whom we haven't got and aren't likely to have unless there's a drastic change in our sex life. Forty is right on the horizon for both of us. And, oh yeah. Carol loves clothes. One look at the way she dresses, and there's no need to ask where her salary goes. She earned it, she says.

Laughing, Carol likes to kid me, "What's yours is mine, Ronnie, and what's mine is mine."

I give in and let Carol have what she wants.

"Hell, yeah, it's a good idea!" Ariel smiles. "Like I told you, I'm getting lonely." She looks at me hard. "Ronnie, live a little, why don't you? I see your hang-dog look around the office. That wife of yours is not delivering the wifely favors, is she? How long's it been?"

I say nothing. She studies my face carefully. "C'mon, how long's it been?"

"What is this, Ariel? Pity or desperation? I don't need the trouble," I say, staring back.

"Boy, it has been a while for you! Look, I'm not out to ruin your home life or anything. It's just that I've got an itch I can't scratch, and you've got one, too, right? What could one time hurt? A little roll, and we both go home happy. That wife of yours, Carol? Think she'll care enough to catch on?"

THEY MET ONCE, Carol and Ariel. It was at a company Christmas party two years ago. Carol agreed to come on the condition that we have one drink, I introduce her to my boss and my cubicle mate, and then we clear out. Ariel came alone. Carol flirted with Hal, my boss, like she never flirted with me. I don't know what she was thinking. Hal is my boss, not hers. It's like they knew each other from somewhere. On the way home, she never mentioned Hal or how or if they knew one another. It was all about Ariel.

"That cubicle-mate of yours, nothing to worry about there, I can see," Carol sneered. "I just think women look desperate when they try to camouflage their mousy brown hair with streaks of blonde. Pathetic."

After we got home from the party, Carol came to me with the idea that I take out a life insurance policy on myself. She was undressing for bed when she told me about it.

"You know, Honey, your boss Hal mentioned something about a benefit you ought to consider. Hal says too many of his people aren't taking advantage of it, so whenever he gets to speak with a spouse, he likes to offer a little advice. That's sweet, don't you think?"

"So," I ask, "what's Hal's advice?"

"Supplemental life insurance, a term policy at employee rates. Corn Belt issues the policy, and the employee pays through regular payroll deductions. I think it's a great idea."

She turns from the mirror, pearl necklace in hand, and looks at me.

"He says you could get five hundred thousand in death benefit coverage for just fifty bucks a month from your check. Sounds good, doesn't it?"

So, I think, if I die early, Carol gets the payoff she'll never get from my measly 401K. A supplemental life insurance policy is probably not a bad idea. Well, if it makes her happy...

"So, who did Hal say I needed to speak to? HR?"

"Oh, no. I think you could just talk with Hal."
Un-hunh! Ohhh!

Ariel is coming around. She sits up carefully, holding her head, her eyes downcast, tightly shut. She tenses, whimpers, opens her eyes cautiously and lets out a shriek.

Jesus, where are my clothes?!

Ariel wraps her arms around whatever little she can cover and spies me out of one eye. "Jesus, Ronnie, I'm laying here, out cold with my cootch in the air, and you don't even cover me up? What the hell kind of boyfriend are you?"

"With what?" I say, pointing to my own nakedness. "I just came around myself."

"Hey, this isn't where we were," says Ariel, looking around, bewildered. "We were skinny-dipping in that little lake we found. How in the hell did we get here?"

Ariel and I have been lovers since that night she invited me to the Tool Factory for a drink. If I've learned anything about her, it's that she loves doing things that are a bit exotic. Our first was at the motel two blocks down from the bar. Then it was the back seat of her car, the front seat of mine, over the copy machine while both of us were on break, then in the rear john of a Boeing 767 during a flight to Florida to settle storm damage claims. In Florida, we stretched a two-night stay into a week, citing an additional claim load beyond what we anticipated so we could get more time alone together. Hal hesitated for a moment when we called him for approval, then authorized the extra days.

This most recent time, we were headed to Henryville to check on a complaint a claimant filed against a contractor we hired to rebuild a barn destroyed by a tornado. On the way back to our Indianapolis office, we detour through Clark State Forest. Ariel looks around like a kid stealing candy, points toward an access road and tells me to turn.

Ahead, I see a small clearing with a lake beyond. As soon as I apply the brakes, Ariel begins peeling off her clothes.

"Beat you to the water!" She laughs and jumps out the door.

In two steps, she is wading in.

I am right behind her. Soon, we are in chest-deep water, embracing. A black bear could have splashed into that lake, and we wouldn't have heard a thing.

***

"The last thing I remember is standing in that lake with you, then the lights went out," Ariel says, rubbing her head again. "I feel groggy as hell. Were we drugged or something?"

I feel the welt on my hip. I'm groggy, too, like I'm coming out of anesthesia. I look around. This was not the little lake in the Clark State Forest, not even close. We are in a stand of weeds along a drainage ditch, and the place does not look familiar.

"We've gotta get out of here," I say, looking around. "Thank God it's early in the morning. Let's head for cover, that place over there." I point to a small equipment barn about 30 yards from us, with no other structures nearby. "Maybe we can hide there before people get up and head off to work."

We take off along the drainage ditch as far as we can go, then break into a barefoot run, hopping and hobbling over the terrain until we come to the barn. We look around, and both of us spot the same thing—a lawn tractor sitting alongside the barn, covered with a blue plastic tarp. Ariel runs to the mower and begins pulling the tarp away carefully to keep it from rustling. I come around to the other side and climb into the seat. It's a Dixie Chopper Classic, almost brand new. Ariel hops onto my lap and pulls the tarp around us.

"Leave the tarp," I say as I cross my fingers, turn the key, and push the ignition button.

"Why? We can't go riding around like a couple of naked idiots!"

"It'll just get in the way. Besides, if we leave something behind, anything, maybe it'll signal that we're not stealing this thing, just borrowing it." I smile weakly, aware of how quickly my transgressions are piling up.

The engine fires. I put the transmission into gear, and we drive away. Ariel looks over my shoulder, keeping an eye out for any sign that people might be around.

"Now, where are we going?" Ariel asks me over the tractor's whine. I look around nervously. I begin to recognize my surroundings, and a plan takes shape in my mind. I'm not far from my home, maybe four or five miles away.

"My place. A few miles away. It'll take about a half-hour or so on this thing, but most people aren't up yet. We should be able to slip right into the drive; then I'll park this thing behind the mini barn out back. We can hide there until we're sure Carol is gone. Any ideas about how we got from Clark State Forest to here?"

"Nope, but I've got to get out of this sun! It's hotter than hell!"

We are both sweating, naked, and clinging to each other to keep from slipping off the seat built for one. An early morning breeze helps a bit. I spot my house, drapes drawn and shades down. *Carol may still be here!* I think to myself. I guide the tractor onto the drive, scraping the mower deck on the curb as I start up the incline. I keep the tractor moving until I can park it between the mini-barn and our backyard fence. We climb off the seat and place our butts onto the cool, dewy grass. The mini barn offers a bit of shade, and things are quiet. We both calm down a bit.

"Hello, Hal?" Carol is standing on the patio, speaking into her cell phone, her voice breaking through the early morning stillness. *Did she hear the tractor? Why was she calling Hal?*

Ariel gives me a worried glance. I try to look reassuring.

Carol is just trying to protect my job, I think to myself, *like any decent spouse would do. I really am a heel, having an affair while Carol is covering for me. And here I sit, stark naked, in my own backyard with my stark-naked girlfriend right next to me. If any guy ever deserved to be busted…*

"What's happening? Did things work out?" Carol was trying to keep her voice down, but Ariel and I can hear every word in the still morning air.

"Don't tell me to be patient, Hal! I'm scared to death. I've never done anything like this before. Those two clowns you hired – they couldn't kill flies, let alone people. Why would you hire losers like that? Hey, don't hang up on me!" Carol throws her phone onto a table and bursts into angry tears.

A moment passes, then we hear the back door open and shut. We sit tight for several more minutes. The garage door opens, and an engine starts. A moment later, Carol backs down the drive, and the garage door closes. We wait a few minutes longer for good measure, then trot quietly to my back door before the rest of the neighborhood is up and moving around. I retrieve a key I keep hidden behind a downspout and let us both in. Ariel heads for the shower while I get her a pair of my jeans, a dress shirt, and a pair of sneakers. Ariel and Carol are about the same size, but I don't want Carol finding any of her stuff missing and get suspicious. I wrap a towel around myself and head for the den to investigate. I think Carol has known Hal a lot longer than just one company party.

Hal once told me he was from southwest Michigan, but he didn't say where. On the bookshelf, I take down Carol's senior yearbook, thumb through the pages, and put it back. I scan the shelf again. I spot something I never noticed before, a memory book from Camp Paw-Paw summer camp in southern Michigan. I thumb through the pages and find two pictures, side-by-side, of people I recognize immediately. Hal and Carol. They spent one summer together there as camp counselors. A summer romance, perhaps?

What's up?" says Ariel, standing barefoot next to me, tucking the shirt into the ample jeans I gave her. "I'm going to need a belt. I sure wish you'd let me wear some of your wife's clothes. Man, has she got expensive taste."

I show Ariel the yearbook. "I never knew Carol and Hal knew each other. I thought I had introduced them. You heard Carol's end of that phone call, just like I did. I think they're planning to have us killed."

"Now, wait a minute, Ronnie. That's kind of a stretch, don't you think? I mean, if she caught you and me, wouldn't she be better off divorcing you and taking half of everything? I mean, what's her motive? It's easy to screw up a murder. It's hard to kill somebody without somebody else finding out about it. And besides, what's Hal's motive?"

"How about a supplemental life policy worth 500 grand, plus the payout from my employee life policy benefit? Would that be motive enough, especially if she gives him a share? Hal is the guy who got Carol to convince me to sign up for that supplemental policy. Besides, how else can you explain the two of us in a lake in Clark State Forest at midday, then waking up the next morning, naked and drugged, laying alongside a drainage ditch, with no idea how we got there?"

"I don't know," says Ariel, "but you better get a shower and get dressed. I'm still feeling kinda loopy."

WHEN I COME out of the shower, Ariel is still barefoot. "Can't I borrow a pair of your wife's shoes? The sneakers you gave me are too big."

"I'll get you a pair of her sandals. Maybe she won't notice them missing. We need to clean things up and get out of here, so we can figure out our next move. If they are planning to kill us, we don't want them catching us in this house."

I pull on some clothes and grab a pair of Carol's sandals to give to Ariel. We both hear a car door slam, then voices. Ariel hurries to slip on the sandals, and I crouch low near the window to see if I can spot whoever it is. It couldn't be Carol. We just heard her leave for work. I see Frank escorting Estelle toward the door. "My in-laws!" I say to

Ariel. "Stay down. When they see there's nobody home, they'll leave. They don't have a key."

Carol's parents, Frank and Estelle, have never liked me. They are rich, religious, and live in Michigan. Carol goes there for weekends every three months, and they come to see her. When they do, I get treated with painful courtesy, like the nosy neighbor who has disturbed their peace. In my own house, no less! I get the idea that they think Carol deserves better than me, a cubicle rat who will never amount to anything.

———

WE HEAR a key rustle into the lock. The door opens, and in comes Carol, with Frank and Estelle behind. Estelle is speaking breathlessly, "Oh, Carol, dear, when you called and told us Ronald had gone missing, we just knew we had to come right down... *Oh, My God!*"

Ariel stands up slowly from her crouched position behind the Barcalounger. I stand barefoot and surprised in the middle of the floor. Carol plants herself in front of me, hands on hips, every inch the woman wronged. Estelle covers her mouth with both hands.

Frank looks at me, stern and menacing. "Ronald, what have you done to our daughter's reputation? We are good Christian people, and this fooling around has no place in our family!"

"What fooling around, Frank? This is my colleague from work, Ariel."

"She's wearing my shoes!" Carol hisses, her eyes fixed on Ariel's feet.

"Don't kid with me, Mister Ronald!" Frank demands, "What's she doing in a man's shirt and pants? They're yours, I presume? Tell me you're not having an affair with this woman!"

"Oh, oh yeah, well—whatever!" I throw up my hands.

It is all I can think of to say. Ariel lets out a worried little whimper.

Another knock comes at the door. I open it to two county sheriff's deputies.

"Do you know who owns that lawn mower behind the barn out back?"

"Officers, I can explain…" I stammer nervously.

"The contractor who owns it called us this morning to report it stolen. That thing's worth fifteen thousand bucks. Then we get a report from a retired couple that two naked people went riding past their place early today on a lawn tractor. We've been tracking it down all morning. Looks like you stole it. Which of these women was on that tractor naked with you?"

Ariel steps through the door, a guilty look on her face.

The deputy doing the talking is a short and stocky woman, mid-forties, with the permanent scowl of someone supervising detention hall. She glares at us while her partner pats us down, Mirandizes us, and handcuffs us. Her name tag reads, 'O'Doul.'

"Get in the prowler. Back seat. We're headed to the Sherriff's Department."

"Officer, I really can explain," I say through the mesh cage while settling into the seat.

"Oh, geez, that'll be a big help. Save it for when we get to the Sherriff's."

She radios ahead to report that the tractor has been located and requests a car hauler to pick it up. Then O'Doul slides into the driver's seat with her partner on the passenger's side, and we take off for Jeffersonville to the County Sherriff's office.

O'Doul and her partner let us out of the back seat and usher us, still handcuffed, into a holding cell. In time, we are taken to an interrogation room and told to sit at the table.

A plainclothes officer walks into the room with O'Doul, and she removes our cuffs.

"Right now, we've got two people joy riding in the nude on a stolen lawn tractor worth fifteen thousand bucks," says O'Doul, "That's felony stealing. Then there's the public nudity. You said you could explain. Still wanna do that, or do you want an attorney? Up to you."

They both sit down and stare across the table at us.

I hesitate, then look at Ariel, who nods back at me. I tell the officers about the trip Ariel and I made to Henryville, skinny dipping in the lake, waking up beside the drainage ditch, borrowing the tractor, all of it. Plainclothes leans over and whispers something in O'Doul's ear.

"Sit tight," Plainclothes says. They both leave.

Soon, a deputy comes back with a county nurse and an EMT to examine us and take blood and urine samples. I get led off into one exam room and Ariel to another. I am instructed to pee in a cup, then told to strip so the EMT can check me for injuries. He stops at my left hip.

"Something bite you here? You've got bruising and what looks like a small puncture wound."

I tell him about waking up in a mental fog after what appeared to be several hours and explain that Ariel went through the same. Both of us have sore spots, me on the left hip and her on her backside. He checks the area for discharge and takes a picture. Then he tells me to get dressed. A few minutes later, I'm headed back to a cell to wait for the results of the lab tests and if we're going to be charged with anything. Ariel is taken to a separate cell.

THE FOLLOWING MORNING, a deputy tells me to get up because someone needs to speak with me. My visitor is from the county prosecutor's office, waiting for me in the same interrogation room where Ariel and I were questioned the day before. He introduces himself as Ben Taggart and tells me he's an investigator.

"I've got some questions. First, do you use prescription fentanyl for anything? Pain management, perhaps?" I tell him no.

"Well, you've got it in your bloodstream, and so does your girl-friend. Where did you get it? Out partying, perhaps? Stuff makes you crazy, like stripping off your clothes, stealing a lawn mower, and riding around on it with your naked girlfriend crazy. It can kill you, too. That dose we found in your bloodstream was strong. Doesn't take much."

I shook my head. "No, sir. I don't do drugs. Neither does Ariel."

"Well, I just wanted to hear you say that. I'm not saying I believe you, but there's an injection wound on your left hip and one on her butt. Users don't normally stick themselves there. It's too difficult to reach, and it hurts too much when you sit down. Now, do you know these two guys?"

He motions me to look at the two photos he places before me. I have no idea who they are and tell him so. He nods his head.

"Ever hear of a guy named Hal Deeft?"

"Yes. He's my boss."

"That's right. He's your boss. Are you married to Carol Truax?"

"Yes, I am," I respond.

"The deputies tell me you've been real cooperative, and that's smart. You've been telling them everything you know and didn't ask for legal counsel. But now's the time. Better call one, or the court can appoint one. You don't want to be without an attorney now. Know what I mean?"

I know what Ben Taggart means. Their attention is shifting away from me and Ariel and onto whoever tried to kill us. And their names are Hal Deeft and Carol Truax. But without an attorney to guide me through the legal shitstorm that's coming, I am vulnerable. I'm the guy cheating on his wife with his cubicle mate. I'm the guy who stole a fifteen-thousand-dollar lawn tractor. I'm the guy they found with fentanyl in his veins. I need good legal cover to protect myself as much as possible until the county prosecutor can build a case against the two prime suspects. And, like Ben Taggart said, "I'm not saying I believe you."

I'm a claims man. I know attorneys. I call for a jail deputy and ask to use a phone.

An hour later, the deputy tells me I've got another visitor. He unlocks the cell door and escorts me to the interrogation room. Salonika Katsikas is seated at the table with her briefcase open and her hands folded. My case file lays open on the table.

"Hello, Ronnie! Glad you called. It's been a while since I've worked with a case involving Corn Belt. How's it hangin'?"

A smirk crosses her lips and vanishes.

I smile politely. Salonika is a great criminal defense attorney with a wicked sense of humor. She loves needling people she knows. She smiles back.

"So," Salonika begins, "I've been looking into your case. The prosecutor's office is scrambling to make sense of the evidence they collected, which is considerable. They found your clothes and your car, by the way, right where you left them, at Oak Lake in the state forest. That part of your story checks out. Say, that was pretty risky, you and your girlfriend, -Ariel, is it? - you and your girlfriend volunteering to talk without an attorney present. Not smart, Ron, but you figured if you could just explain everything, things would be alright, yes?"

I nod, dejected. More sins pile onto my already ruined reputation.

"Lucky for you, things seem to be breaking in your favor. Then the deputies got the tractor's owner to identify the property as his. When he did, they asked him if he wanted to press charges. Guy named Len Blankenship. He says he knows you?"

"Yes, I hired Len to repair landscapes after that last Henryville tornado." I say, "That was a big claim. Man, I can't believe I didn't recognize his property!"

"Yeah, we'll get to that in a minute. But back to Len Blankenship. Naturally, he wanted to know who took his lawn tractor and why, so they told him about you and your girlfriend out riding around on it, stark naked. He laughed like hell!" Salonkia says, flashing a saucy grin.

"About Len Blankenship...," I say.

"Sure, sure. He's not pressing charges. Says since he got his property back in one piece, he figures he owes you one for the business you gave him. No felony theft charge."

"Man, that is a relief! I never intended to steal it, I..."

Salonika said softly, "Relax, Ronnie, this is all gonna work out for you."

I nod. "I appreciate the help, Salonika. I really do. How is Ariel?"

"She's OK, from what they tell me. She hasn't lawyered up yet because you've been doing all the talking. Let's go through the rest of this."

Salonika continued, "And now for the fentanyl in your system. Stuff makes you crazy, Ron. Bet you didn't even know where you were when you woke up. But that's working in your favor, too. After you were picked up yesterday, the state police caught two guys dealing fentanyl in Jeffersonville. How they caught them is not important to us, but what happened after they caught them is. The cops searched their van for drugs and found a Crosman Cap-Chur dart rifle, a box of tranquilizer darts, and fentanyl. They also found traces of DNA on a tarp in the van's cargo area. Naked people leave lots of DNA around. The DNA is being tested, and we should be getting the results back in a few weeks. When the state cops heard about your case and the wounds on your hip and her butt, they put the two together. From what I'm told, both guys are plenty scared and talking. According to them, the plan was to inject you both with a lethal dose of fentanyl, then move you from the site to another location where you would be found, so it would look like the two of you were partying and overdosed yourselves. They tailed you to Oak Lake. The people who hired them wanted you both dead and humiliated, but the way these two guys went about this was half-assed.

Lucky for you. The prosecutor says there are grounds for attempted murder."

"I talked to Ben Taggart from the prosecutor's office this morning. He asked me if I knew Hal Deeft and if I was married to Carol Truax," I tell her.

"Hot damn! That's good news!"

Salonika laughs, pleased with the direction the evidence has taken. I laugh, too. I'm feeling good for the first time since all this began.

Salonika explains that the county prosecutor has decided the evidence at hand is enough to release us without charges, not even for public nudity. But we may be called to testify when charges are brought against the two fentanyl dealers and whoever hired them.

"And," Salonika tells me, "the primary suspects are Hal Deeft and Carol Truax."

I'm saddened but not surprised. My marriage to Carol was finished a long time ago, but I didn't want to admit it, and neither did she. We both thought having affairs would be easier. But why murder?

Salonika arranges for Ariel and me to be released. I receive my street clothes, and a deputy leads me to the discharge area where Salonika and Ariel are waiting. We are discharged, and Salonika takes us to Ariel's place.

Carol is arrested by the sheriff's deputies the next day. The Indianapolis police arrest Hal and turn him over to Clark County for arraignment along with Carol.

The trial date is set for six months from the arraignment to give the defense time to prepare. Meanwhile, the attorneys are busy trying to cut deals with the county prosecutor. The report on our DNA samples proves that Ariel and I were in the back of that van. The fentanyl dealers, facing attempted murder charges of their own, are cooperating to help their attorneys' efforts at plea bargaining. Deals are struck, and the case never goes to trial.

SALONIKA ASKS to meet with me and Ariel as soon as the prosecutor's office informs her of the settlement, to explain it all.

Carol and her attorney agree to 30 years with the possibility of parole after 20 years for her part in the solicitation-for-murder scheme. Her attorney convinces the judge assigned to the case that Hal masterminded the plot, despite his attorney's attempts to pin it all on Carol. Hal and his attorney agree to 50 years, but with the possibility for parole after 30 since Ariel and I are both still alive and well. The attorney for the two guys makes a deal for a more lenient sentence for attempted murder since they screwed up the dose and made it non-lethal. Turns out they make more by selling it on the street than from killing someone with it. Pure dumb luck for them and us. They get the same deal as Carol, 30 years apiece, but with the possibility for parole after 20 years.

Carol gives me a divorce, uncontested. Her relationship with Hal started up again shortly after our wedding. They kept it going with trysts in Michigan and Indiana. When Carol learned about me and Ariel, they started planning to get rid of us and set themselves up for life.

"And that," Salonika says to us, "is that."

Corn Belt Independent Life and Property Indemnity launches a full-scale investigation into the system of bribes and kickbacks paid to adjusters by contractors in exchange for consideration for business—and blame all of it on Hal. He hasn't been formally charged yet, but Corn Belt needs someone to take the heat, and Hal is their man.

I am sitting at the Tool Factory, alone. I haven't seen Ariel in weeks. On paper, my job is intact, but everybody is on edge over the kickback investigation, and frankly, I spend little time in the office. I'm staring at my drink and don't notice her until I feel her index finger stroke my chin.

"Hey, want to fool around? I got some cash put away. You do, too, right? What do you say we spend it?" I look up into her beautiful smile.

"Let's," I say.

Corn Belt Independent Life and Property Indemnity Company receive our resignations by registered mail. We're halfway across the world, where we can feel the heat of the sun. Ariel sighs with contentment as I massage her with oil. "That feels good," she says as she rolls over on her back and looks up at me, desire in her eyes. Ariel gets what she wants.

DEATH US DO PART
BY STEPHEN TERRELL

The smell of old wood, dusty files and stale cigarette smoke wafted through the Sheriff's office, carried on an early summer breeze through a large window. The fresh air was a blessed comfort from the June heat in the old jail.

Sheriff Frankie Cline sat in his creaking swivel chair, his boots propped up on his battered desk. A tall, broad-shouldered man with sharp features, he wore his hair in a close-cropped crewcut. Well-known throughout the county as a World War II hero, he was six months into his second term, one of the few Democrats in rural Indiana to survive Dwight Eisenhower's landslide election the previous November.

Across the desk, leaning back in a wooden chair that Cline thought might collapse at any second, was his brother-in-law, Jerry Halstead. Two years into his first term, Cline hired his wife's youngest brother as a deputy to keep him out of the Korean War draft. Happy wife, happy life.

Outside the Sheriff's office, in the area open to the public, Cline could hear a couple of old gossips playing checkers. They were department retirees who now spent their days either at the jail or the courthouse, trying to pick up a story worth spreading. *Better than just waiting to die.*

"So, think that's what we'll be like when we get that old?" Halstead said. "Playing checkers and spreading bushwa?"

A knock on the door frame to the office interrupted Cline before he could respond. Grady Puckett and Quentin Reece stuck their heads in past the open door. Grady was a tall, lanky man in his fifties, missing two fingers from his left hand, something not uncommon among area farmers. Quentin Reece was a compact, wiry man somewhere past 70 – maybe approaching 80 – with leathery skin from a lifetime of working his fields. Cline knew that despite Quentin's age, he still outworked and out-produced men half his age.

"You got a minute, Sheriff?" Grady said.

"Door's open," Cline said. Cline pointed to several wooden straight-back chairs lined against a wall. "You know my brother-in-law, don't ya?"

Each man doffed their wide-brimmed straw hats, typical headgear for farmers during summer. "Sure, we know Jerry," Grady said with a pleasant smile. "How you doing?"

"Sweeter'n milk from an old fat heifer," Jerry responded.

"You mean a cow or you talking about that girl down at Molly Fuller's place?" Quentin said with a smirk.

The room burst into laughter as Jerry's face turned red. Molly Fuller was known for running a whorehouse filled with over-aged, overweight girls, none of them locals. The brothel was located in a dilapidated tourist camp on the only highway in the county with enough truck traffic to keep her in business. No one lived nearby, so no one complained. But everyone, even the high school kids, knew about it.

"So, boys, what can I do for you?"

Grady pulled out a cigarette and lit up, then began to talk in a raspy voice. "You know Virgil Bagley, don't you? Has that farm over by Quentin and me."

Cline nodded. "I know him." Like most rural county officeholders, he knew almost everyone in the county. "He and his wife got two grown boys that still live at home. I had to go out there a couple years back. Census taker was concerned that maybe his wife wasn't doing well. He thought Virgil might be beating up on her."

"I've wondered that myself," Grady said. "You never see her out except when she's feeding the chickens."

Cline scratched at his chin. "If I remember right, one of them boys is a little touched in the head."

"That's him. Boy got kicked in the head by a cow when he was young. Ain't been right since. But that ain't the problem. It's old man Bagley."

"Go on."

Quentin Reece jumped in. "We been havin' trouble with him for years. He treats my property — Grady's, too — like a dump heap for his farm. He's been doing it for years. But it's just getting worse."

"So what has he done that's brought you in here?"

Grady lit a cigarette off the one he had just finished. "It's the pigs and that pond he built."

Cline leaned back further in his chair. "Tell me about it."

"He built a new pig lot. It's right across the property line from my house and across the road from Quentin's."

Cline sat up and put a smile on his face trying to diffuse tensions. "I thought that if you asked a farmer what pig shit smells like, he'd say, 'money.'"

"Ain't so when it's up against your house," Grady snapped. "And they ain't your pigs."

"That's only part of it," Quentin said. "He damned up Slippery Creek a couple of years back. It created a pond on his property and cut off water to mine. Now when we get a big rain, water flows out of that pond, through his pig lot, and onto Grady's front yard. Mine, too. We get our yards flooded and covered in pig shit."

"Did you try talking to him?"

"You ever try to talk to Virgil?" Grady said. "Quentin and me, we went over there yesterday. Virgil called us every swear word I ever heard, and some I ain't. Ran us off his property with a shotgun. His boys was standing beside him, holding an axe and sledge like they was gonna start pounding on us. That's why we came here."

Cline slid his boots off the desk and sat upright in his chair. "I don't know what I can do about his pigs or the water, but I'll go talk to Virgil about pointing a shotgun. If nothing else, it'd be a good reason to check on Mrs. Bagley again. Make sure she's doing all right. As for the rest of this, sounds more like something you need to talk to a lawyer about."

Quentin sneered. "Lawyers. Might as well go talk to my jackass. And I wouldn't have to pay my jackass to listen to me."

———

THE FOLLOWING AFTERNOON, Jerry Halstead was walking by the Sheriff's open door when Cline yelled out at him. "Hey, Jerry! Call up Sandy and tell her you'll be late for supper. I want you to ride with me up to the Bagley farm at about six o'clock. I need to talk to Virgil about pulling that shotgun on Grady and Quentin."

"Why don't we go now? I ain't got nothing to do right now."

"Best time to catch a farmer is supper time. Otherwise, they're most likely out in the fields."

Shortly before six o'clock, Cline and Halstead got in the Sheriff's new Ford Customline with the police package Mercury engine, Cline's one gift to himself for his reelection. They headed west out of town on the twenty-minute drive to the Bagley farm.

The Bagleys lived in a turn-of-the-century, two-story white farmhouse that was showing wear. A chicken coop was not far from the house, and chickens wandered about the yard, pecking for insects and grubs. Behind the house was a barn in serious need of paint.

Virgil Bagley opened the front door as Cline and Halstead made their way up the steps to the porch. Maybe 65, perhaps older, Virgil was short, no more than five-foot five-inches, with a round bald head, heavy jowls, and almost no neck.

"Howdy, Sheriff. What brings you out here?"

"Need to talk with you for a few minutes, Virgil. This is my deputy, Jerry Halstead. Can we come in and talk a spell?"

"Sure, Sheriff. You're always welcome here." Virgil turned and let them into the house, walking with a distinct limp from a farm accident when he was a young man.

The front room, a parlor, was dark, with windows covered by heavy maroon curtains. The scuffed wood floor creaked under foot. The room smelled unpleasant, of dust and cooking odors, stale cigarettes and old farts. Three worn overstuffed chairs were crowded into the room, their armrests decorated with dime-store doilies. Bagley's adult sons, Jim and Lenny, occupied two chairs. Still wearing work clothes and muddy farm boots, they blankly looked straight ahead, taking no notice of the Sheriff and his deputy.

Virgil pointed to a floral-covered davenport next to a heavy walnut cabinet that held a Philco radio. "Have a seat." Virgil sat in the one empty chair while Cline and Halstead sat on the sofa.

"Ida," Virgil bellowed. When there was no immediate response, he yelled louder. "Ida!"

A frail white-haired woman hurried in, wiping her hands on an apron tied at her waist. "You need something, Virgil."

"Bring some coffee for the Sheriff and his deputy." It was not a request.

"There ain't any made," Ida said in a submissive voice. "I'll have to make some."

"Don't make any for us, Mrs. Bagley," Cline said gently. "We're just going to be a few minutes. By the way, how are you doing these days?"

Ida Bagley lowered her head. "Passable," she said.

"Make it anyway," Virgil demanded, cutting off anything else his wife might say. "I might want some with supper."

Ida nodded, then turned and hurried out of the room.

Virgil sat in what obviously was his chair by the way it conformed to his shape then seemed to swallow him. To Cline, the farmer looked like a toad with a flap of skin hanging from his chin and two bulging eyes protruding from his yellow-green-tinged face.

"We don't want to interrupt your supper," Cline said, knowing fully well that was precisely his intent.

"No, never mind, Sheriff. What can I do for you?"

Cline leaned forward, hands on his thighs. "I understand you've been having some trouble with your neighbors."

Virgil grunted. "You mean old Quentin Reece and that Grady Puckett. I don't consider them neighbors. They's always causing trouble for me."

"That's not how they see it."

"They's goddamn liars. That's what they are." Virgil lifted a butt cheek a let go with a thunderous fart as if emphasizing what he thought of Reece and Puckett. "They can't take care of their own farms, so they's always blaming me for something."

"Pa's right," chimed in one of the sons. Cline thought it was Jim, the older one.

"Settle down," Cline said. "I'm not here to settle any dispute about your property or your farming. That's up to the judge if someone takes it to court. What bothers me is threatening someone with a shotgun, or anything else, for that matter."

"It's a damned lie," Virgil barked. This time, his two sons were nodding in agreement. "I was coming back from shooting a coyote that's been bothering my chickens when they come up to me. They was the ones threatening me. I never pointed my gun at them. No, sir."

"I'm not here to decide whether it happened or not," Cline said. "I'm not here to arrest anyone. But when I get reports of someone waiving a shotgun, I got to look into it."

"Them sons of bitches is lying," Virgil said. "Ain't that right, boys?" Jim and Lenny vigorously nodded.

"That's right, Pa," Lenny said with a thick voice.

"See," Virgil said. "That's three against two. It didn't happen."

Cline and Halstead both struggled to suppress laughs. "That's not the way it works," Cline said. "It's not something I take a vote on. But look here, if I get any more reports of you waiving your gun at someone or one of your sons making threats, I'm going to have to do something. I just want to make myself clear on that before someone gets in real trouble."

Virgil shook his head. "Ain't us causing the trouble. But we ain't gonna let them tell us how to run our farm, neither."

Cline stood, and Halstead followed. "Just stay on your own property, and don't do anything that's gonna cause problems for your neighbors."

"You tell them to stay off my property. And I'm gonna farm any damned way I want."

CLINE AND HALSTEAD rode in silence, heading back to the county seat. They were halfway back to the jail when Halstead broke the silence. "Is it just me, or are those people strange?"

"They're plenty strange, all right. Keep to themselves, almost like hermits. As far as I know, they don't socialize with anyone."

"I couldn't believe he ripped off that fart right in front of us."

"That's Virgil."

"Them boys got an odd look to them. Something about the set of their eyes. I know the one got kicked in the head, but even the other one looks odd."

"Jim, the older one, was married once. People say she was back home within a month. Nobody ever said what happened, but she got a divorce, and the whole family moved away."

"Well, just don't ever send me out there."

"Jerry, that's why I brought you out here with me. If you're gonna be a deputy, you gotta learn to deal with all types of people. I wanted you to get an idea who we are dealing with in case you have to make the trip out here by yourself next time." Cline glanced over at his deputy. "And I'm sure as shit that we're going to be going out there again."

***

On Thursday afternoon of the following week, Deputy Halstead walked into Sheriff Cline's office, where the Sheriff was hunched over a ledger book. "Frankie, we got another issue out at the Bagley property."

Cline looked up. "What now?"

"Martha just took a call from Dolores Puckett, Grady's wife. It seems Virgil and his boys started using their tractor to drag all their pig and cow manure over to the edge of their property and dump it just across the fence line from the Puckett's house. Grady and Quentin headed over there a couple of hours ago. They ain't been back home, and she's worried. Wanted to see if we could check on them."

"Damn! I told them not to go over there!" the Sheriff said, slapping his hand on his desk. "Jerry, I have to meet with the County Council this afternoon to review the budget. I'm trying to get them to fund two new deputies. I can't miss that meeting. Can you drive out there and see what's going on? Tell Grady and Quentin to get back to their own homes and stay there. I'll come out sometime tomorrow and talk to all of them."

"What if they won't go?"

"Arrest Grady and Quentin for trespassing on Bagley's property. Then bring them back here. But don't put them in a cell. If they're here when I get out of the Council meeting, I'll have a talk with them, then send them home without their supper."

"Sounds like you're scolding a couple of three-year-olds."

Cline gave a short laugh. "That's what it's like sometimes when these farmers around here get to squabbling."

Halstead nodded and started out the door.

"Jerry?" the Sheriff called after him.

Halstead stopped and turned.

"I don't think this is much more than bickering. But watch yourself. Every farmer in this county carries a shotgun. If things get heated, back away and radio for assistance. Don't get in over your head."

"Sure, Chief." And with that, Halstead was gone.

HALSTEAD PULLED his deputy's car, a worn post-war Ford that got passed on to the deputy with the least seniority, into the long two-track drive that led up to the Bagley's house. He stopped behind a battered farm truck and turned off the engine. He heard the sound of machinery running someplace behind the house in the direction of the barn. Halstead stepped outside his car, slipped on his broad-rimmed Sheriff's hat, and put on his most serious cop face. He walked around the side of the house toward the mechanical noise. That was where he expected to find Virgil and his sons, likely finishing the day's work before supper.

A few chickens pecked in the grass for insects. They scattered in front of Halstead's purposeful strides. As he approached the barn, he could tell the noise was coming from behind the barn. Halstead turned the corner of the barn and saw Jim Bagley sitting on an Allis-Chalmers tractor with a bush hog attached. Jim ran the machine back and forth over the small stretch of ground long since cleared of any brush. A few feet away, Lenny Bagley was wielding an axe, chopping at something.

Halstead was confused about why the boys would run a bush hog over a smooth stretch of ground. Then, as Jim raised the implement, Halstead saw blood and pieces of bone covering the vegetation.

Swine flu. That was Halstead's first thought. The deadly disease had decimated droves of hogs on several farms in nearby counties. But why would the Bagleys be grinding up dead hogs?

As he looked closer to where Lenny was working with his axe, Halstead realized Lenny was hacking at a human torso. A few feet away was a severed head. It was Grady Puckett.

Halstead tried to pull his revolver from his holster, but a sickness overcame him. He fumbled the gun, and it fell into the dirt. As it did, Halstead spewed vomit across the grass. Without bothering to wipe his mouth, he grabbed his gun. Shaking, he pointed it toward the two Bagley boys. "Stop!"

It was clear that Lenny and Jim could not hear him over the grinding machinery. Halsted pointed his gun in the air and fired.

The shot got the attention of the two boys. "Shut down that machine and drop that axe," Halstead shouted as loud as he could. But neither Lenny nor Jim moved. The roar of the bush hog continued.

Halstead didn't hear the footfalls behind him. He heard a click, barely registering it as a shotgun being cocked an instant before Virgil Bagley pulled the trigger, sending a deer slug through Halstead's brain.

***

FRANKIE CLINE, his stomach full of his wife Madge's meatloaf and mashed potatoes, settled into his Barcalounger chair in front of their Admiral TV he had only recently purchased from the Guarantee Auto store. He was going to watch his favorite show, *Dragnet*. The familiar four-note opening sounded, followed by Jack Webb's voice over the image of a police badge: "This is the city, Los Angeles, California." But as Webb finished, Madge walked into the room. "Frankie, it's Sandy on the phone. Jerry's not home yet. Do you know anything about it?"

Cline looked up. "No. I had to meet with the County Council today, so I sent him out to the Bagley farm about five o'clock. Virgil ruffled his neighbors' feathers again. When I got out of the Council meeting, I saw he hadn't brought Grady and Quentin back to the jail, so I figured everything was calmed down. He should have been home a couple of hours ago."

"Well, he's not, and my sister is beside herself."

Cline got up. "Tell Sandy that Jerry's car probably broke down. He's got the department's clunker for a squad car. It's always breaking down. I'll go out and start looking at the route he would have taken."

Madge's face reflected concern, but she passed along her husband's message over the phone to her sister. "I'll call as soon as I hear something. But call me if he walks in the door." After Madge hung up, she turned to her husband, who was strapping on his gun belt.

"Do you really think that he just broke down?" Madge said. "Wouldn't he just call in on his police radio or walk to a neighbor and call?"

"I don't know, Madge. If the battery is dead, the radio won't work. And there's still a lot of farm folks that don't have phones. But I'll go see."

"I don't like this, Frankie,"

Cline gave her a small kiss on the cheek. "I don't either." Then he was out the door.

Cline drove back to the jail, then traced the route to the Bagley farm. He drove slowly, swinging the car's spotlight from side to side, then back again, checking the roadside ditches, fields and dirt paths for a broken-down police car. What was usually a twenty-minute drive took nearly twice that time. It was approaching ten o'clock when Cline pulled into the Bagley's long driveway.

Unease overtook him. He swung the spotlight across the yard in front of the house. A battered farm truck and a green Hudson Commodore that Virgil used when he drove to town were parked in the drive. There was no sign of Halstead or his car.

Cline keyed his radio. "This is the Sheriff. I'm out at the Bagley farm trying to find Jerry. There's no sign of him or his car. I have a bad feeling."

"Sheriff, are you in trouble?" said the night dispatcher over a crackling radio.

"I don't think so. It's probably nothing. But if you don't hear back from me in twenty minutes, call the state police and let them know what's going on."

"Sheriff..."

"Out," he said and turned the radio off. Cline unsnapped the strap holding his revolver in place, then stepped out of the car. He walked to the trunk, opened it, and removed his shotgun, cracking it open and sighting down the barrels to make sure it was loaded. He grabbed a fist full of shells from a box and slid them into a jacket pocket for insurance.

As he shut the trunk, Cline saw the porch light go on, and a small, frail figure stepped onto the front stoop. Ida Bagley was wearing a pink robe. At her side, she held a shotgun pointing toward the ground.

"That you, Sheriff?" she shouted out in a thin voice.

"Yes, ma'am. It surely is."

"I was expecting you."

"Now, Mrs. Bagley, I don't know exactly what's going on here, but do you know how to break that shotgun open?"

"I surely do. My daddy taught me to hunt when I was little. But it's not loaded."

Cline continued to stand next to his car. He trained the spotlight on the old woman. "I'm sure you're telling the truth, but I need you to open the breach and dump out any shells in it."

"Sure, Sheriff." Mrs. Bagley did as she was directed, but no shells fell from the gun. "I didn't mean to startle you."

"That's fine," Cline said, his voice as reassuring as he could make it. "Now toss the gun away from you a bit."

Cline watched as Mrs. Bagley followed his directions, using a two-handed motion to toss the shotgun off the porch. "You're safe, Sheriff. You can come on up."

"Where's your husband and the boys?"

"Virgil's in the living room. The boys are out back. Ain't none of them gonna hurt you."

Cline walked forward, holding his shotgun pointing down, but in a way he could quickly raise it and fire if needed. As he reached the porch steps, Mrs. Bagley turned, opened the door, and held it for the Sheriff. "Won't you step inside," she said with an inviting smile.

Cline took the door and directed Mrs. Bagley to enter in front of him. Cline followed.

What hit him first was the lingering scent of spent gunpowder and death. It was a smell he was all too familiar with from his combat service during WWII. Then what he saw stopped him in his tracks.

Virgil Bagley sat in his chair, his mouth frozen open, a massive hole in his chest. He was covered in blood that pooled on his lap and dripped onto the floor.

As Cline stared at the corpse, Mrs. Bagley turned, still wearing a pleasant smile. "I'm sorry I didn't call you, Sheriff. I just didn't know what to say. And I figured you'd eventually make your way out here."

Cline shook his head in disbelief. "What happened? Did Jerry shoot him?"

"Oh, no, Sheriff," Mrs. Bagley said softly, the smile never disappearing. "I did. The boys, too. They're out back."

"Dead?"

"Oh, yes. I'm sorry, but so is your deputy. Mr. Puckett and Mr. Reece are dead, too, although they are quite ground up by now. But I didn't have anything to do with that."

All his years in combat and the eight intervening years as a policeman had not prepared Cline for this docile woman describing the carnage. The room swirled about him. Cline placed his hand on a nearby table, trying to steady himself.

"I'm sorry for my language, Mrs. Bagley, but just what the hell happened?"

"Have a seat here at the dinner table. Would you like some coffee?"

Cline sat down heavily and removed his hat, leaning his shotgun against his leg, still close enough to grab it if need be. "Mrs. Bagley, I don't need any coffee. Just sit here with me and tell me what happened."

Mrs. Bagley delicately sat and began her story. "About four o'clock, Mr. Puckett and Mr. Reece came by. I could tell they were really irritated when they came to the door."

"Virgil and the boys was in the barn, but I said they were out in the fields and wouldn't be back 'till after dark. I hoped they'd go away and simmer down, but they didn't. I guess they heard Virgil and the boys working out back 'cause when Mr. Puckett and Mr. Reece walked from the house, they headed toward the barn."

"What happened then?"

"They got into quite a ruckus. I seen it all from the kitchen window. When Puckett and Reece yelled at Virgil, Lenny came out of the barn with a big hammer and just walked up behind Mr. Puckett and hit him right on the crown of his head. He crumpled like a sack of potatoes. Then Jim knocked Mr. Reece on the ground, grabbed the hammer from Lenny and pounded on Mr. Reece a couple of times."

"What did your husband do?"

"I learned over the years about Virgil. If I ever spoke back, or disagreed, or didn't have supper ready when he wanted it, he'd just smack me across the room. Butchering hogs never meant much to Virgil. People, neither, I guess. And he taught them boys to be just like him."

"Did the boys hit you, too?"

"Not as much as Virgil, but once they got growed, they did. And they was gettin' worse."

"What about my deputy, Jerry? What happened to him?"

"I wished I could have stopped that. But I was upstairs when I heard the shot. I looked out the window and saw Virgil standing there with his shotgun. Your deputy was on the ground, blood pouring out of his head. Then Virgil yelled at the boys to move the deputy's car to the barn, and they'd get rid of it tonight. That's when I knew I had to do something."

Cline involuntarily gulped. "What did you do?"

"Virgil came in, leaving the boys to finish chopping Mr. Puckett and Mr. Reece into pieces." Again, Ida gave an indecorous smile. "I guess they was going to spread them on the fields or dump them in the hog pen or something. Virgil was settin' in his chair, expecting me to fix dinner like I always do. I saw the shotgun where he left it when he came in, leaning against the kitchen door. I loaded it and walked into the living room. When he looked up at me, I shot him. Then I reloaded and went out back where the boys was working. And I shot them, too. They didn't even see me."

Cline gave a deep sign. "Oh, Mrs. Bagley. I wish you had just called me. You didn't have to do all this."

"I did," she said quietly. "Virgil's been like that for years. And the boys was just like him. That's why Jim's wife left him so soon after they got married. He was just like his paw. She was smarter than I was and got out. So when Virgil and the boys killed them men, I knew I couldn't take no more. I had to stop it. I figured I just needed to take care of it myself."

"I'm going to have to arrest you and take you to jail. You know that."

"I do, Sheriff," Mrs. Bagley gave an odd smile. "I'm sorry about your deputy. If I could have done anything to save him, I would have. As for arresting me, I'm okay about the jail. Except for once a month for groceries, I ain't been off this farm in probably twenty years. It'll be something new. Least ways, nobody is gonna be screaming for me to fix dinner or hittin' on me 'cause they don't like what I fix. Now, can I go upstairs and change? I don't want to be traipsing around in my night clothes."

Cline nodded. He sat silently for several minutes, contemplating how he would tell his sister-in-law that her husband was dead. As time passed, he began to wonder what was taking Mrs. Bagley such a long time to change clothes. Finally, he stood and shouted, "Mrs. Bagley?"

From upstairs, the Sheriff heard a single shot crack followed by a thump as a body hit the floor.

AMERICAN REBEL
BY ELIZABETH PERONA

The last time I saw Pat in Indiana, he was in the back seat of a dusty Ford pickup truck bound for 'Idaho.' He gave a brief wave as I watched from the front yard of my parents' farmhouse. He feigned disinterest, as though he couldn't care less that his 'uncle' had abruptly put the farm up for sale in the middle of summer, 1971, to move, leaving a charred, collapsed barn and dead livestock behind. I knew two things: first, Pat was tired of moving, and second, I'd lost a personal hero, a true American rebel. In the denseness that only self-absorbed middle-school boys can envelope themselves, I never realized I had caused it.

Or that I might one day make up for it.

Pat wore his glasses like Clark Kent, smart but not nerdy, with discerning brown eyes that watched everything. When I first met him, he was seventeen years old to my twelve, and without a brother, I took to him like one. He was self-assured in a defiant sort of way, with an intensity that threatened to erupt at any moment. His shoulders were square and muscular, and the fact he worked hard on their farm was evident in the way his shirt sleeves swelled when he moved his arms. I immediately wanted to be just like him.

"You're in high school, ain't you?" I asked. My parents had moved into the adjacent farmhouse, and we'd come to meet the next-door neighbors, although next door meant a half mile down a county road.

"Aren't you," he said, correcting my grammar. That's what I meant about him being smart. He never had to think twice like I did, about whether the language I'd grown up with would lose me points on an English essay. Later I would come to learn just how smart he really was.

"Okay. Aren't you?"

"Yeah. I'm a senior."

We sat on hay bales outside the chicken coop, not too far from the screened-in back porch where my parents and his pa were getting acquainted. We boys had been sent out to find something to do.

"You play any sports?" I'd asked this in the hope that we might establish something in common, like baseball or basketball, two activities that were almost a religion in rural Indiana.

"Lacrosse," he said. It took me a moment to realize he wasn't speaking French.

"What's that?"

Pat stood. "One of those fancy field games they play out east. I played when we lived in Jersey."

I wanted to clue him in I was smart. I may have grown up saying 'warsh' instead of 'wash' and 'crick' instead of 'creek,' but it didn't mean I was dumb. "You mean New Jersey?"

"Yeah. We weren't there long. Just another stop on this long journey here." He shrugged and headed toward the barn. I followed. From the strong, pungent smell, I figured it was their pig barn. Pigs have a recognizable smell you'd like to forget but never do. The minute even a hint of that overpowering, irritating odor hits, you know exactly what it is.

"Where you going, boys?" his pa called from the porch. He had a slight accent I couldn't place. His stocky figure loomed through the screen.

Pat pushed his glasses back up the bridge of his nose. The July heat and humidity may have stuck our shirts to our chests, but it made the hard, plastic eyewear slide. "I'm going to feed the hogs," he said in a defiant tone, as though feeding the hogs would constitute a crime. He never turned around to speak to him, just continued toward the barn.

"Why don't you and Bobby check the coop for eggs? I'm sure Bobby's seen plenty of pigs."

Pat shrugged and waved at me to follow. I hadn't moved since his pa's reprimand so I scurried to catch up, tripping on a rare patch of grass in a yard made barren by the lack of July rain.

"I don't mind helping feed the pigs," I said.

"Doesn't matter. He said not to. I like to let Kurt think he controls me." He spat on the ground forcefully, like he had aimed at something, but there was nothing in the hardscrabble grass but clover. "For now," he added, a wicked smile on his face.

"What's that mean?" I asked.

"It means the thing he doesn't want you to see, you'll see, if you stick around long enough."

There was something I wasn't supposed to see? If I needed any more encouragement to follow this guy with his James Dean attitude, that was it. Plus, I loved the implication that he wanted me to come back, though I wasn't sure at that point if he considered me a friend or an ally. Actually, I was good with either.

Later that night, I overheard Mom and Pop talking about Kurt, Pat's pa. "Something's wrong with that man, don't you think?" Mom said.

I stood rock still on the staircase leading up to my room, eavesdropping. Our farmhouse, built in 1910, had old age settling in on it, and though I only weighed 100 pounds, the stairs still complained.

"If'n you mean he's arrogant for a pig farmer, I'd go along with you."

"He did seem to feel too good for us." Mom was around the corner from where I stood, so I couldn't see her, but I knew she'd crossed her arms at that point and propped them up on top of her belly. "Friendly for outward appearances' sake. 'Course, he is a widower. You got to make allowances for that."

Mom always gave a person the benefit of doubt, especially if a non-traditional status was involved. Not having a wife was one of them.

"What do you think about the boy?" Mom continued.

"Brooding," Pop said.

"Like James Dean." Mom was into James Dean. "'Course, what seventeen-year-old boy doesn't brood?"

"He seems older than that to me."

"Well, I hope Bobby doesn't turn into a brooder."

So they didn't like his pa and had reservations about Pat. I found myself worried they might stop me from seeing him. I found myself holding my breath.

"The boy seems to be a hard worker, though. Bobby could learn from that." Pop was coming through for me. I didn't stop to resent the implication that I was somehow lazy. "Probably just need to keep an eye on them."

Mom was quiet and I couldn't tell from the silence if she agreed or disagreed. I wanted to peek around the corner and gain a clue from how she was standing, but I couldn't risk the creaking of the stairs.

Finally Mom said, "Mark my words, there's something odd going on over there."

Moments later I heard rattling in the kitchen, so I scurried upstairs.

Two days later, I rushed to finish my chores early. I jumped on my bike and headed over to Pat's. Pop had just nodded his head after lunch when I told him I was going for a ride. He was absorbed with weather reports on the dry summer, and Mom was hanging laundry outside. They knew I hadn't tired of riding the three-speed Schwinn they got me for my birthday in May, so I figured they wouldn't think more of it.

Pat's farm was pretty quiet. My tires crunched gravel on the driveway as I pulled up by the house. No one answered when I knocked loudly three separate times. I went around to the back and surveyed the land.

The doors to the pig barn were open. I hesitated to go back there since I'd been warned off, but I thought if Pat was there, I'd be fine.

I made noise on my way just in case Pat's pa was there so he'd know I was coming. No one came out, though. I put the kickstand down and stopped the bike well back of the wide red doors. The pig stink was bad but no worse than anything I'd encountered at our place. I moved forward, stopping at the doors and letting my eyes adjust to the darkness.

The pigs were sick, or at least most of them were. They were coughing as they rutted around, not very active. Many of the bigger ones looked skinny, like they'd lost weight. Snot ran from their noses. Swine flu, I thought, 'cause I'd seen it in our herd last year. But right away Mom and Pop separated out the infected ones and killed them. Said it spread quickly, so we had to be careful.

I wondered at the timing, too. At our farm, it'd been early winter. In the height of summer, it didn't seem possible. And why were the pigs inside, anyway? They would all catch it if nobody did anything.

Back outside, I got all the way to my bicycle when I saw Kurt coming around the side of the chicken coop. My eyes widened. Last person I hoped to see. At least I was now far enough from the pig barn for him to be uncertain if I'd been inside or not.

I waved and tried not to sound scared. "Pat around?" I called.

Even being several hundred feet away I could tell he was scowling. Was I in trouble? He looked to be assessing the situation before he said, "Come here."

I thought about hopping on my bike and tearing out of there as fast as I could, but his "come here" hadn't sounded threatening. Plus, I wanted to maintain the illusion I hadn't done anything wrong. I walked my bike over to where he stood holding a bucket of chicken feed.

"What are you doing here?" he asked, his voice bathed in curiosity with an undertone of menace.

"Looking for Pat," I gulped. "That's all."

"Why didn't you try the house?"

"I did, but no one answered."

He crossed his arms over his chest. "Why did you come back here?"

"I saw the barn doors open and I thought maybe Pat might be back here."

"You're sure no one was in the house? How many times did you knock?"

"Three times."

Kurt snorted. "Only three? He probably couldn't hear you over the goddamn music."

I sucked in a breath. Mom and Pop never talked that way. We were God-fearing people and went to Mass every Sunday. I was an altar boy. Kurt's demeanor changed when he saw my reaction.

"Go up to the house," he said. "This time bang loudly at least six times. And yell for him. He'll come down eventually."

I didn't need another invitation. I jumped on my bike and sped to the farmhouse, trying not to spray gravel at Pat's pa. Having gotten away with viewing the sick pigs, I didn't want to jeopardize any tolerance he had toward me.

I parked my bike in the grass and climbed the steps to the porch. This time I could faintly hear music. I banged and yelled for Pat eleven times. Finally, the front door opened, the screen door between us. When he realized it was me, he smiled vaguely. He glanced at my bike. I think it occurred to him then I'd pedaled all the way over to see him. "Hey," he said. "What brings you here?"

"Want to do something?" I asked.

"Just a minute." He ducked back into the house, looked through a few windows and came back. "You seen Kurt?"

"You mean your pa?"

He hesitated. "Yeah. Seen him?"

"Back by the chicken coop," I said.

"Really?" He held the door open for me. "C'mon in."

I don't know what I expected, but the small entryway looked nothing like the neatly kept space Mom had at our house. There was a mat to wipe my shoes on, but that was the extent of any niceties. Odd-looking glassware and other medical stuff was scattered around, the kind I'd seen in the hospital several years ago when I'd had my tonsils taken out.

"Step around it," he said, watching me navigate the minefield. He plowed up the stairs, his longer legs taking them two at a time. I pounded behind him, single-staired.

At the top, Pat led us to the back bedroom. He slid a key in the lock. "I know Kurt gets in here, but I like to keep up the illusion of privacy."

The room was a tribute to rebellion. Posters lined the wall. Some were of movies like "Rebel without a Cause" or "Billy Jack," others were of protest musicians like Pete Seger or counter-culture icons like Woodstock. Pat put a finger to his lips to indicate I should be quiet. He put an album on his stereo and it began blaring the sound-track from Woodstock. I perused his bookshelf, packed with well-worn paperbacks and a few hard-cover books. Pat was well-read, but his tastes tended toward underground science fiction and fantasy. I picked up Robert A. Heinlein's "Stranger in a Strange Land," which I'd tried to get at the library. The librarian had sniffed at my request and told me it wasn't "literature." If I'd thought Pat was cool, I now thought he was super-cool.

"Can I read this?" I asked.

"If you give it back."

I carried it around, looking at everything while he sang along to Ritchie Haven's "Freedom." Pat could carry a tune but he mostly screamed the lyrics. "Kurt hates it when I do this," he said, his eyes flashing. I couldn't tell if it was in anger or amusement.

"Why do you call him 'Kurt,' and not 'Pa'?"

"Figure it out, Einstein."

I stopped and considered the facts. They didn't look anything alike. Still, I phrased it as a question. "He ain't your pa?"

Pat nodded. "Isn't, but yeah."

"Then who is he?"

Pat gave me an impish smile. Then he said something in another language, two words with several syllables and a lot of hard consonants. "That's his name," he added.

Russian, I thought. Or German.

"You can't tell anyone," he said. "Not your parents, no one."

"So, what's going on? You got a barn full of sick pigs. You're living here with someone who ain't—isn't—your pa, yet you want everyone to believe he is. And who're you? Is your name even Pat?"

His eyes opened wide. "You saw inside the barn? Oh, man, did Kurt catch you?"

"In a manner a' speaking. I was out of the barn before he saw me. I think he can't decide if I was in there or not. I didn't admit to it."

Pat stroked his chin like an adult. "He'll assume the worst-case scenario. That could be bad for you. Make sure you're with me anytime you're here. If you knock and I don't answer, get back on your bike and head home. Don't let Kurt ever find you alone."

"Why? What's going on here?"

"I love this song," he said, avoiding my question. "Have you heard it?"

"No."

"It's the Fish Cheer, by Country Joe MacDonald. Get ready. Sing it with me."

I had no idea what was coming.

"Give me an 'F,'" he yelled.

"F," I screamed back.

"U!"

"U!"

"C!"

My eyes practically bugged out of my head when it suddenly dawned on me what we were spelling. I stopped shouting.

Country Joe sang the final letter.

"Go ahead," Pat shrieked. "Let it out. It'll feel good."

It wouldn't feel good when my mouth got washed with soap, which would happen if Mom ever learned I even spelled it. Pat laughed like he knew what I was thinking.

"Your folks will never know. You think Kurt's going to tell them?"

I paused to contemplate Pat and his defiance of all things held decent by parents. At that moment, he seemed larger than life, even bigger than I had thought two days ago. I opened my mouth. The word almost came out.

His eyes lit up with amusement. "Say it! Say it loud!"

I did, but in a whisper, and waited for legions of angels to descend from heaven and cast me into hell.

He grabbed my shoulders. "Shout it! You sound like you're apologizing for it."

I *was* apologizing. Lightning should've struck me right then and there.

On the other hand, nothing had happened yet. I yelled it.

"Better," he said triumphantly. The song finished, so he plopped the needle back at the beginning. We sang it over and over until we were laughing so hard we had to stop.

He turned off the record player. "I want to show you something," he said conspiratorially.

He opened the door and looked around. No sign of Kurt. We crept down the stairs. They creaked like mine, making me hold my breath.

We reached the first-floor landing and he motioned me to remain still. He disappeared into the parlor looking for Kurt. He reappeared at the end of the corridor and motioned for me. I tiptoed through the laboratory equipment to get to him.

"I don't see Kurt anywhere," he whispered into my ear, "but we need to be quiet just in case."

We stood close to what I guessed was a dining room table, but it was covered with books and papers. Squinting, I could see the books were not written in English.

Pat pulled at my arm. He led me down a back corridor. At the end was a door with three locks on it. He pulled out a wad of keys. It took him a bit to find the right three that unlocked the door. I followed him downstairs into the dark cellar, gulping nervously. When we reached the bottom, he turned on a light switch. It might have been the previous darkness or the now-noticeable abundance of lights, but I felt like he'd turned on the sun. This was not like any cellar I'd been in before. I stepped off the bottom stair and gaped.

It was larger and deeper than ours. The brick walls were painted white, the floor was a very clean, white linoleum, and light fixtures covered nearly every inch of the ceiling.

There were eggs everywhere, placed individually in glass dishes. "Hen's eggs," Pat whispered. "It's how the virus gets produced."

I'd learned about viruses in science class, but I didn't get a chance to ask which virus. An alarm went off. It wasn't deafening but persistent enough I stopped and looked up at the ceiling where the noise came from.

Pat clenched his teeth so hard I could practically hear them grind. "Kurt's coming in from the barn," he hissed. He pushed me up the stairs, hurtling me toward the door. I barely had time to turn the knob before I found myself through it. "Upstairs to my room, as fast as you can."

I didn't need any encouragement. I hit the first stair and bounded up them like I'd been launched from Cape Canaveral. But when I got to Pat's room I discovered he'd locked the door. I twisted and twisted the knob but it didn't open. Pat wasn't behind me. I had no idea where he was but I could feel my heart beat in my chest.

What was going on at this farm?

I had no time to process what I'd seen before Pat dashed up the stairs, two at a time. His hand was out and he had the key in it. He fumbled it in the lock before it finally caught and the door swung open.

"I had to lock the basement door and that took a while." Then his head jerked up. "Damn. I forgot about the lights."

He eased the door behind him noiselessly, then dashed to his stereo and turned it on. "Act normal," he said, "and for God's sake don't tell anyone what you just saw."

"I got no idea what I saw."

And there would be no explanation, at least not then, because Pat set the needle in the middle of the "Fish Cheer," and started screaming the words. A wave of his hand indicated I should do the same.

Act normal? This would never feel normal. Still, I tried not to sound scared or apologetic. I focused on the moment. The door swung open.

"Turn off the goddamn music," Kurt said, looking as angry as ever. Pat continued to let the music play, singing along solo, since I'd stopped the instant he'd walked in the room.

The two of them looked at each other. Pat shouted the Fish Cheer.

Kurt walked over and scraped the needle off the record. In one quick movement, he threw the record on the floor and smashed it with the heel of his boot. The room became eerily quiet. "Where you boys been?"

"In here," Pat said. "Where else would we be?"

"In the basement, where the lights are still burning."

"I must've left them on when I was down there earlier."

Kurt cast a suspicious eye at me. "How much does he know?"

"I don't know nothing about anything." I backed up against the wall. I hadn't felt such coldness in anyone's presence in my life. I think he could have killed me.

Pat jumped between us. "He told you himself, he doesn't know anything."

Out of nowhere, Kurt's hand lurched for Pat's throat. Pat's forearm came up as though he'd been expecting it and knocked it away. Pat followed it up with a side kick to Kurt's groin. Kurt shifted his position lightning fast and Pat's foot sailed past. Kurt threw a karate chop into Pat's back and I heard Pat grunt. Kurt's blow knocked him onto the floor but he rolled back up.

The fight had me riveted. I felt like I was in the middle of a Bruce Lee movie. I was scared and entranced at the same time.

Kurt and Pat began a strange dance of kicks and punches, each stopping the other's blows. I'd seen it on television. They knew karate. Pat maneuvered Kurt around so that I had an unobstructed way to the doorway, and beyond it, the staircase. "Get out of here, Bobby."

I felt bad about leaving him, but I wasn't about to take chances. I made it out the door and down the stairs, my heart beating wildly. Behind me I heard heaves and groans. I cleared the front door, jumped on my bike, and sped down the driveway.

The country road was deserted. No way to get help. I rode home as fast as I could.

I threw my bike on the grass in front of our house. I scoured the house, the barn, and anywhere else I could think of, looking for Mom or Pop. I finally found Pop coming out of the fields behind our home.

I was so frightened my story came out garbled. Pop gave me a look that was at once confused and concerned. "Settle down now." He put his hand on my shoulder and knelt beside me. "You say Kurt is not Pat's father? And they have a herd of sick pigs? Why would they keep those?"

"But we've got to do something! The two of them were karate fighting. I'm afraid Kurt's gonna kill Pat. Pat fought to get me out of there."

"Why would you think Kurt would do something to Pat?"

"He was threatening me before Pat stopped him."

"What did he say?"

I tried to think back. "I guess all he asked was how much I knew. And I said I didn't know nothing, which was true."

Pop thought a moment. "I believe you saw this, but maybe you didn't understand what you saw. Maybe Pat was hiding something from his dad? Maybe that's why his father was upset?"

I could see in Pop's eyes that Pat was the rebel here.

"We need to go back. To make sure Pat's okay."

"I want to talk to your mom first. It's not good when neighbors get involved in family arguments."

In the end, they did nothing. Mom said we should just stay alert for strange things at that farm. And she forbade me to go back there without her permission, which I was sure would never come. At least I hadn't mentioned the Fish Cheer.

That night there was a knock on my window. I had a bedroom on the second floor, so it scared me at first. I turned on a light and found Pat's face against the screen. "Let me in," he said.

I took out the screen from the inside. He had bruises on his face and arms. He was wearing jeans, so I couldn't be sure if he had bruises on his legs, but I was betting he did. I propped the screen against the wall and he came through. He winced when his feet hit the floor.

"What are you doing here?" I whispered. Mom and Pop had the bedroom next to mine.

Pat had a hard, determined look on his face. "I killed him."

"You killed who?" I asked, incredulous he would say anything like that.

"Kurt. I killed Kurt." He prowled my room like a skittish barnyard cat, looking to and fro.

"Your pa?"

"Do you not understand? He's not my father."

"Whoever he was, I know you didn't kill him."

He pulled me so close I had to look him in the eye. He was shaking. He was scared. "Just before I came here. With my bare hands. I caught him while he was sleeping. He needed killing."

I blinked in disbelief. "No."

Pat let me go. "You have no idea who they are. Who I am. Who I was."

"Who were you?"

"I was an orphan. Smart, but no parents, no country to claim me when they took hold of me, to use me. Now," he stood a little straighter, "I'm an American rebel."

I heard Mom stirring in the next room. She was a light sleeper. "Is that you, Bobby?" she called.

My eyes lit up. I knew Mom. She'd be in here in a minute. I started looking for places for Pat to hide. I grabbed him by the arm. "Under the bed," I muttered into his ear.

"Yeah, Mom, it's me." Pat got down and rolled under the bed skirt. A dust bunny rolled out the other end.

"Are you okay?" Mom asked. I could hear her right outside my door.

"Fine. Just go back to sleep."

"Are you having a nightmare?"

That would be an understatement. "I'm fine, Mom. Really. You should go back to bed."

"I thought I heard another voice in there."

"Must be your imagination."

The door opened anyway. Immediately she spotted the open window with the screen against the wall. Walking over, she looked out the window. "You haven't been climbing out on the roof, have you?"

I tried to sound like she'd caught me. "Yeah." I shuffled my feet. "I know I shouldn't do that."

A sneeze came from under the bed. Mom turned toward it, nearly hyperventilating. "Who is under that bed?" she screamed.

Of course, that woke up Pop, who came running in clad in only his boxer shorts, carrying the shotgun he hid under his bed.

Mom pointed. "Under there," she said.

"It's Pat from next door," I said, jumping in front of Pop's double barrel. "He needs help."

"I'm coming out," Pat said.

He rolled out, patches of dust attached to his shirt and jeans.

Mom took one look at the bruises on his face and arms and her demeanor immediately changed. She gently touched the dark spots on his face. "My child," she said. "What has happened to you? Who did this?"

"His pa," I said. "I saw his pa hit him earlier today. I told that to Pop this afternoon, but you said we weren't going to get involved."

"That was before I saw this," Pop said, pointing toward Pat's bruises. "You don't beat women, and you don't beat children. I'm going to go see him."

"In the middle of the night?" Mom said.

Pop exhaled noisily and considered the options. "No. I guess it can wait until morning. Let's find somewhere for this young man to sleep."

"He can stay here with me. I'll get out the cot."

In the end, Mom and Pop agreed it was the best course of action. When they were back in the other room, I rolled to the edge of the bed so I could whisper with Pat. "You didn't really kill him, did you?"

"Go to sleep, Bobby."

I kept asking questions, so he rolled on his side away from me. It was dark in the bedroom and I couldn't see if he was asleep. After a while I clutched my pillow and closed my eyes. I didn't think I could sleep after all this, but I did finally.

I awoke the next morning to the sound of fire trucks. Pat was gone from my bedroom, and the barn at his farm, the one that housed the sick pigs, was ablaze, along with the chicken coop. All the animals perished.

We found Pat at the farm, but not Kurt. Kurt—or his body if Pat had truly killed him—was nowhere to be found, and never would be. Instead, 'Uncle Craig' was there. Pat strained to call him "uncle." I understood right then that Craig was no more his uncle than Kurt was his pa.

Pat pulled me aside and told me to forget the eggs, the sick hogs and the laboratory and never speak to anyone about it. He acted like my life depended on it.

Two days later, the farmland went up for sale and they left for 'Idaho.' At least that's what Craig told Pop.

I did see Pat one last time. It was February 1976, and my family was in Trenton, New Jersey, visiting a cousin stationed at Fort Dix, about 16 miles south. But a deadly outbreak of what would be called "swine flu" had quarantined the base. We stayed a day or two longer than planned, waiting to hear if my cousin had been affected.

Mom and Pop waited anxiously in the hotel room by the phone. I was concerned, of course, but found myself more interested in the video arcade across the street. I had spent a good portion of my allowance learning how to defeat "Breakout" when a young man came in, acting disinterested in the gaming experience but nonetheless trying to lose himself in the crowd. He radiated a James Dean persona with a brown leather jacket, a cigarette dangling from pouty lips, and walked with a cocky strut that said if someone dared to swing at him, they'd have their hands full. Slung over one shoulder was a backpack like hikers use.

The James Dean thing made me think of Pat. I came up behind him. I had grown quite a bit during the four years and now was about an inch taller than he, but it had to be him. I said, "Hi, Pat."

His back stiffened but he kept walking. "Pat, it's me, Bobby." He sped up. I did, too. He walked out of the arcade before he turned around. Our eyes met and there was immediate recognition. He grabbed me by my coat and pulled me out of sight around the side of the building.

"Bobby, what are you doing here?" His voice was impatient but relieved. Whoever he *didn't* want to see, it wasn't me.

"My cousin is in Fort Dix. It's in quarantine."

He pulled the cigarette from his mouth and blew smoke. "Don't I know it."

I waited for him to explain but he didn't. Not at first. Then he glanced from side to side, checking the surroundings even though we were in an alleyway between buildings with no one around.

"The virus jumps from pigs to humans," he said. "They developed it."

He didn't specify who 'they' were, and I didn't ask. I had put two and two together some time ago.

"Will it kill the soldiers?" I asked, thinking of my cousin.

"The ones who already have it, maybe. The rest will be all right if I have anything to say about it." The backpack came off his shoulder. He shoved a hand into it and pulled out a small duffel. He showed it to me like it was a prized object.

"What's in there?" I asked.

"A vaccine. I've been working on it for years in secret. I knew they were aiming for the Fort."

I didn't have to ask what a vaccine was. I'd had one for polio.

"I have to get out of here," he said. "They're looking for me."

"Mom and Pop are across the street. Let me get them. They'll drive you out of here."

He shook his head. "Too dangerous for them. And anyway, this needs to get to the State Department. They're expecting it. Sort of."

"Can I help?"

He considered me for a moment. "It might be risky."

I didn't have any idea what he considered risky, but he still had my allegiance, and I wanted to help. "I don't care." And to emphasize my point, I said the Fish Cheer.

That got him to laugh. "You've grown up."

"And my English is better."

He pulled me back inside the arcade and into their public restroom. He did a quick search. No one there. "I'm changing outfits," he said. He pulled clothes from the bottom of his backpack, handing me the duffel. The place smelled strongly of urine. I noticed it had a metal trough instead of a urinal. No wonder.

Pat zipped up his pants and bent down to put on sneakers. "Here's what I want you to do. Two streets to the south there's an alleyway. Carry the duffel to the end. You'll find a limo blocking the street. The driver will be wearing a black beret. Knock on his window. He'll roll it down. Ask him if it's legal to block the street like that. He'll get out and open the passenger door behind him. No matter what, do not get in. Just throw the duffel in and get away fast as you can. Disappear into a crowd. Then get back to your hotel and stay with your mom and dad." He put on round, wire-rim glasses.

Pat had totally transformed. The would-be James Dean was now a would-be John Denver. "What about you?" I asked.

"It's safer for me that you're doing this, and I can get a head start on my own disappearance." He pushed me out of the restroom. We left the arcade and crept along the side of the building until we reached the street. "Now go," he said.

"Will I ever see you again?" I asked.

No answer. He spotted a group of teenagers on the move and hurried to join them. He blended in.

He was still my hero.

I tried not to look like I was running as I made my way to the alley he'd told me about. Once in the shadow of the buildings on either side, I ran to the end. As he said, there was a limo blocking the street. I did everything exactly as he said.

The driver got out, his chauffeur outfit too tight to be believed. I was in cross country. I knew I could outrun this guy if it came to that.

He opened the back door.

I didn't get close. I threw the duffel in from a distance.

He stepped toward me. "Get in," he said.

I shook my head, backpedaling as I did, keeping my gaze on him. "That's all you need."

He launched toward me, but I stayed far from his grasp. "You're not the guy I'm supposed to meet," he said.

"I'm not."

"Then who are you?"

I didn't need to think. I turned to run, twisting my head back over my shoulder, shouting, unconcerned who heard. I had become one with my hero.

"An American rebel."

AUTHOR BIOGRAPHIES

Roberta J. Barmore was born after Zeppelins stopped flying but before cars had seatbelts. She has been reading from the time she realized those wonderful marks in books told stories. She began writing fiction in grade school, usually instead of doing homework. She shares her Indianapolis home with one lodger, two very large tomcats and a few thousand books. Her day job is doing arcane technical things for a TV station.

Mary Bischoff is a native Hoosier who spent her childhood romping through cemeteries and reading 1930s comics in courthouse basements while her parents did genealogical research. Among the jobs in her past, she has been a licensed claims representative, a reservations agent for a major airline, owned her own medical legal transcription/proofreading business and worked in an Indianapolis hospital during the Covid years. Now happily retired, she loves spending more time with her family, reading, traveling, knitting and playing Pokemon Go.

J. Paul Burroughs, aka Jon Paul Burroughs is a retired IPS schoolteacher. He writes detective fiction: online, the Nick Mahoney PI adventures and the paranormal series, Karma and Crime. Karma and Crisis, the sequel, will be published later this year by Per Bastet Press. He has stories in the *Homicide for the Holidays*, *Murder 20/20*, and *Trick or Treats* anthologies. He performs as Hoosier poet James Whitcomb Riley, for the Riley Birthplace Museum. He lives in a historic home in Greenfield with his wife of 40 years, Ronda, and their adorable (but mischievous) pug, Pip.

N.W. Campbell is a Hoosier transplant who grew up in northwestern Pennsylvania. He is a Navy veteran and husband and father and grandfather, and a former technical writer and retired pastor who currently teaches composition at Ivy Tech Community College in Indianapolis. Campbell has been a member of Speed City Sisters in Crime since 2013, and has published two stories in Blue River Press anthologies: "Tumbling Crows" in *Decades of Dirt: Murder, Mystery, and Mayhem from the Crossroads of Crime* (2015) and "Ceilings" in *The Fine Art of Murder* (2016).

Ross Carley's first four novels feature PI and computer hacker Wolf Ruger, an Iraq vet with PTSD. *Dead Drive* (2016) and *Formula Murder,* set in the formula racing industry (2017) are murder mysteries. Cyberthrillers *Cyberkill* (2018) and *Cryptokill* (2020) are books one and two of the *Cybercode Chronicles*. His fifth novel, *The Three-Legged Assassin*, featuring assassin Lance Garrett, was released in February 2022. He also has short stories in the three latest Speed City Sisters in Crime anthologies. Ross is an artificial intelligence and cybersecurity consultant. He and his wife Francie split their time between Indiana and Florida. www.RossCarleyBooks.com, Instagram @RossCarleyAuthor

Diana Catt has 20+ short stories appearing in anthologies published by Blue River Press, Red Coyote Press, Pill Hill Press, Wolfmont Press, The Four Horseman Press, Speed City Press, and Level Best Books. Her collection, *Below the Line*, is available on Amazon. Her debut novel is *Death Map* (Per Bastet Publications, LLC, 2022), and she is working on two sequels. Diana is a microbiologist and is the owner/operator of an environmental microbiology lab. She is often hunting in scary places for mold and finding unexpected and mysterious things that wind up in her stories. www.dianacatt.com

Leanne Edelen's writing journey has just begun in the past few years. During that time, her poems and stories have been selected as a winner of the Kentucky Monthly 9th Annual Penned contest and the 2021 Beartooth Anthony Campfire contest. Leanne was also an invited speaker at the 21st Kentucky Writers Day Celebration. Her short story "Playing Possum" will soon appear in the *Strangely Funny X* collection of stories of horror gone wrong. Leanne currently lives in Louisville, KY with her loving husband. She is blessed to be a mother and stepmother to three wonderful children.

Lillie Evans is an author, playwright, and storyteller. Evans wrote the play *Take My Hand: A Blues Man's Path to Gospel*, which was selected for a reading at the prestigious National Black Theatre Festival, and she later produced the play for the 2018 Indy Onyx Fest.

Ms. Evans, writing as L. Barnett Evans has co-written two plays with fellow author/playwright Crystal Rhodes, *Stake Out* and *Grandmother Incorporated*. The play *Grandmothers Incorporated* is based on the characters from their popular cozy mystery book series of the same name. The books include *Grandmothers, Incorporated, Sin City, There's Something Wrong with Miss Zelda,* and *Whose Knife is it anyway?* The play, *Grandmothers Incorporated*, recently won the 2023 Mature Ladies Playwriting Competition sponsored by the City of Evanston, Illinois.

Evans is also co-editor of Speed City Sisters in Crime anthology, *Murder 20/20*. (www.lilliebarnettevans.com and www.grandmothersinc.com)

Shari Held is an award-winning fiction author who spins tales of mystery/crime, horror, romance, and fantasy. Her short stories have been published in dozens of magazines and anthologies, including *Hoosier Noir, Yellow Mama, Asinine Assassins, The Big Fang,* and *Murder 20/20,* for which she served as co-editor. Visit her website, www.shariheld.com, for more information about her and her stories.

Ramona G. Henderson has an MSN from Indiana University and is a former assistant professor of nursing. She has always had a great passion for writing. Much of her inspiration comes from her native southwestern Indiana and places where she has traveled. Her comedy *Operation Farley* was performed at the 2018 Divafest and her dark comedy *The Malicious Bird Feeder* was performed at the 2022 Indiana Ten Minute Play Festival. Her favorite genre is mystery and some of her short stories have been published in the Speed City Sisters in Crime Anthologies. She has served on the board of the Speed City Sisters in Crime chapter. She is a member of the Indiana Writers Center, The Indiana Playwrights Circle, Speed City Sisters in Crime, and Sisters in Crime National.

C.A. Paddock wrote her first mystery, *Mystery Adventure of Jimmy Hashburger*, as a first grader. She has three short stories published in Speed City Sisters in Crime anthologies: "The Making of a Masterpiece" in *The Fine Art of Murder* (2016, Blue River Press), "Into the Light Darkness Falls" in *Homicide for the Holidays* (2018, Blue River Press) and "The Woman in Black" in *Trick or Treats: Tales of All Hallows Eve* (2021, Speed City Press). Her personal essay, "Doing What Comes Naturally," was recently published in the *Gal's Guide Anthology: Journey* (2023, Gal's Guide Press). She lives in Indianapolis with her husband, Steve.

Elizabeth Perona is the father/daughter writing team of **Tony Perona** and **Liz Dombrosky**. Together they write the Bucket List mystery series and a variety of short stories, one of which, "The Ear Witness," received Honor Roll status in the *Best Mystery Stories of the Year 2021*, edited by Lee Child. Tony is also the author of the Nick Bertetto mystery series and co-editor of the four anthologies including this one, *Amber Waves of Graves*. Liz Dombrosky graduated from Ball State University in the Honors College with a degree in teaching. She is currently a stay-at-home mom and serves as an administrator for her church. Both Liz and Tony are members of

Mystery Writers of America and Sisters in Crime. See more at www.elizabethperona.com.

P.K. Richard is a cyber security analyst when she is not writing poetry and crime fiction. A member of the Derby Rotten Scoundrels and the Speed City Sisters in Crime, she is working on her first novel. She lives in Frankfort, Kentucky, with her husband, Bruce, and in her spare time can often be found hiking, camping, and painting.

Elizabeth A. San Miguel is a new, if not young, writer who lives in Indianapolis, Indiana. She graduated a long time ago from Indiana University, Bloomington with degrees in Journalism, History, and Fine Arts and a minor in Art History. She also received a Certificate of Applied Computer Science from Indiana University-Purdue University at Indianapolis (IUPUI). She spends her days coding in the statistical database language SAS and her evenings and weekends amusing herself by thinking up fun ways to kill people, literarily and not literally.

Andrea Smith loves happy endings and kick-butt heroines who help serve up justice. She's published four short stories featuring Chicago police detective Ariel Lawrence, including "A Lesson in Murder," featured in the mystery anthology *Women on the Case*, published by Delacorte. Andrea's short fiction has also been published in *Alfred Hitchcock Mystery Magazine*, *Mary Higgins Clark Mystery Magazine* and five Speed City Indiana Sisters in Crime anthologies. Her short story featuring amateur sleuth Vera Ames was published in *Alfred Hitchcock Mystery Magazine*. Born and raised in Chicago, Andrea holds a bachelor's degree in journalism and a Master of Arts in novel writing and publishing. She's a past president of the Speed City Indiana chapter of Sisters in Crime and past We Love Libraries Coordinator for Sisters in Crime National.

Stephen Terrell is a retired lawyer with a life-long passion for writing. He has written three novels, and his short stories regularly appear in Speed City Sisters in Crime anthologies. His short story "In Deepest Darkness" was selected to the Honor Roll of Best Short Stories of 2021 edited by Lee Child. Stephen writes the regular column, "On Second Thought," for the American Bar Association's Experience Magazine. He is an avid motorcyclist. For more information, www.terrellwrites.com.

Joseph S. Walker lives in Indiana and teaches college literature and composition courses. His short fiction has appeared in *Alfred Hitchcock's Mystery Magazine, Ellery Queen's Mystery Magazine, Mystery Weekly, Tough,* and a number of other magazines and anthologies. His stories have been included in *The Best American Mystery and Suspense* and three consecutive editions of *The Mysterious Bookshop Presents the Best Mystery Stories of the Year.* He has been nominated for the Edgar Award and the Derringer Award and has won the Bill Crider Prize for Short Fiction. He also won the Al Blanchard Award in 2019 and 2021. Follow him on Twitter @JSWalkerAuthor and visit his website at https://jswalkerauthor.com/.